THE
BLACK
MADONNA

THE
BLACK
MADONNA

Louisa Ermelino

SIMON & SCHUSTER

New York   London   Toronto   Sydney   Singapore

SIMON & SCHUSTER
Rockefeller Center
1230 Avenue of the Americas
New York, NY 10020

SIMON & SCHUSTER and colophon are registered trademarks
of Simon & Schuster, Inc.

Designed by Katy Riegel
Manufactured in the United States of America
1 3 5 7 9 0 8 6 4 2

Library of Congress Cataloging-in-Publication Data
Ermelino, Louisa
The Black Madonna / Louisa Ermelino.
p.   cm.
1. Little Italy (New York, N.Y.)—Fiction. 2. Italian American families—Fiction. I. Title.
PS3555.R55 B58 2001
813'.54—dc21
00-058805
ISBN 0-684-87166-1

The author wishes to thank the Ucross Foundation for the gifts of time, support, and wide-open spaces. And for their faith and efforts: Roz Siegel, Elaine Markson, Lutz Wolff, Sara Nelson, and Daniel Richman.

FOR

BINNIE KIRSHENBAUM

AND

FOR CARLO, ALWAYS

. . . on a throne supported by two long shafts, which a dozen men at a time took turns in carrying, came the Madonna. She was a paltry papier mache affair, a copy of the powerful and famous Madonna of Viggiano, with the same black face, and decked out with sumptuous black robes, necklaces, and bracelets. . . . Peasants with baskets of wheat in their hands threw fistfuls of it at the Madonna. . . . The black-faced Madonna, in the shower of wheat, among the animals, the gunfire, and the trumpets, was no sorrowful Mother of God, but rather a subterranean deity, black with the shadows of the bowels of the earth, a peasant Persephone or lower-world goddess.

—*Christ Stopped at Eboli,* by Carlo Levi
(Farrar, Straus and Giroux, 1947)

THE
BLACK
MADONNA

TERESA

1948

Teresa Sabatini always said her Nicky was a good boy, a smart boy. She said he never gave her any trouble, but how could that be?

It was Jumbo. Jumbo weakened the rope, Teresa said. But if Nicky was so smart, like his mother said, how could he have let Jumbo go first? How did it happen?

Jumbo was the biggest baby ever born on Spring Street, or Thompson Street, or anywhere else anyone could remember. He broke the midwife's scale and so she held him up by his feet like a chicken and guessed his weight. "Twenty-three pounds," she said, and Jumbo's father yelled it out the window.

Dante was standing downstairs like always and when he heard it, he went into the candy store and called the *Daily News*. A photographer came and took pictures of Jumbo, who had been carefully dressed in his sister's clothes because nothing his mother had ready would fit him.

Jumbo's mother Antoinette took him the next day to show him to Teresa, who lived downstairs. She put Jumbo next to Teresa's son Nicky, on the couch in the parlor. Nicky was four months old and his mother loved him more than life. Teresa felt proud to see him sitting on the couch, propped up with pillows. "Look at that, will you?" Antoinette said, pointing to Jumbo, "bigger than your Nicky and only just born."

When Jumbo's mother left, Teresa pinned a blessed medal of the Immaculate Conception on Nicky's undershirt. The medal had been blessed by the bishop when he came the May before to raise money for the missions. Teresa had held it up herself when the bishop made a cross in the air with his right hand over the congregation. It was a silver medal but Our Lady's dress was painted blue. Teresa attached it to Nicky's undershirt with a small gold-colored safety pin. She sat on the couch and held him in her lap. She put her mouth in the soft place between his head and his shoulder.

Jumbo's mother cut the picture out of the newspaper with the caption that said BIGGEST BABY BORN and pasted it on the wall near the light switch in the kitchen so that anyone who came in could see it and know she had produced a masterpiece. When it was time for the landlord to paint the apartment, she said no, and took the month's free rent instead so as not to disturb the picture.

Next to Jumbo's picture hung the image of the Madonna that had belonged to Antoinette's mother, the Madonna with the black face, which she had brought with her from the other side. Antoinette's mother had kept the Black Madonna in her bedroom, the gilt frame festooned with blessed palm and silk flowers, but Antoinette kept her in the kitchen so the Madonna could look over the family all together, all the time. The Mangiacarnes were always in the kitchen.

Teresa took consolation in the fact that Antoinette kept a messy house and hid dirty dishes in the bathtub under the porcelain cover. The cover was to make you forget there was a bathtub in the kitchen. It was six feet long, it had clawed feet, but when it was covered, you could forget. You could feel high-class. Teresa remembered how, when she was growing up, before steam heat, the bathtub was exposed and filled with coal. That, she thought, was obscene. She took this apartment on the fifth floor, even though there was one available on the second, because it had a bathroom, a real bathroom off the entrance hall with a narrow tub and a toilet and room for a wooden hamper with a hinged lid where she put Nicky's dirty laundry. Teresa said it was worth the extra stairs, and she never left her dishes in the sink but washed them the same night.

Teresa would bathe Nicky in a laundry tub set on the kitchen table. She would test the temperature of the water with her elbow before she put him in, cradled in one arm so he wouldn't slip. She would press her fingertips over his heart to count the beats. She laid him on a towel, rubbed him dry, kissed the backs of his knees. She made a bunting with the towel, a corner of it falling in a point over his forehead, like a monk's cowl. Then she would put on the wool undershirt, put her ear against his chest, and pin the medal of the Blessed Virgin where his heartbeat was. She didn't trust Jumbo's mother not to overlook him, to call up the evil eye, which would make him sick or crippled or worse. She held Nicky close to her body when she heard Antoinette pass the door on her way downstairs.

On the stoop in the late afternoons before they went upstairs to start dinner, the women would sometimes talk about the state of Antoinette's house. Teresa always wanted to turn the conversation to Jumbo, how big he was, how it wasn't normal, but she never did. She knew the women would think she was jealous, because truly, what was more beautiful than a big fat baby boy?

Instead, the women on the stoop would ask about Nicky's father and Teresa would tell them what she told Nicky as she rocked him to sleep, that Nicky's father was working the ships all over the world, that he sent money from places like Singapore and the Solomon Islands. "See you soon" he always wrote across the piece of paper folded around the money. Teresa would bring down the envelopes that the money had come in and let the women look at the stamps.

Dolls with brown faces and yellow faces dressed in extravagant costumes would arrive. Teresa would open these packages on the stoop and pass the dolls among the women for them to admire before she brought them upstairs and put them on a shelf over the couch in the parlor. Every day she dusted them, and the beginning of each week, she washed and pressed their satin dresses.

Sometimes Nicky's father sent her silk cloth in bright colors with gold threads running through it, and once there were sequined slippers, the toes curled up in front. She folded the silk cloth neatly into her top dresser drawer, next to the slippers, next to the envelopes with stamps from all over the world.

She bought a globe in the five-and-ten-cent store and showed Nicky the places in the world his father would go. She would match the names on the stamps to points on the globe. She would take Nicky's finger and trace the path of his father's ship, watching as it moved nearer to New York, closer to Spring Street. But Angelo Sabatini would come home only once, when Nicky was seven, the time he showed him how to tie the sailor's knot, the time he gave him the ring he had won in a crap game in Hong Kong.

Nicky and Jumbo were friends growing up, which was why they were swinging on the rope. It was Nicky's idea when they found the rope behind the stairs. They were sitting out on Nicky's back fire escape when Nicky told Jumbo he could make a knot so strong that they could do anything with that rope. They could go anywhere. He learned that knot from his father, who was a sailor, a merchant seaman, he told Jumbo, who sailed all over the world.

"You don't have a father," Jumbo said.

"I do too."

"I never saw him."

"He's a seaman. I told you a million times. He goes all over the world."

"Then how'd he show you the knot, if he's never here?"

"He came home once," Nicky said, "and he showed me how to make the knot."

"So what?" Jumbo said. "Who cares if you can make a knot in a rope? Where's that gonna get us?"

"Listen, it'll be great. We tie the rope on the fire escape and we can swing across to the next one, like Tarzan. You know the way Tarzan goes all over the place on those vines? Well, we can go right along the building. If we can rig it up right, we can maybe even get over to Salvatore's, knock on his window. His mother'll go nuts."

"Maybe we could catch her in her slip . . ." Jumbo half-closed his eyes. He ran his tongue over his upper lip as though he were tasting chocolate. He kissed the tips of his fingers.

"Yeah, maybe . . ."

"She ain't his real mother, you know. His real mother's dead from when he was a baby. Magdalena don't look like nobody's mother because she ain't."

"Forget Magdalena. You wanna swing on that rope or what?"

"What else can we do?"

"We can set fire to Mary Ziganetti's cat."

"Forget it. Let's swing on the rope."

Nicky climbed up and knotted the rope on the fire escape above. "You go first," he called down.

"I don't know," Jumbo said. "You think it's safe?"

"Of course it's safe. Watch me." Nicky slid down the rope. "See? It's easy." His palms burned and he pressed them against his legs. He kept smiling so Jumbo wouldn't notice.

"That's different," Jumbo said. "It's not the same thing, coming down like that."

"You're such a Mary," Nicky said. "Here, take the rope." Jumbo held the rope in both hands and Nicky twisted it around Jumbo's wrists and tugged on it to tighten the knot.

"Tarzan just holds on," Jumbo said. "He don't do it like this."

"Tarzan's a pro. We're just starting."

"I'm scared."

"Why? I told you this knot can hold anything. It holds big ships. Now get up on the railing."

"I'm too fat."

"C'mon, Jumbo, just get up there. Grab my hand. I'll hold you."

"Let me step on your knee."

"You'll kill me if you step on my knee. Forget it." Nicky pushed Jumbo aside. "Give me the rope. I'm going first." He tried to unwind the rope from Jumbo's hands but Jumbo clenched his fists.

"No, no, I'll do it. I'll go. Just hold me."

"You're sure."

"I'm sure. I'm sure. C'mon before somebody sees us and makes us get down." Jumbo slipped one hand off the rope and grabbed Nicky's shoulder. There were circles of sweat under his arms. Nicky could see them when Jumbo pulled himself up onto the fire escape railing. Jumbo moved his hand to Nicky's head and pulled at his hair.

"Jumbo . . ."

"What? What?"

"Let go," Nicky said. He put his hands against Jumbo's back, his fingers spread wide, and gave him a shove. Jumbo flew out, propelled by his weight. "Open your eyes," Nicky hollered, but Jumbo didn't and missed his chance to catch hold of the fire escape on the other side. He shrieked as he swung back.

Nicky could see the terror in Jumbo's face. His mouth was a gaping hole; his eyes had disappeared into the flesh of his cheeks. Nicky waited, ready to push him out again anyway. He leaned over the fire escape, arms extended, and when Jumbo came close enough he gave him another push. But his hand caught Jumbo's shoulder and sent him back out over the alley spinning at the end of the rope like a top.

"Now, now," Nicky yelled, and this time Jumbo caught the fire escape with his feet. "Good going. Now climb down. Go ahead. You can do it."

Jumbo started to cry. "I can't. I can't. Oh God, Oh God. Ma!!!!!"

"Quit it. Shut up. Don't be a dope. You're there. You can do it. Just don't look down."

Jumbo left one hand on the rope and stretched the other out toward the railing. Nicky made his voice soft. "Good. Good. You got it. Come on. You got it," and Jumbo grabbed the railing and pulled himself over. He stood on the fire escape, his face red and shiny with sweat. He was panting. Nicky could see his tongue. "You did it. Great," Nicky called out to him.

Jumbo took a deep breath. "I did good, huh?" he shouted. His voice cracked.

"Yeah, yeah, you did great, but now don't let go the rope. Send it back. I'm coming over."

Jumbo had forgotten about the rope, which had caught around his neck and under his arm. He took hold of it now with one hand and pulled up the bottom of his T-shirt with the other and wiped his face. Nicky could see Jumbo's huge chest heaving. The rolls of white flesh above his waist quivered.

Nicky whistled through his fingers. "Send it back," he yelled.

"Okay . . . Hold your horses."

Nicky was anxious now, excited. He was proud of himself, proud of his father. The knot had held. If the knot could hold Jumbo, it could hold anything, he figured, just like his father had said.

Jumbo flung the rope to him and Nicky caught it easily and leaped off the fire escape in one smooth motion. He held the rope tight between his knees and raised one arm in the air. He yelled at the top of his lungs, euphoric, and swung far out over the alley.

But not far enough. Nicky never reached the fire escape where Jumbo waited to catch hold of him but missed it by a mile, and swung back, away from the fire escape, away from Jumbo, far out over the alley. And that was when the rope broke.

Nicky went down three stories. The fire escape outside Vicky Palermo's window on the second floor broke his fall. He smashed her pots of basil when he landed. Blood and small sounds came out of his mouth.

The sun was strong and Jumbo couldn't see. He put a hand up to shade his eyes and he looked for Nicky down in the alley. He thought he might be dead falling so far. He should be splattered all over but he wasn't even there, not a trace of him, not that Jumbo could see. Jumbo looked over at the fire escape Nicky had jumped from and down into the alley one more time before he shrugged his massive shoulders and went home for lunch.

Outside Vicky Palermo's window, Nicky lay on the fire escape and moaned from deep in his throat and called for his mother. He crawled up to the windowsill and fell in the open window. He was covered with blood and dirt. He smelled of basil.

Vicky Palermo was bleaching her hair with peroxide at the kitchen sink. When she saw him she ran out into the hall and down the stairs and into the street screaming that something had come through her window and was dying in her kitchen. Dante was standing outside the building like always and she pulled on his arm and made him go upstairs. He tried to make her come with him but she wouldn't.

Dante carried Nicky down in his arms, talking to him all the way while JoJo Santulli got his uncle's car and drove them to the emergency room at St. Vincent's. Dante liked Nicky. "I wish I had ten of him," he was always telling Nicky's mother Teresa, although she was the only one who believed it was true.

At the hospital, a pretty red-haired nurse held Nicky's hand while the doctor set the bones and sewed up the wounds. They thought Dante was the father and made him sign a paper. They told him they didn't know what would happen, how or if Nicky would walk again. Bring him back in a week, the doctor said, and

Excellent Book ✓

they would see. Nicky held the red-haired nurse's hand all the way out to the car and only let go when Dante had to shut the door so they could drive back to Spring Street.

Nicky's mother was downstairs waiting for them when JoJo Santulli pulled the car as close as he could to the curb. She led Dante up the four flights of stairs to the apartment and tried to give him money before he left. She put Nicky in her bed with the quilted satin coverlet and in the corners of the room she put flat dishes filled with olive oil to protect him, to create a place for him safe from malevolent spirits.

In the morning she brought a basin of water to the bedroom and washed Nicky in the bed. She wiped the dried blood from around the wounds on his legs and kept the cloth. She laid it on the windowsill in the sun and when it was dry she folded it and put it in her top dresser drawer, underneath the squares of silk her husband had sent from Singapore and the Solomon Islands. She never asked Nicky what happened. She only planned how she would make him whole again and keep him to herself.

Dante stood downstairs outside the building where he always stood and told whoever passed what had happened, as much as he knew, about Vicky Palermo's kitchen and JoJo Santulli taking them to St. Vincent's and how he had signed the paper for them to fix Nicky's legs. He mentioned the red-haired nurse and said that if he ever got married, that was the kind of girl he could go for. Everyone he told nodded at this, even though everyone knew that Dante would never get married.

What Dante would do was stand outside the building on Spring Street. He was always there if you needed him, unless it rained. Then you would find him in the candy store, sitting on the wooden folding chair in the back next to the red icebox full of soda bottles.

At noon Dante's mother would bring down his lunch and a small carafe of red wine and he would go over to the park bench on the corner to eat it. When he was finished, he had a coffee in the café next to Benvenuto's Bar and Restaurant. This had been going on now for a long time, as long as anyone could remember.

Dante's mother talked with the other women on the stoop about Dante's *condition*. "When he goes far away," she would tell them, "he gets dizzy, sees little black dots. Up the block, he's okay, maybe, but he can't cross too many streets. My poor Dante," she always said, "such a strong healthy boy."

The women would click their tongues in sympathy. They would silently thank God for their men, but they would tell Dante's mother that it was not the worst thing in a son. No daughter-in-law would curse her old age. And they would smile but mean it.

Nicky's legs swelled and his knees filled with water. The doctor had sewn crosses in black thread across his legs and Teresa washed around the stitches with wet cotton. When he was healed, she broke the threads with her teeth, and kept them with the bloody cloth, underneath the squares of silk her husband had sent her from halfway around the world.

Dante didn't tell Nicky's mother what the doctor had said about Nicky's legs. "Why should I?" he told everyone else at the end of the story. "What do they know, after all?" If Nicky's mother heard, she never let on.

And Nicky didn't tell his mother about the rope and the knot his father had said could hold anything. "We were playing on the fire escape. Nicky fell," Jumbo told Teresa even though she didn't ask. Jumbo's mother had sent him to talk to Nicky's mother because she was afraid.

"It pays to be careful," Antoinette said to the women on the stoop, "you never really know." She crossed herself and spat three times.

The women on the stoop told Nicky's mother to thank God that Vicky Palermo was in her kitchen, that Dante was standing outside, that JoJo Santulli had his uncle's car. They put a hand on her shoulder and asked if Nicky's father was coming home. Teresa looked at them, wiped her eyes with a corner of the handkerchief she had balled up in her fist. "He's on his ship. He's halfway around the world. How could he come?"

Teresa kept Nicky in the house. Everyone could see him sitting in the front window where she had carried him so he could watch the street. Sometimes he sat in the back window and looked across to Salvatore's building. Salvatore would wave and shout at him across the alley.

Nicky's mother kept him home from school. When the truant officer came, she bandaged Nicky's head so that only one eye showed. She left a small space for him to breathe. She led the truant officer into the bedroom and showed him her son. "He fell three stories," she whispered in his ear.

Nicky joined the list of the mysteriously afflicted on Spring Street. His mother said he was going to stay home from now on. She would keep him there. "I'm not taking any chances," Teresa told the women on the stoop. "The next time he could get killed."

After the fall, Nicky's legs healed but they didn't work. His mother massaged them. She rubbed them with olive oil that she heated in a pot on the stove. For weeks and weeks she did this, twice a day, but when Nicky tried to walk, he fell. Teresa made him stop. "You'll hit your head," she told him, and carried him everywhere.

"Take me downstairs," he asked her. "I'll sit on the stoop."

"You can't," she said. "There's only women on the stoop. How can they talk with you there? Use your head."

"Take me on the corner, then. I'll sit in the park."

"I can't stay there all day and watch you."

"I can stay alone."

"You can't."

"Dante can watch me, then. He's always outside."

"You can't impose on Dante. Use your head."

"C'mon, Ma, I wanna go out."

She sat next to him, reached over and pulled down the shade on the kitchen window. She put her hands on his shoulders and rubbed the back of his neck. "You will, *caro,* when you can walk, when you can protect yourself. They can't see you like this. You've got to be strong. Who knows what could happen now? What they could do to you?"

"Who, Ma? Who's *they?* You're making me crazy. I just wanna sit downstairs."

"Shh . . ." she said. She closed his eyes with her fingers, covered his mouth with her hands. "You want to walk again, you listen to me."

Jumbo stayed away and Nicky's mother was glad of that. She attached a holy-water font in the shape of a seashell inside her door, and when she heard Jumbo or his mother leave the house, she sprinkled the holy water onto the landing and down the stairwell.

Salvatore came by often and sat with Nicky on the couch in the parlor under the shelf of dolls in extravagant costumes. Teresa would put out dishes of nuts and hard candies, even though Salvatore would bring Nicky jawbreakers and lemon ice from the candy store downstairs where Dante sat when it rained. When Teresa saw Salvatore, she would touch his cheek; she would push the hair back from his forehead with her hand. She wanted to, but did not, wet her fingers and smooth the cowlick that sprouted at his part. He had been hers for a little while; he had been like her own. But he didn't remember, couldn't have remembered, and now he was grown, a big boy, like her Nicky.

Salvatore would smile at Teresa's attentions. He was used to being fawned over. Magdalena spoiled him, would pet him until he blushed. But Salvatore came here to see Nicky. He would make Nicky tell him over and over again about the rope and the knot and how he fell the three stories onto Vicky Palermo's fire escape.

"I could show you how to knot the rope," Nicky told Salvatore. "You could swing across the alley to see me, climb right up the fire escape to my window. You wouldn't have to come all the way down and across and up again. You could come anytime, three o'clock in the morning if you wanted, and no one would know.

We could smoke butts out the window. If my legs worked and I had the rope, I'd come over and see you tonight."

Salvatore shook his head. "How could you still wanna do that?"

"The knot was perfect," Nicky said. "It was Jumbo. He busted the rope. If it wasn't for Jumbo, we'd be swinging all over the alleyways with that rope."

Salvatore squeezed the pleated cup to get at the last of the lemon ice. "When are you gonna walk, Nicky? When are you gonna get out of here?"

"Who knows? 'Soon,' my mother keeps telling me. 'Any day,' she says."

"You went to the doctor?"

"Yeah, but he didn't say much. My mother's mad at Dante and JoJo Santulli for taking me to the hospital but everybody thinks they're heroes so she won't say nothing." Nicky shrugged. "At least I don't have to go to school."

"You'll go," Salvatore said, "but you'll get left back and you'll be in Fat Augustina's class for two years. She'll get to beat the shit out of you for two years instead of just one."

"Nah," Nicky said. "I'm a cripple. She'll treat me good, and anyway then I'll be with you and Jumbo and nobody can say I got left back on purpose."

After three months when the truant officer stopped coming and Nicky wasn't walking, his mother went to see the woman on Bedford Street who had the power. Teresa brought her oranges and grapefruits and the money that had come that morning in an envelope from the Suez.

"My son can't walk," Teresa told the woman. "What can you do?"

"I can do everything," Donna Rubina Fiore said. She lit candles and put the money in the front pocket of her dress. She kept her hand over the pocket where the money was. "First," she told Nicky's mother, "we call the good spirits in. It's not enough just to keep the evil out. It's already here. That's why your son can't walk." Teresa nodded and touched Donna Rubina's hand to show her respect. "Fill a glass with water, cover it with a dish, and burn a candle," Donna Rubina said. "When the candle's finished, write your son's name . . ."

"Nicola. His name's Nicola . . ."

"Write 'Nicola,' then, on a strip of paper, fold it four times . . ." Donna Rubina leaned across the table, "for the four elements . . . and put it in the dish. The glass of water goes on top. Leave it at the foot of his bed and come to see me when the glass is empty."

Nicky's mother repeated the instructions to herself on the way home. She did all that Donna Rubina told her to do, and when the glass was empty she went back to Bedford Street.

Donna Rubina sat in her darkened parlor. She was laying out a deck of picture cards. "The water's gone," Teresa told her.

"Good, the spirits have drunk it. I come soon to see the boy."

Donna Rubina came to Spring Street the next week and climbed the four flights to Teresa's house. She crossed herself at the holy-water font when she came through the door. She leaned over Nicky, who was sitting up in bed. He could see her gold tooth. She smelled of must and camphor. Nicky was only twelve but he wasn't stupid. "Ma . . ." he said.

Teresa stood beside him. "Shh," she told him. She pulled his ear. "Keep quiet and listen."

Donna Rubina carried a black bag big enough to hold a baby. She put it on the table and opened the gold clasp. From inside she took out a square of white linen and a glass jar with a thin layer of dirt at the bottom. She showed the jar to Teresa. "From the ceme-tery," she told her, "on All Souls Day." Donna Rubina emptied the dirt into the center of the cloth, twisted the ends around the lump of earth, and strung it around Nicky's neck with a cord. He hated the way it smelled but saw his mother smile.

"Lay down," Donna Rubina told Nicky, and she closed his eyes with her fingers. She put her hands on his forehead and rubbed his temples. She outlined his eyebrows, his nose, his mouth. Her hands were rough and smelled of dead things like the cloth bag she had placed around his neck. She spoke low in an ancient dialect he couldn't understand and then she put her two fingers hard into his eyes. Nicky sat up and yelled at his mother. Donna Rubina slapped his face. "No wonder," she said. "An ungrateful son . . ."

Teresa moved close to Donna Rubina. "He's sorry," she said, and poked Nicky hard in his ribs with her finger. "Forgive him." She put four tightly rolled bills into Donna Rubina's hand. Donna Rubina took them without looking down and dropped them into her front pocket. She had explained to Teresa that the money must be rolled up tight, as slim as cigarettes, disguised to fool the spirits.

Teresa bent to kiss the old woman's hand. "*Mille grazie,* Donna Rubina," she said, and she stood back up and put a hand on Nicky's shoulder. Nicky felt his mother's nails dig into his skin.

"Thanks," Nicky said. He blew out his anger in a sigh. His mother led Donna Rubina to the door and he heard them whispering.

When Donna Rubina was gone, when the hallway door downstairs had slammed behind her, Teresa came back and sat beside him on the bed. She smoothed back his hair. She ran a hand down his arm and over his legs. He looked away from her. "When you walk, you'll thank me," she told him.

"Yeah," he said, "except I'll be blind."

Nicky's mother waited for her miracle. She lit candles and stood Nicky up from the chair in the kitchen. She did this only at night, making sure the window shades were pulled down, the chain secure in its slot across the door. She closed her door after all the other doors on the landing had closed. She listened for the doors in the rest of the building to close. When she came down the narrow hallway of her apartment to unhook the string that looped around the doorknob and held her door open, she was the last one.

After the house was secure, after the door was shut, she would help Nicky up from the chair and stand in front of him. She would coax him forward. *"Cammina, cammina,"* she would say in a soft voice. She would close her eyes halfway and mutter a prayer and Nicky would hold out his arms to her and try to move his legs. She would step back, calling to him, whispering his name, and then he would fall.

Once he knocked her down and fell on top of her. The two of them lay there, Nicky tangled in her skirts. She smacked him that time and said he wasn't trying, but then she enclosed his head in her arms, his chin caught in the bend of her elbow, and pressed him against her. She held him this way and petted him until he complained that he couldn't breathe.

Nicky was bored with the rituals and the amulets and the smell of the olive oil that she worked into his legs. After Donna Rubina had stuck her fingers in his eyes, he wouldn't let his mother bring her to the house. Donna Rubina told her there was little she could do from a distance, that the demons were very clever, convincing Nicky to refuse her help. Donna Rubina smelled failure and took care for her reputation. She promised Teresa she would hold Nicky in her special prayers. "He's a very young boy," she told her. "Miracles take time." Donna Rubina scratched her chin with the thumb of her right hand. "There is something . . ." she said to Teresa, who had come to see her with gifts of pignoli cookies and figs soaked in brandy.

Teresa stood very still. She put her palms together, fingers laced in supplication. Donna Rubina hesitated. She curled her bottom lip under her front teeth. ". . . something I can give you," she said, and she pulled a small leather case from her pocketbook. Inside, next to a scapular of green felt, was a holy card with an image of the Madonna, a gold Madonna with a black face. She held a black-faced infant and they wore gold crowns and garlands of flowers. *Patrona e Regina della Lucania* was printed along the bottom of the card. The sky behind the Madonna was blue.

"From our province," Donna Rubina said. "Magnificent, no?" Teresa nodded, afraid to do more. Donna Rubina handed the card to Teresa. "For you," she said. Teresa closed her hand over the picture of the Black Madonna. "Keep her hidden," Donna Rubina said. "Keep her hidden for yourself and your son." Teresa reached into her pocket but Donna Rubina stopped her. "No, no," she said. She smiled. "Next time."

When Teresa got home she put the holy card with the picture of the Black Madonna in her top dresser drawer, between the folds of silk cloth from halfway around the world.

Get me crutches," Nicky told his mother, "so I can go downstairs. I can go up the block. I can go to school."

"How can you do that? You can't walk."

"If you get me crutches, I can."

"You think you gonna crawl, Nicky? Forget it. When you walk, you go downstairs. You crawl, you stay home."

"But I can't walk. You just said I can't."

"You will. I promise," she told him and then she made a sound, a long, low wail, a cry, until he promised to stop asking her and give her more time before he hobbled around outside like a cripple, like the boy in the movie she took him to see every Christmas at the Loew's Sheridan. "There's still Our Lady of Mount Carmel, *La Madonna Bruna*," she said. "The Madonna who answers. I'll do the novena. I'll walk barefoot in the procession to 115th Street with a lighted candle. I'll go on my knees. Then we'll get our miracle. You wait. Have patience. I promise you."

She cut him a piece of bread and covered it with butter. She poured him a glass of milk and held it while he drank. When he was finished she made him spit on a corner of the handkerchief she pulled from under her sleeve and then she wiped the corners of his mouth.

Nicky told all this to Salvatore, who came now to see him almost every day after school unless he had to work for his father. Salvatore's father was an important man, a *padrone*. He had a shelf of books in his house and could add columns of numbers in his head. The neighborhood was always talking about just what he was worth.

If Salvatore saw Nicky in the front window, he would go up and knock on the door. But usually in the afternoon when school got out, Nicky's mother sat him in the back. "You don't want them to see you in the window all the time with your tongue hanging out," she said, and Nicky didn't complain because he knew Salvatore would see him in the back window and would climb up the back fire escape and sit outside the window and they would talk. Teresa never objected to Salvatore. When he would come to see Nicky in the window, she would bring them glasses of water tinted with wine. Nicky would ask him about the rope, but Salvatore always said he couldn't find one, not the right kind anyway, the kind Nicky said he needed, but he said he would try and figure something out. What Salvatore figured out was a platform on wheels that Nicky could sit on and pull himself around the apartment. Salvatore got the idea from the go-carts they would make with a crate and a two-by-four piece of wood and a roller skate. Teresa was not unhappy about Nicky's new freedom. She said as long as no one saw him wheeling himself around like a circus freak, it was not a bad thing. When Salvatore arrived with the contraption under his arm, Teresa had nodded her head and raised her eyebrows, secretly pleased at Salvatore's cleverness. Nicky kept his "chair" under the bed and out of sight, and used it when his mother was not around.

Teresa came downstairs one night after supper when the weather was starting to get warm. The women made room for her on the stoop. They asked about Nicky's legs. They had seen Donna Rubina come and go. Nicky's mother shook her head. "Bad luck sticks," she told the women. "It's hard to shake."

The women looked down. They rocked back and forth, their skirts tucked behind their knees, and they agreed with Teresa, but one young woman stood up. It was Magdalena, Salvatore's stepmother. "This is America," she told them. "You can make your destiny." The women looked at her. Magdalena seldom sat on the stoop, didn't gossip, never put her head together with theirs, but while they were wary of her, they listened, because behind their suspicions was a grudging respect.

If magic didn't work, she said, maybe Nicky needed a doctor, a special kind of doctor. "You ask my husband," she told Teresa. "He knows all kinds of people. He has business outside, away from here."

"Yes, yes," the women told Teresa. "Listen to her. Her husband Amadeo is a smart man."

Teresa looked down at the women and then faced Magdalena. "I know your husband," she said. "Long before you came here, I knew him."

Magdalena clicked her tongue against the roof of her mouth. She raised her chin. "Come with me now," she said, and she took Teresa's arm and pulled her off the stoop. Magdalena linked her arm with Teresa's and held her close. Teresa stiffened but Magdalena held tight and led her around the corner to her house. It wasn't a tenement, but a private house, and she and Amadeo and Salvatore lived in all of it.

"She was lucky," the women on the stoop said, talking about Magdalena, "to hook a man like that. He started with nothing like the rest of us but now he has a house with chandeliers hanging from every ceiling."

"And a bathroom with colored tiles on the wall," one of the women said to another in a low voice, "pink and green, laid in a pattern, like a checkerboard."

"How do you know?" someone asked.

"What do you mean by that? You think I'm lying? Tony the plumber told my husband."

The women argued about who knew what and who told whom, but they all agreed that whatever the color of the bathroom tiles, Magdalena had fallen in good. "If things had gone different," one of them said, "it could have been Teresa living in that house."

But Mary Ziganetti shook her head. "Teresa never had the luck. Some people, they got a horseshoe up their ass, but not Teresa."

Amadeo Pavese was surprised when Magdalena brought Teresa into the house. He stood up when the women came into the parlor. It was the room where he and Teresa had spent Sundays, where Salvatore and Nicky had played. They were so tiny then; just little boys. Amadeo remembered how Teresa would put them down on the rug by her feet, one then the other, and how they would grab at her skirt with their fists and pull themselves up. They only wanted to be in her lap, he remembered, a long time ago.

Amadeo came to Teresa and took her hand. "How good to see you," he said. He felt awkward, uncomfortable. If Teresa could tell, she gave him no sign. She said nothing.

Magdalena sat down in one of the big chairs. She leaned forward, legs apart, her elbows resting on her knees. "Teresa needs a doctor, Amo. A good one, the best, to make Nicola walk. I told her you would know, that you would help."

Teresa looked over at Magdalena. Such a girl, she thought. But a girl with power, who knew how to make her way in the world.

"Of course," Amadeo said. "Why didn't you come before, Teresa? You know I would help you, always."

Teresa inclined her head. She half-closed her eyes. "I didn't think," she said.

Magdalena stood up. "Good. It's done. Come, Teresa. Have something with us."

"No, no. Thank you, but Nicky's alone. I have to be with him. He needs me all the time. You understand." She turned to go.

Magdalena nodded. She followed Teresa to the door, but before she let her out, she touched Teresa's arm. "Amadeo will pay," she told her. "You don't worry about nothing but Nicola."

Teresa shook her head. "I don't worry," she said. "Nicola has a father. His father will pay."

Amadeo Pavese had said he would find Teresa a doctor and a few days later there was a paper for her behind the counter in the candy store downstairs. On it was a doctor's name, a Fifth Avenue address, and a phone number. Teresa called the doctor from the phone in the candy store to ask for an appointment. "Three weeks from today," she told the women on the stoop.

"Such a long wait," they said, impressed.

"He's a very big doctor," Teresa told them.

"He must be good," they said.

Teresa waved a hand in the air over their heads. "The best," she said. "Nothing but the best for my Nicky."

Three weeks later, Teresa got all dressed up and they took a cab to the doctor's office. There were Persian rugs on the floor. The furniture was antique. *"Alt'Italia,"* Nicky's mother whispered in Nicky's ear when the doctor came into the room. *"Toscano, genovese."* She sniffed in disapproval.

"Look at his shoes," Nicky told his mother. "You get me a pair like that and I'll walk in hell." Teresa made a face as if to smack him but would never do it in front of the Fifth Avenue doctor. Instead she twisted the tip of his ear in her gloved fingers and threatened him when he screwed up his face with the pain.

The doctor examined Nicky and talked to them for a long time. Teresa thought she might faint. She sat straight, her back not touching the chair. The bones of her corset dug into her sides. Her smile covered her teeth. The doctor talked about Nicky's spine and nerves and muscles and said things she didn't understand.

"Can you make him walk?" she asked the doctor when she thought he was finished.

"He needs an operation," the doctor said.

"And you swear to me he'll walk?"

"Signora, forgive me. I'm not God."

Teresa stood up. She touched the painted wooden cherries on the brim of her black straw hat. It was from an Easter long ago, before she was married, and she worried that it had lost its shape after all those years in the box under the bed where she had stored it. "Don't worry about God," she said. "I'll take care of God. What can *you* do?"

The doctor put a hand on Nicky's knee. "I'll do my best."

Like an *amerigane,* this doctor talks, Teresa said to herself, and this gave her confidence in him. Wasn't America the greatest country in the world?

The doctor sat back. "You have to consent to the operation, sign papers, and the boy has to want it."

"I want it. I want it," Nicky said. "Anything beats this. I can't do anything. I can't go downstairs. I can't go to school . . ."

The doctor looked from Nicky to Teresa. "Why doesn't he go to school?"

"How much does the operation cost?" she said.

"He needs to be in school," the doctor said.

"He needs to walk," Teresa told him.

"His father?"

"His father's away at sea, halfway around the world . . . Singapore, the Solomon Islands . . ." She tried to remember other names she had read off the stamps to the women on the stoop. "Suez," she said after a moment.

"You decide, *signora* . . . You call me, and I'll make all the arrangements."

When they got outside, Nicky's mother pulled his hair. She yanked it so hard Nicky thought she'd snapped his neck. "You keep quiet," she said to him. "You don't tell people your business. Life is hard enough without giving them things to use against you, a knife to stick in your heart." She twisted Nicky's ear and when she let go it was red like a summer tomato. "Who knows why this happened?" She looked up and shook her fist at the sky. "Only God knows why He did this."

Nicky started crying. "It wasn't God. It was Jumbo," he said.

"Jumbo weakened the rope and when it was my turn it broke. The rope broke and I fell." Nicky was bawling now, his eyes shut tight, tears caught in his lashes.

A woman in a fur coat stopped in front of him. Colored feathers stuck out of her hat. "What is it?" she said to Teresa. "What are you doing to him?"

"You mind your own business, you." Teresa waved her away. "He's my son. I'll do whatever I want with him." Teresa pulled Nicky upright and stuck her hand out, pushing Nicky into the cab that pulled up at the curb of Sixty-fourth and Fifth. She got in after him. "Worry about yourself," she told the woman in the fur coat through the window. Teresa muttered to herself as the cab pulled away. She pushed her handkerchief in Nicky's face. "Here," she said. "Blow your nose."

All the way downtown, Teresa held her breath. She held it until she saw the bell tower of St. Anthony of Padua church and knew Spring Street was only two blocks away.

Dante helped Teresa get him upstairs, and when Nicky was in his chair at the kitchen table, she took off her hat and filled the coffeepot. She asked Dante to sit down but he said it was too nice a day to be inside, which made Nicky cry like before.

"He's fine," Teresa told Dante. "He's just excited." She put a hand on Nicky's forehead to check for fever and Dante gave him a piece of gum. When Dante left, she shut the door and pulled the chain. She boiled the milk for the coffee. Nicky made a face when the skin of the milk went into his cup.

"What?" she said.

"I hate the *scuma*."

"You don't know what's good for you," she told him, and took the cup for herself.

"The *scuma*'s good for me?"

"Of course. It's got all the vitamins."

"You always say that. You say everything bad is good. You say the apple core's the best part."

"That's right. It is. What do you know?"

"How could it be the best part? How? How?"

"You're just spoiled," she said. "When I was your age, I ate everything and I said thank you. I never talked back." She poured coffee into his milk and stirred in three spoonfuls of sugar. She gave him a plate of anisette biscuits and ran a hand through his hair. She kissed the streaks of dirt the tears had made on his face and then she sat down with a pencil and paper and wrote numbers in columns.

"Whatcha doing?" Nicky wanted to know.

"Nothing. Dunk your biscotti."

"Can I go down?" he said. "The doctor said I could. He said I should go to school."

"He's up Fifth Avenue. What does he know about here? You stay in the house. When you walk, you can go all over. I don't care where you go. Now be quiet. I got things to figure out."

"Am I getting the operation?"

"The doctor said you needed the operation?"

"Yeah, but . . ."

"Just eat your biscotti. Leave everything else to me. I'm your mother, no?"

$\mathbf{T}$eresa left early the next morning. She was wearing the black straw hat with the painted wooden cherries and her corset. Before she left, she stood by the side of the bed where Nicky slept and she pushed back his hair and made the sign of the cross on his forehead with her thumb. He pretended to be asleep, and lay still until he heard the door shut and her footsteps on the stairs. He said three Hail Marys to measure time before he pulled himself over to the front window and watched his mother turn the corner up Sullivan. Then he made his way to the back to call Salvatore.

Salvatore's bedroom window was open. Nicky could see him in front of the mirror over his dresser knotting the blue tie he wore to school. His hair was wet and slicked back. Magdalena was shouting for him to hurry. Her voice carried across the alley.

Nicky cupped his hands around his mouth and yelled Salvatore's name over the din of voices and sounds from the open windows. Salvatore turned when he heard him and waved.

"Come over," Nicky said.

Salvatore leaned out the window and looked up. "I'm late, Nicky. What is it?"

"I said, come over. Don't go to school. My mother's gone. See if you can find Jumbo."

"Jumbo? That's easy. He's in Sam and Al's stealing candy. He's in there every morning, pays for three Hersheys and takes six."

"So get him and come over."

"I don't know, Nicky. I got caught cutting school last week."

"C'mon, Sally. I can't take it in here much longer. Besides, the old lady's gone for the whole day."

"How do you know that?"

"She told me she was going uptown, to see that doctor about my legs."

Magdalena shouted, louder than before. "I gotta go," Salvatore said. "Before she gets serious."

"You coming over?"

"Okay, okay."

Nicky went to the front window to wait. He pulled the shade up as high as it would go. He put a pillow under his elbows and leaned far over the windowsill and looked out on to the street. He didn't care who saw him with his tongue hanging out.

On the corner of Prince and Sullivan, Salvatore caught up with Jumbo and his five sisters. Before they turned down the street toward the subway, Jumbo's sisters petted and kissed him goodbye until he cried. When they left, Salvatore had to give him a handkerchief to wipe off all the lipstick. "Christ, Jumbo, I'd whack them if I was you." Jumbo didn't answer. He took the wrapper off a Mounds bar. "I thought you ate Hersheys in the morning."

Jumbo shrugged. "I mix it up."

"We're cutting school," Salvatore said. "We're going over Nicky's."

Jumbo nodded. His mouth was full of coconut. He was looking over Salvatore's shoulder. "Oh, shit," he said. "Fat Augustina . . ."

Salvatore turned and saw the seventh-grade nun coming down Sullivan Street. Her arms were folded across her chest, her hands hidden in the sleeves of her habit. A silver crucifix swung at the end of the oversized black rosary she wore wrapped around her waist.

Sister Augustina was built like the truck that delivered coal, and they called her Il Duce behind her back. Jumbo said she was bald underneath the veil and Nicky had drawn cartoons of her naked on the wall in the boys' bathroom.

She had always been a "boys' nun," and after Father Tom mixed the classes, she was never really happy again. She sat the boys and the girls on opposite sides of the room in an effort to recapture the past. Some years she put the boys in front and the girls in back. The girls annoyed her. They made her wince. They fawned and whined and went home to cry to their mothers.

Salvatore pulled Jumbo into LaCapria's building and they ditched their books under the stairs and doubled back through the alleys and up the fire escape ladder of Nicky's building. Jumbo stopped in front of Vicky Palermo's window on the second floor to catch his breath. She had nailed it shut after Nicky's fall. She said she didn't want any more surprises.

Jumbo was breathing hard. He grabbed Salvatore's arm and held him back. "Did she see us?" Jumbo said. A drop of sweat hung at the end of his nose, another at his chin.

"No point worrying about it now," Salvatore told him. He kept climbing. He was on the third-floor fire escape when Jumbo yelled for him to wait. Windows opened around the alley. Gracie Petrussi was hanging sheets. Jumbo flattened himself against Vicky Palermo's window. He jammed his fingers into a pocket and felt for his last Hershey bar. By the curve of it, he knew it had almonds.

"C'mon," Salvatore called down. "What are you waiting for?"

"Shh, Gracie Petrussi . . . She'll see us. She'll tell my mother." Jumbo slid down along the window and sat on the ledge. He unwrapped the Hershey bar and bit into it, sucked the chocolate around the almonds until they were dry and chalky in his mouth. He decided to stay where he was. He was afraid of heights. He had been ever since Nicky fell. "Good thing it wasn't you," his mother told him later. "Your size, you would have gone through the earth. We would have found you in China."

Salvatore had to come all the way back down to get Jumbo and stand right behind him on the way up, so close that Jumbo could lean back and feel Salvatore's body against his own, like a wall.

Salvatore pushed Jumbo in through Nicky's window. Jumbo scraped his knee and left chocolate handprints on the curtains where he had grabbed at them. "You sure your mother's gone for the whole day?" he asked Nicky, spitting on his fingers and rubbing the blood off his knee. Jumbo was afraid of Nicky's mother.

"She'll overlook you in a minute, say something, do something to bring you harm. She's out to get you," Jumbo's mother would tell him. His five sisters would nod in agreement. Only this morning, while Jumbo's mother was tying a white silk scarf around his neck to protect him from drafts, she had stabbed a finger at the floor. "That *strega* on the fifth floor, she's jealous of you, your big strong legs. She blames you for what happened to her fatherless son."

"He's got a father," Jumbo said.

"Where? Who says? Who sees him?" Antoinette said.

"He told me."

"Never mind. You just stay away. They go right. You go left."

Jumbo's five sisters bowed their heads. They worried about their baby brother. He was like their own child. They would give him nickels and licorice whips. They would hide jelly-filled candies and cherries wrapped in red foil in their clothes. Jumbo would press his body against theirs, each sister in turn, and search for the candy. He would dig his fingers into their sides and under their breasts. He tickled them until they screamed. "Oh, baby," they would say and kiss the top of his head.

Jumbo stood inside the window, afraid to sit. "Relax," Nicky said. "She's gone."

"Where?"

"Uptown, to see that fancy doctor on Fifth Avenue that's going to make me walk, the one Salvatore's father knows."

"You sure that's gonna take all day?"

"You kidding? You know how *far* uptown is? I been there. It's a long ways away from here, lemme tell you." Nicky frowned. "Why're you so nervous?"

"I don't know. She don't like me, your mother. She never liked me."

"Forget this bullshit," Salvatore said. He took out a collection of cigarette butts and lined them up on the coffee table. Some of them were two inches long. He sent Jumbo into the kitchen to get matches. Jumbo came back with a dish of eggplant.

"Whatta you got?"

"It was on the table, Nicky."

"My mother must have left it for lunch."

"Can I have it?"

"Now, Jumbo? It's for lunch," Salvatore said. He picked a cigarette butt off the table and sat back on the couch. He put his feet up.

"So, I'm hungry now. That's a crime? Jeez, Sally."

"Eat it, Jumbo," Nicky said. "Take whatever you want. If it's gone, my mother'll be happy." He leaned over the coffee table, took one of the longer cigarette butts and put it in his mouth.

"Where's the matches?"

Salvatore looked at Jumbo. "The matches, you went in the kitchen for matches, you came back with eggplant. You got us sitting here like dopes."

"Big deal," Jumbo said. His mouth was full. "Whatta you want? Can't you see I'm eating?"

Salvatore stood up. "I'll get them," he said.

"There's wine in the kitchen," Nicky called after him, "in the corner under the sink, you want to get it."

Salvatore came back from the kitchen with a bottle and three glasses. "The hell with the wine," he said. "Look what I found." He held up a bottle of grappa, labeled with adhesive tape marked with the date it was made. He took the matches out of his pocket and lit his cigarette and Nicky's. He inhaled, blew out a stream of smoke, and then three perfect smoke rings. He filled their glasses, and proposed a toast to Sister Augustina. They gave the fascist salute and fell back on the couch.

They were very glad that Nicky's mother had gone uptown, that Nicky had no brothers or sisters, that they were alone in the apartment. "You're the luckiest guy in the world," Jumbo told Nicky. "You don't go to school, you got no brothers or sisters busting your balls. Just you and your mother . . . imagine if she went to work. We'd have the whole place to ourselves all the time. We could get some girls to come over." Jumbo hoisted up his pants. "Rosanna Montenegro . . ." He moved his tongue over his lips.

Rosanna Montenegro had come from Italy and was put three grades back because she couldn't speak English. She was a big girl, she had tits, and Salvatore swore he had seen a stain on her uniform skirt one morning when they were pledging allegiance to the flag. Sister Augustina had sent her home right after prayers.

"Rosanna Montenegro?" Salvatore said. "What would you do with Rosanna Montenegro? Eat her lunch?"

"You're right," Jumbo said. "What would I want with Rosanna Montenegro? Your sister's easier."

"I don't have a sister."

"If you did, she'd be a mattress."

"Well, I wouldn't want your fat-ass sisters if they were all laying here naked with bows on."

"How about Marielena?" Nicky said.

"Marielena? She's flat like an ironing board."

"She smells."

"Her socks are dirty."

"Maureen?" Nicky said.

"The Irish one?"

"All Maureens are Irish, stupid."

"What's so great about Maureen?"

Nicky leaned back and closed his eyes. He conjured up Maureen. "She's got blue eyes and . . ."

Salvatore put his hand around his throat and pretended to choke himself. "Give me a break," he said. "She's got all those disgusting freckles."

"Yeah," Jumbo said. "They look like dirt."

Nicky sat up. "Well, anyway, you can forget it. My mother's not getting no job. Why would she? My father takes care of everything. He sends us money all the time. He's always sending presents." Nicky pointed to the dolls on the shelf above their heads. "Look at that," he said. "The house is full of stuff he sends."

"Yeah, your old man's great, Nicky," Salvatore said, "but listen . . ." He refilled their glasses. "I figured out how to get you a crutch."

"Where? How? Not a bum. Not from some Bowery bum."

"Naw, there's this old guy on Sullivan Street, Orlando. I deliver his groceries from the store. The thing is, I wanted to find you two crutches, but Orlando's only got one."

"Didn't he get two?"

"Yeah, but he lost one. That's my point. If this one disappears, he'll think he lost it."

"One crutch?"

"He gets around good with it. If he can, you can."

"I never seen him."

"No one sees him. He don't go out."

"How come?"

"He don't want nobody to call him a cripple."

"That makes sense. I can understand that," Jumbo said.

"You and my mother," Nicky said. "So how you gonna get it?"

"When he's watching television."

"He's got a television?" Jumbo said.

"Yeah, my father got it for him since he's stuck in the house all the time."

"Christ, I wish I had a television."

"Shut up, Jumbo. This is important," Nicky said, turning to Salvatore. "So how you gonna get the crutch?"

"Easy. Orlando's in love with Milton Berle. You know how he dresses up on the show like a woman"

"Yeah?"

"Well, when Uncle Miltie's in drag, Orlando thinks it's really a woman, just his kind of woman, I guess, because he goes nuts. He starts throwing kisses, loud smacks you can hear all the way in the kitchen. His eyes water. He hates when Milton Berle comes back on as a man. Then he starts cursing at the television. He gets so excited and mad that he don't even hear me when I leave. He don't even know I'm gone."

"So what about the crutch?"

"He lays it on the floor by his chair. I'll just slide it out while he's smooching with Uncle Miltie."

"You think he's a homo?" Jumbo said. He had found biscotti in the kitchen and was dunking them in his grappa.

"Who? Milton Berle?"

"No, this old guy, Orlando. You should tell your father. He should know."

"Jumbo, you are a real *mamaluke*. It's a good thing you eat all the time 'cause the things that come out of your mouth . . ." Salvatore flipped his cigarette butt out the back window and lit another.

"What if you get caught?" Nicky said. "Won't he know it's you?"

"Nah, he's half gone. I'm telling you. He combs his mop. He gives it haircuts."

"Was he a barber?"

Salvatore shook his head. "He just likes things neat."

"When can you get it?"

"This afternoon, tomorrow, first chance I get."

"Where will I keep it?"

"In Jumbo's house."

"Why my house?"

"Your house's such a mess, nobody will know it's there."

"Hey . . ."

"Take it easy, Jumbo. It's no reflection on you. All of you stuffed in those three rooms. Your mother alone could fill it up. You're a big family."

"In more ways than one . . ." Nicky started to giggle. "I'm sorry . . ." he said.

Salvatore was laughing now too. So was Jumbo. The bottle of grappa was almost empty. They couldn't stop laughing. Salvatore poured the last of it into his glass and tipped the bottle over on the floor. "One dead soldier," he said. The three of them screamed. Jumbo fell off the couch and rolled under the table. And then they heard Matty J.

Matty J had opened the window in his mother's bedroom. His mother had made the front room her bedroom, the room that looked out over Spring Street. Matty J had opened the window without the fire escape as far as it could go and he was straddling the window ledge, one leg dangling over the head of the gargoyle that decorated the line of windows along the top floor.

"I'm going to jump," he shouted until every window on both sides of the street opened. People pushed each other to see, they leaned out their windows to watch. Matty J shouted until the people who lived in the back ran outside or into the front apartments without knocking to see what was going on. A crowd gathered in the street and stood there looking up.

No one on Spring Street had ever jumped out a window. Cesare Garibaldi's wife had fallen out shaking her dust mop, and a super had gone down hooking up a new clothesline. Charlie Esposito threatened to jump when his wife died, but that had just been talk.

Salvatore and Jumbo ran to the front window, dragging Nicky along between them. They had the best seats in the house. Matty J was out the window on the fifth floor of the building directly across from them. Matty J's mother screamed as loudly as Matty J.

Matty J's father pulled on his arm. Matty J pulled back and tilted farther out the window and his shoe fell off and hit Margie from the second floor on her forehead as she was looking up. The shoe was a loafer, soft as butter. Only this morning, his mother had shined it with a soft cloth. Matty J was shaking his fist at the sky and cursing God.

"He lost at the track," Luisa Carelli told Annamaria Petrino. They were standing downstairs looking up. "Last week it was a card game." She blew her nose and put the handkerchief in the front pocket of her apron.

Annamaria Petrino made a face. "His wife spoils him," she said. "He's getting worse. He never tried to jump before. Sometimes he bangs his head against the door downstairs but he never tried to jump."

"He always goes up the roof when he loses."

"Yeah, but only to be nearer to God, to curse Him from a closer distance."

Inside, the boys elbowed each other out of the window. "Matty J's crazy," Salvatore said.

"Crazy like a fox," Jumbo answered. "He's forty-five years old and he's never had a job. That's my kind of crazy."

"Here come the cops," Nicky said. "What are they gonna do?"

"Talk him in," Salvatore said.

"I didn't know cops did things like that."

"Yeah, they're regular good Samaritans when they're not breaking heads."

"Shh," Nicky said. "I want to hear what's going on."

Nicky listened to the policemen cajole Matty J. There were two of them. They were tall and blond. He imagined their nameplates said Donovan and Murphy. They talked to Matty J until he stopped screaming and then they took his arm and pulled him inside.

Matty J's mother was kissing the policeman's hand, the one that held Matty J's arm. "You saved my son," she said. "You brought him back from the edge of hell, the jaws of death." She covered the policeman's hands with her own. Her husband wiped the tears from her eyes with his handkerchief.

"We have to take him to Bellevue," the cop said, "for observation."

Matty J's mother was a small woman. She looked up at the big, blond policeman. "You crazy?" she screamed, and she bit him. She dug her teeth into the hand she had been caressing. Her husband held her shoulders. The policeman was shouting. His partner was pulling him out the door. Matty J's mother followed them down the stairs and into the street. "You leave my son where he is. You don't touch my son. Murderers. Killers." The policemen worked their way through the crowd and got into their car. Everyone watched them drive away. "The nerve . . ." Matty J's mother said when the police car turned the corner. Everyone surrounded her in sympathy.

Margie from the second floor gave her Matty J's shoe. An hour later, Matty J was outside the building with the racing form. He was clean-shaven, his loafers polished to a dull sheen.

The three boys hung out the window until the street was back to normal. Salvatore looked at Nicky and Jumbo. "You know what those cops are saying?"

"Dumb guineas," Jumbo said.

"Crazy wops," Nicky answered.

"Sick dagos."

"Dopey greasers."

They hit and pushed each other. They laughed when Nicky fell over. "I'm going to be a cop," Nicky told them. Jumbo choked. Salvatore bent double. The door grated against the chain.

"Shit shit shit," Jumbo said. "It's your mother." He crossed himself. Salvatore was out the back window. Jumbo caught his foot between the radiator and the wall. "Help me, help me."

Salvatore turned back to pull at Jumbo's leg. "We can't leave Nicky like this," he said to him. "Get back in."

"No, No. I can't. The *malocchio*. She'll get me. She hates me." He looked over his shoulder, yanked at his foot. "You know that, Nicky. Your mother hates me, the truth. She wishes me dead." His foot pulled free.

"Nicky's mother doesn't make the *malocchio*. What's the matter with you?" Salvatore said.

"She'll get the woman on Bedford Street. They're in cahoots. She comes here all the time. My mother sees her. You don't know. You don't live in this building. You don't see what goes on."

"For chrissakes, Jumbo."

"No, go ahead," Nicky said. "I'll be okay."

"You sure?" Salvatore said.

"Yeah, go on. I mean it." The last thing Nicky saw was the crack of Jumbo's ass where his shirt had worked its way out of his pants.

Nicky's mother banged on the door. "Nicola . . . you in there?" Nicky pulled himself over and took the chain off the door. "Why you don't answer?" she said. "Why you got the chain on?" He didn't say anything and she shut the door behind her. She closed the front window and pulled down the shade.

"Mama," Nicky said. "You missed it. Matty J tried to jump out the window. The cops saved him."

Teresa took off her hat and sat down on the couch. She made a face when she saw the cigarettes and the glasses. She kicked the empty bottle that rolled near her foot. She went over to Nicky and pulled him up by the ear. "All alike," she said, "all of you." She pushed him back onto the chair and he started to cry.

The dolls sat above her head, the fading sunlight caught on the garish colors of their dresses. She sat somber and black beneath them. She followed Nicky's eyes and looked up at the dolls as if she were seeing them for the first time.

"The doctor, Mama. What did the doctor say?"

"In a month."

"I'll walk, Mama. He said that?"

"He'll do the operation. He'll do his best. That's what he said." She took off her good shoes and rolled her stockings to under the knee. She went into the bedroom to change her clothes, and when she came out, in her arms were the squares of silk and the sequined slippers and the envelopes with stamps from all over the world. She took the dolls off the shelf and put them in a paper bag.

"What are you doing?" Nicky asked her.

"I'm going out," she said. "You lock the door. Go to bed." She carried everything down the stairs and walked east on Spring Street, beyond West Broadway, through the darkened streets of rag factories and paper warehouses, and as she went she dumped her treasures bit by bit into the giant bins by the loading platforms where the bums slept in cardboard boxes. It was very late when Nicky felt the weight of her in the bed beside him.

That morning Teresa had left the house wearing her corset and the black straw hat with the wooden cherries; she didn't go to see the doctor on Fifth Avenue. Where she went was to the Merchant Seamen's Union Hall to find Nicky's father, to find out why the money had stopped, to tell him about his son, about the operation and the fancy doctor, and to ask him to come home and do something to make Nicky walk.

Teresa had never tried to reach him before, there had never been a reason, but now Nicky needed him. After the doctor, whom she doubted, all she had left was the Madonna. She couldn't put all her hopes on heaven. Not even the Mother of God was completely dependable. Sometimes a boy needed his father.

There was no guarantee her prayers would be answered. This she knew. God always answered, the priest would say when the women cried, but sometimes the answer was no.

At the union hall she gave the name to the man at the counter and waited while he looked in the file cabinets lined up along the wall behind him. "Sabatini . . . Sabatini . . . Angelo . . . Angelo Sabatini . . ." He pulled the card and came back to the counter. "His last ship docked two months ago."

"Impossible," Teresa said. She stood taller and straighter than before and shook her head until the wooden cherries rattled against the brim of the black straw hat and she felt foolish.

"What can I tell you, lady? It says so right here."

"But I just got this," she said, and handed him the last envelope she had received. It was postmarked the Maldive Islands.

He turned it over a few times and gave it back to her. "This is fine, lady, but I'm telling you, Angelo Sabatini ain't at sea. He's in the Bronx. Leastwise, that's where the union's sending his disability checks."

Nicky's mother looked down at her envelope. The stamps were particularly large and beautiful. They showed bright blue fish flying out of the foam at the tip of an ocean wave. "What's the date on the postmark?" the man behind the counter asked, leaning over. "When did you get that letter? Sometimes . . ."

"It doesn't matter," she said. She put the envelope face down on the counter between them. "If he's not at sea, he's not at sea. If he's in the Bronx, he's in the Bronx."

"That's not what I said."

"Yes, you said that."

"I said his checks are going to the Bronx."

Nicky's mother didn't move. She stood there, staring, her hands folded on the counter like a schoolteacher waiting for her class to quiet.

"Listen. How about I give you the address?"

"Where he's living in the Bronx?"

"I don't know where he's living. All I know is where the checks are going. It says here on the card that the checks are going to the Bronx. Look, it's right on the card." He held it out to her but she stared straight ahead. "I'll write it down for you," he told her, and wrote the address on the back of the envelope from the Maldive Islands and pushed it across the counter to her. "Go see for yourself. What do I know? I just pull the files."

"Thank you," she said.

"Who are you?" he asked her.

"His wife."

The man looked down at the card in his hand. "Cynthia, right?" He smiled at her. He had a front tooth outlined in gold. "The union knows everything," he said.

Teresa smiled back at him. Behind the smile her teeth bit into her bottom lip. Cynthia . . . Teresa thought. What kind of a name was that? Angelo was with a woman named Cynthia, his wife, the card said. Teresa closed her hand around the envelope until the edges of it cut into her skin. Her betrayal was complete. There was a sudden bad taste in her mouth. "Thank you," she said again. She turned and left the building.

She went down the nearest subway and studied the map. She asked the man in the change booth how to get to the Bronx and he told her the Bronx was a big place.

She showed him the address and he told her to go to Houston Street and take the Third Avenue El. She thanked him and felt lucky.

It was a long ride. "Liar, cheat, thief," she mumbled to herself, but when the sun cut through the grime on the windows, she forgot about her son's father. She looked out the window and imagined that she was going away somewhere, somewhere nice. She expected that the train would pass out of this city and into the country and she thought that she might open the window and smell the fresh air.

There was an old woman sitting next to her who asked where she was going, and Teresa showed her the envelope with the address on it. "Get off at Fordham Road," she said, and asked Teresa for the stamps. Without hesitating, Teresa tore them off the envelope and gave them to her. Without the stamps, the envelope looked ugly and unimportant.

The train came into Fordham Road and Teresa got off and waited on the wooden platform until it pulled away. The old woman waved through the window, the stamps in her hand, and Teresa waved back. She looked down at the remnant of the envelope she held. It was nothing, she thought, dirty paper, and after she had studied the address written on the back of it until she could close her eyes and still see it, she tore the envelope into small pieces and threw them into one of the square metal garbage containers that hung under the gum dispensers.

Down all the steps to the street, she thought about finding Nicky's father. She slowed her pace. She thought about going back up the stairs on the other side and taking the train down to Spring Street and forgetting about him but then she was in the street and her mind cleared. She had been taking care of herself and Nicky for a long time. When she found the dirty rotten sonofabitch . . . She closed her eyes then cast them up to heaven and asked the Madonna that he die spitting blood. She imagined him, his face no longer handsome, red spittle dried on his lips, and she felt better. She would know what to do when she found him. She trusted herself.

This neighborhood was similar to her own, she noticed. There were faces like her own; she knew the language and the sounds on the street. It was no Park Avenue. She walked slowly, watching for the numbers on the buildings.

Outside a doorway, where a group of men sat on kitchen chairs, she stopped. They were talking, smoking, watching the street. One man ground out his cigar. It was an Italian stogie, a guinea stinker. She could smell it from where she stood. She watched him pull off the burnt end with his fingers and chew the stub.

"*Signori*," she said, standing at a respectful distance. The man chewing the cigar stub raised his hat to her.

"I'm looking," she said, "for Angelo Sabatini."

"Sabatini? Angelo?" The man scratched his head before he replaced his hat. "You mean Angie Kiwi? . . . The sailor?" Nicky's mother clenched her hands into fists, her nails dug into her palms.

"Maybe," she said. "He's a merchant seaman?"

"Yeah, Angie Kiwi . . . I don't know why they call him that. Who remembers these things?"

"There's a bar he hung out in," another man said. He was leaning against the building, his legs crossed at the ankles. "A sailor's joint, the Kiwi. Maybe that's how he got the name."

"Funny name."

"Yeah, must come from someplace them sailors go. They go some crazy places . . ."

Nicky's mother shifted her weight. Her feet hurt. "He's lived here long?" she said, her voice low, friendly.

"Long enough, yeah. He married a girl from around here. Ain't that right, Vinny?"

"Yeah, he's married to Damiano's daughter Cynthia."

"Damiano the undertaker?"

"Yeah."

"Where'd she get that name? I never heard nobody with that name."

"It's Celestina, but you know. They all want to be up-to-date today so she calls herself Cynthia."

"What a name . . . Cynthia." The old man with the cigar butt sighed and spat out some black juice and coughed. He turned to the man sitting next to him, who was dozing in the sun. "Ain't that right?" he said, nudging him with his elbow. "Angie Kiwi's married to Celestina Damiano? The one with the big earrings?"

His friend opened his eyes, brushed aside a fly that had landed on the top of his very large ear. "Yeah, yeah," he said. "They live over there"—and he pointed across the street—"on the top floor. Celestina, she's always complaining about the stairs."

"Her name's Cynthia," the man leaning against the building said.

"Well, I call her Celestina. I ain't up-to-date like some people."

"You can call her what you want, but Angie Kiwi's not there." This from a fourth man, young and handsome. He looked at Teresa, his eyes careful. It was what he did with women.

"Well, that figures. Sailors are never home. My mother always said they made good husbands. 'And if you're lucky,' she used to say, 'they die young and leave a pension.'"

"What does your mother know? Your father drove an elevator."

"That don't mean she didn't have dreams."

"Angie Kiwi's in the hospital," the young man said. He lit a cigarette that he took from a silver case.

"No . . . what are you telling me?" the old man chewing the cigar said.

"It's his ticker. They brought him in a few days ago."

"How do you like that? Guy survives all them years going all over the place, makes it through the war, finally gets home, and bang, his ticker goes."

"Ain't that always the way?"

"But it got him off the ships."

"Nah, that was a fugazy. Celestina's brother made a connection in the union. Angie Kiwi put in a disability claim, said he hurt his back, and the brother pushed it through. They can't prove nothing about your back. It's the best way to go. Worst thing, you carry a cane a few years till they settle. My brother-in-law got ten gees, moved to Florida."

"You're right, I remember. Angie Kiwi told my brother Charlie he had to stay flat on his back all the way from Singapore to make the story stick. Told him it almost wasn't worth it, missing all them slanty-eyes on the way home. Said when them girls heard Angie Kiwi wasn't coming back, they cried for days."

"He's full of shit," the young man said.

The man standing against the building laughed. The old man chewing the cigar stub spat out tobacco juice. The young man checked his shoes.

The old one swatting flies raised his hand. "Shut up," he said. "The lady, she don't want to hear you." He tipped back his chair and tipped his hat to Nicky's mother. "*Scusate, signora . . .*" he said, extending his hand.

"*Niente,*" Teresa said. She smiled a little bit. She had wanted them to forget she was there. She felt the young man's eyes on her and she swayed slightly, rocking back and forth on the heels of her shoes. She wasn't used to going long distances in shoes with such high heels, such delicate soles, but her feet had stopped hurting. She couldn't feel anything but the flush of triumph and revenge.

Angelo Sabatini, her husband, who had another wife, another name . . . Angie Kiwi, they called him up here, who made girls from halfway around the world cry, was lying in the hospital with a bad heart. She said a sudden prayer to the Virgin that he should not get off so easily. Not a heart attack, she begged. He should die in agony, but, she added, not before she found him, not before she told him the way things were.

The men had forgotten her again. She waited and listened, but they were discussing a bocce game now, and someone named Gianni Michalini's accident. She stepped forward. "Poor Angelo," she said softly. "Do you know where he is? What hospital?"

They all looked up, as though surprised to see her still standing there, and the handsome young man shrugged his shoulders and pulled on the sleeves of his jacket so that they fell just right over his shirt cuffs. "Where could he be?" he said. "The hospital we all go to."

The cigar chewer pointed up the street. It's not far," he said. "Keep walking straight. You can't miss it."

The old man chewing the cigar stub laughed out loud. He was missing teeth. Nicky's mother could see this when he laughed. "He's a good guy, that Kiwi. If you see him, tell him Frankie Moe sends his regards."

"Life is funny," one of the men said. "You never know what's coming next."

"Celestina must wear Angie out every time he comes home. This time his ticker couldn't take it." The man on the bench bit into his apple.

"Yeah, maybe Celestina's got something those slanty-eyed girls don't."

"Hey, you forgetting about this lady?" The fly swatter turned his head.

But Teresa was gone. She had left and no one had seen her go, not even the handsome young man who had watched her so carefully from the start.

Teresa found the hospital easily enough. It was a great cavernous building that took up a city block. When she got inside, she felt dizzy and out of breath. She could hear her heart beating. She sat down on a bench against the wall and waited for the feeling to pass.

She spoke to no one but sat with her eyes straight ahead. She thought about Nicky alone in the apartment but it was still early in the day, she reminded herself, and she relaxed, unlacing her fingers, which she held tightly together in her lap. She had left Nicky lunch, and Dante was downstairs, standing watch outside the building. It was a beautiful day.

At the main desk she got the room number of Angelo Sabatini with no trouble at all. He was in the men's ward, they told her, on the second floor. The halls of the second floor were crowded with men in chairs, in pieces, suspended on metal racks. The smell of illness, the smell of them, made her hold her breath, but then she was in front of his room. She stopped and made herself small outside the door. She didn't see him at first. There were two rows of iron beds and she looked carefully from one bed to the other at the faces of the men. She was straining to see clearly and still stay hidden.

She saw him finally in the last bed, by the window. Even here, she thought, he managed to find a way. Thirty men and Angelo Sabatini gets the window, the light, the air, the view. She stepped inside. The room went silent for an instant while the men closest to the door looked her over. There was a card game going on near the center of the room, wheelchairs pushed together. The men raised their heads.

She walked softly toward Angelo's bed at the end of the row, the last bed, the one by the window. She smiled at the men who stopped what they were doing to look at her, count her steps, realize she was not there for them.

Angelo was asleep. She stood there at the side of his bed. His hair was as black as she remembered. His beard made a shadow along the hollows of his cheeks. He looked the same to her except he was thinner. She could see that now, standing over him. He was still handsome, more handsome a man than she would be expected to have. She knew that. She had heard the whispers.

For that moment, she forgot what he had done, forgot her curses, her son at home with no father and legs that didn't work. She conjured up the color of his eyes behind the closed lids. Nicky had those blue eyes. Everyone had said they would change. "All babies have blue eyes when they're born," Jumbo's mother had insisted down at the stoop, rubbing her belly, amazing them all with its size such a short time into her pregnancy. But Nicky's eyes hadn't changed, except to get more blue. Jumbo's mother would never join in when the other women went on about them. Teresa would nod at the compliments and cross her fingers behind her back. It never hurt to be too careful.

Teresa reached out her hand and shook her husband's arm. He turned his face away from her in his sleep. This made her angry and she dug her fingers into the soft space between his neck and his shoulder. The cotton of his pajamas was smooth and finely woven. They were his own. Cynthia must have brought them, Teresa thought, washed them, pressed them in her Bronx apartment, standing near the open window to catch the breeze.

"Angelo," Teresa hissed, and his eyes opened. He stared at her, blinked, wrinkled his forehead. His reaction startled her. Had she gotten so old, so ugly? "You bastard," she said to him. "You don't know who I am?"

He looked at her. He sat up in the bed. His eyes were wide. His mouth opened but he didn't speak. Then the surprise passed and he smiled at her. "Teresa . . ." he said. "*Madonna!* I must be dreaming. Am I in heaven?" He held out his arms. "Come here, let me kiss you. You're so beautiful. I don't believe you're really here." When she stood still, he put down his arms. "How are you?" he said. "Me, I'm sick. I'm not myself. I'm good for nothing. Look at me. Remember how strong I used to be? Forget me. Come here . . . Let me look at you. You look wonderful . . . Teresa . . ."

She smacked him hard across the face. He started to say something but she smacked him again, this time with the back of her hand. Her pocketbook flew off her arm, everything inside spilling into the aisle between the beds. Two young boys came from nowhere and scrambled to collect the change and the pocket mirror. They ran off with them into the hall.

No one moved but heads turned. She hit him again on the side of the head and then once more. She scraped his face with her fingernails. "Dog," she said. "Son of a pig." She put her face close to his. "Your mother pushed you out from her ass," she whispered. "That whore you're with should get cancer. She should die without her tongue."

"Teresa . . ." he said. He was crying. He took her hand and kissed her fingers. His blood was caught under her nails. He looked in her face for some sign of forgiveness.

"I wish you dead, Angelo, crippled in the street, claws for hands, broken under a train."

"Ah, Teresa . . ." he said again, fighting for his breath. "What are you talking about? Listen to me for a minute."

"It's not true? You're gonna tell me it's not true what I know? Just because you fooled me all these years, Angelo, don't think I'm stupid."

"Okay, okay." Sobs caught in his throat. "But the truth, Teresa, did I take care of you? The money . . . did you get the money every month? No matter where I was? No matter what? I sent you things. I always sent you presents."

"You left Nicky and me alone on Spring Street, just me and Nicky, and you never came."

"I did come."

"Once . . . you came once in all those years. Who remembers once? 'She has no husband,' they say. 'Nicky has no father. *Il figlio di nessuno.*' They forget you exist, you come once in all those years. They forget and they whisper that Nicky's a bastard. They say things about me behind my back. 'Where is he?' they say . . . 'this

Angelo Sabatini?'" She pulled her hand away. It was wet from his lips and his tears and she wiped it on his bedsheet in disgust.

"Things happen," he told her. "I don't know why. Look at me. God paid me back. I'm finished. My ticker's bad . . ." And he started to cry again.

"Who cares about you, Angelo? Nicky and I manage good enough, but you stopped the money. That whore you live with is getting it, no? From my son's mouth to her pocket."

"Please, Teresa, she's a good woman. You two would get along, believe me. You'd like her."

Nicky's mother spat in his face. He closed his eyes. "And you married her, didn't you, Angelo? You stupid. You know you go to jail for that in this country?"

"If you'd listen, Teresa . . ."

"I'm not listening to nothing. You listen. I'm going to your house in the Bronx, to your wife in the Bronx. I'm gonna take Nicky with me. I'm gonna tell her some things. And then I'm gonna pull out every hair on her head."

"I don't know, Teresa. You were so sweet, such a sweet girl. What happened to you? Remember how you used to sing for me, and I would . . ."

"Shut up," she said, "before I kill you. If I had a father . . . brothers . . . anybody . . ."

"Okay, okay. What do you want? What am I supposed to do? You want to kill me? Go ahead. I'm half-dead as it is. Tell me. Anything. I'll make it up to you. But Teresa, the truth. Did you and Nicky want for anything? Who on Spring Street's got better than you?"

"Nicky can't walk," she told him.

"What? What happened?"

"He had an accident."

"Oh God. How? What?"

"I need money . . . for an operation to make him walk."

"Look at me, Teresa. I got no money. I can't work no more. I'm shot."

"Nicky needs the operation."

"I got no money," he told her. "I'd give it to you in a minute. You know that. For Nicky I'd do anything. He's all I got."

"The disability . . ."

"How much you think that is? What do you think I get? It's nothing."

"Your wife," she said, "the other one. Get the money from her."

"My wife?"

"Yeah, Angelo. Cynthia, Celestina, whatever you call her, the undertaker's daughter. She must have money. Whoever heard of a poor undertaker? Ask *her* for the money for your son."

"Where'd you get all this from?"

"Never mind."

He held his head in his hands. "Go ahead, Teresa," he said. "Choke me. Ruin me. That's why you came, right? I'm not sick enough. I'm not half-dead already. You wanna finish the job."

"I want the money for Nicky's operation," she said.

"At least you have to give me some time. Let me get out of here . . ."

". . . and then you come down to the neighborhood. You spend a few days on Spring Street. You come all dressed up with presents for me and Nicky. You walk all around and you take us to Bleecker Street for ice cream and pastries. You show everybody Nicky's got a father, Teresa Sabatini's got a husband, and then you can go. You can say you're shipping out and you can go for good."

Angelo's tears had dried. He reached for her.

"You want me to come down to Spring Street and stay with you, Teresa? Like the old days? Like we was before? Like nothing's changed? You still look good, Teresa. You look good to me."

Nicky's mother stepped up close to the bed. She leaned over her husband and he lifted his face to her. She caught up the collar of his soft cotton pajamas in both hands. "You never talk to me like that again," she said. "You do like I tell you and then you leave. Everything's changed. Anything I do now, I do for Nicky."

Angelo leaned back into the pillow. She pulled at him, ripped his collar, and when she let go, he fingered the torn cloth. His eyes were wet again. She turned to go. The men in the room looked down suddenly, pretending to see the cards, the letters, the magazines they held in their hands.

"Teresa," Angelo called. His voice was hoarse.

"Don't forget," she said. "I know where to find you."

Teresa took the El back downtown. She was on Spring Street before she knew it. Until she climbed the four flights to the apartment, she didn't realize how much her feet hurt.

The morning after she had thrown away her treasures, Teresa lay in bed until noon. Nicky had been awake for hours but he lay there, waiting for her to move, to say something. He was frightened that she was dead and he was afraid to look at her, to touch her. He cried silently, his hand over his mouth. He was hungry. He had to pee. He was sure she was dead. He was almost hysterical when she turned to him in the bed and touched his face.

"Nicola," she said. "What is it?" He didn't answer and she pulled him against her. She kissed his face and his ears and his fingers. She lifted the covers and kissed his feet.

He giggled when she did this, but then he was angry. "Why did you do that?" he said.

"What?"

"Stay asleep so long. I thought you was dead. I have to pee."

"So why didn't you go pee?"

"I was scared. Why'd you scare me?"

"So what?" she told him. "So I slept a long time, so you thought I was dead. What does it matter? I'm alive now, no? It's a miracle. Why are you crying? You're such a baby. I don't have a son. I have a little girl." She laughed at him, grabbed him between his legs. "Let me see," she teased him. "Are you a little girl?"

He lay in her arms and she stroked his hair. She sang him a Neapolitan song, a song about women. *You're like a cup of coffee,* the lover sings, *bitter until I stir you and the sugar comes to the top.*

"It's going to be okay, Nicola," she told him.

"But you took everything, the stuff my father sent. What'd you do with it?"

"We don't need any of it," she said. "Your father's coming back. He's coming back to see you, from halfway around the world, all the way back to Spring Street."

Nicky sat up and stared at her. She put pillows behind his head, ran her fingers along his arm. "He's going to bring the money for your operation. He's going to buy you toys and ice cream and say hello to all your friends."

"You saw him? He's coming here?"

"He's coming, for sure."

"When?"

"Soon." She took his hands, kissed his open palms, and held them against her face. "I'll make you breakfast," she said, getting up, "coffee and milk, with an egg in it."

"And sugar."

"Spoonfuls of sugar . . . and you can sit by the window on Spring Street and call your friend Salvatore to come over. He's a good boy, that one, just like you."

"And Jumbo . . ."

"No," she said. "He's bad luck, that one. He's no good."

"Mama . . ."

"No," she said, helping him out of the bed. "Don't bother me. I said 'no.' "

Teresa went down that evening to sit on the stoop. Jumbo's mother Antoinette was sitting at the bottom, and when Teresa saw her there, she stopped and sat on the top step next to Magdalena. She told Magdalena that Nicky's father was coming home. There was no keeping him at sea, she said, after he heard about what had happened to his boy.

She said this loudly enough for all the women to hear. They stopped talking and looked up at her. This was news. They could talk about Loretta Pagliani's fallen womb anytime.

The women moved nearer to her, except for Antoinette, who stayed where she was, and even slid a little farther away and looked out into the street.

"When he heard about the accident," Teresa said, "he made plans to come right home."

Antoinette blew her nose into a dirty handkerchief and stuck it in a big black pocketbook that swung from her arm. "Why now?" she said. "What took him so long?"

"What difference does it make?" Vicky Palermo said. "He's coming, isn't he?"

"Well, I'll believe it when I see it."

"It takes a long time to find a man at sea," Teresa said. She kept her gaze level as though no one of importance sat below her. "He's halfway around the world. It takes a long time."

Magdalena put a hand on Teresa's shoulder. "You have a good man," she told her. "He's always taken care of you and Nicky."

Antoinette opened her pocketbook, took out her handkerchief, and blew her nose again. Then she stood up. "I'm going in," she said. "It's getting too windy down here." She pushed past the women. "Excuse me," she said, climbing over them. She stepped on the hem of Teresa's dress.

"Going to clean your house?" Teresa called after her, but Antoinette kept going.

Teresa started talking again about how Nicky's father was coming back and about all the places he would take them and all the presents he would bring. But before anyone could answer, she stood up and said good night.

When the door had shut behind her, Mary Ziganetti shook her head. "This I want to see," she said.

Magdalena turned to her. "If she says he's coming, why shouldn't he come? Why would she lie?"

"Ah, Magdalena," Annamaria Petrino said. "You're still a girl. You don't know anything about life."

"So you say," Magdalena answered. She stood up when she said this. Vicky Palermo laughed and tugged at the hem of her dress to get her to sit down again but Magdalena caught her dress and held it against her legs. She walked down the steps, careful not to step on fingers and toes.

"And you, of all people to stick up for her. There's no love lost between you two, believe me," Mary Ziganetti said to Magdalena's back. "She thought that boy was hers before you came. Who knows what she had in her mind or what went on?"

Magdalena turned and narrowed her eyes at them. She raised her arm and made a screwing motion into the air with her hand before she went on down the street.

"Eh," Annamaria Petrino said. "In Sicily, they don't leave a man and a woman in the same room alone. They're no fools."

"What can you do?" Mary Ziganetti said when Magdalena had gone. "Naive, that's what she is."

"That's not what I hear," Annamaria Petrino whispered.

"You're terrible," Mary Ziganetti said. "Filthy-minded. Now tell me, what do you hear about her?" And Vicky Palermo moved down a step, closer to Mary Ziganetti.

The next morning Teresa went to the phone booth in the luncheonette on Varick Street and called the hospital in the Bronx.

"Deceased," the man at the other end of the line said.

"He's dead?"

"Dead."

"No," Teresa told him. "It can't be. I just saw him. I was talking to him yesterday."

"Well, you ain't gonna talk to him today."

"Check again. Angelo . . . Angelo Sabatini . . . S-A-B-A-T-I-N-I."

"Lady, he's dead . . . this morning . . . heart attack."

"How could you tell me this?"

"Listen, lady, you called me. I didn't call you."

Teresa leaned against the wall of the phone booth. She clenched her teeth. "That sonofabitch," she said. "Now he had to go and die? He couldn't wait a few weeks?" She slammed down the receiver and slid into the seat in the corner of the phone booth. A woman outside knocked on the glass door and pointed to the watch on her arm. Teresa turned her back to her and put another coin in the telephone and called back the hospital.

"Where is he?" she said.

"Who?"

"Angelo Sabatini. Where did they take him?"

"Is that you again, lady?"

"Where did you say he was?"

The man at the other end sighed. "Wait a minute," he said and dropped the phone. The woman outside the phone booth banged on the glass door and made faces. Teresa made an obscene gesture with her free hand. "Body was released to Damiano's Funeral Home," the man at the other end of the line told her.

"Where is it?"

"Damiano's, Burke Avenue in the Bronx. Got it? Satisfied?"

"Thank you," Teresa said. She hung up, put in more money, called the candy store under her house, and asked for Dante. The woman outside the phone booth pushed against the glass door. Teresa held it closed with her foot.

She lifted her face to get the breeze from the little ceiling fan up in the corner of the booth, closed her eyes, and waited for Dante to come to the phone. By the time he got there, she had to put in another nickel to keep the connection, and then she asked him if he would look out for Nicky. She told him to buy a ham-and-cheese sandwich in Virginia's on Sullivan Street and one for himself, and to tell Virginia to put it on her bill, and to tell Nicky not to worry, that she would be home early, before dinner. She had to go uptown to see the doctor again, she told Dante. "You tell that to Nicky," she said.

She opened the door of the phone booth and stepped on the foot of the woman who had banged on the glass. She pushed past the line of people waiting and she ignored the things they said to her. She walked east on Houston Street and rode the El up to Fordham Road. It was familiar now and she stopped the first person she met on the street and asked how to get to Damiano's Funeral Home.

"A few blocks down," he told her, and when she found it, she stood outside across the street and admired the entrance. The name was in stained glass above the double doors: Damiano Funeral Home, it said, established 1895.

Inside the entrance lobby, a man sat behind a desk off to the right, and across from him was a young woman, her eyes red, a handkerchief in her hand. She kept wiping her nose, twisting the handkerchief around in her fingers.

Teresa stepped up to the desk. "Excuse me," she said.

"One moment, *signora,*" the man said.

Teresa turned to the woman. "Sorry," she said to her. "I just want to ask a question." The woman looked up. Confused, Teresa thought, almost terrified.

"Please," the man said. "I'll be with you in a minute. My daughter's just lost her husband. We're . . ."

Teresa couldn't believe her good luck. She felt a sudden affection for the Bronx. "You're Damiano, the undertaker," she said. "Am I right? And you . . ." she said to the woman, "you're Celestina, Angelo Sabatini's wife."

The undertaker stood up and came from around the desk. "How can I help you?" he said. "Who are you?"

"Me? I'm Angelo Sabatini's wife, the real one."

"This is ridiculous," Damiano said. "Get out."

But Teresa stood there, secure in her position, empowered, as confident as the devil. She would congratulate herself later. She took out the piece of paper, folded many times, that she had been carrying with her, her marriage certificate. She handed it to Damiano, and with it a wedding photo. She stood next to Angelo in the photo, in the white wedding gown they had bought in a second-hand store on the Lower East Side for fifteen dollars, Angelo in the black suit that was still hanging in the closet on Spring Street.

Celestina Sabatini stood up. She pulled the picture from her father's hand. The marriage certificate floated to the floor. Her tears had dried. "What is this? Who are you?" she screamed at Teresa.

"I told you. Angelo's real wife." Teresa's tone was even, almost pleasant. "And I'm only sorry he had such an easy death."

Celestina Sabatini put her hands in her hair and pulled. She opened her mouth and wailed. She rocked in her chair until it fell over and she toppled to the floor. Damiano the undertaker, her father, knelt over her, fumbling for the smelling salts he kept in his pocket to revive grieving widows. "Madonna," he cried out to heaven, then, "Celestina . . . Celestina . . . I told you from the beginning that sonofabitch was no good. What'd you ever get from him? He should rot in hell."

Damiano held his daughter's head off the floor and stroked her face. She sobbed in his arms. The sleeve of his jacket was wet and slimy. He looked up at Teresa. "What'd you come here for?" he asked her. "Trouble? What do you want? You think he had something? He was a broken-down valise."

"I want the body," Nicky's mother told him.

They stared at her.

"No," Celestina shouted. "Never . . . the disgrace . . . what would people say?"

"Exactly why I want the body," Teresa said.

Damiano looked at her closely. "Why should we do that? Give you the body?"

"Because he was my husband, my legal husband, and I should bury him. And then . . ." She paused. "There's the Social Security, the pension. It's mine if I want it. Your daughter gets nothing."

"Get her out. Witch . . . devil . . . whore," Celestina was shouting while her father held her up.

Teresa looked her over. Scrawny, she thought, and no children. She turned to Damiano. "Give me the body," she said. "Pay for the nice funeral I'm gonna give Angelo and I say nothing. Your daughter can have the Social Security. It's a good country, America, no? She can even have the pension. We forget everything and everybody's happy."

Teresa had been paying an insurance policy on Angelo for years. She would put aside money every week and when Mr. Schimel would come to collect it the first Friday of the month, she would make him a cup of tea. He would hold the sugar cube in his teeth while he drank it. He was a nice man, Mr. Schimel, rumored to be the father of certain neighborhood children, all boys. Teresa liked him. Because of Mr. Schimel, she could take care of herself.

Teresa's feet hurt. She sat down on one of the chairs against the wall meant for the mourners. She crossed her legs at the ankle and reached over and took a peppermint from a glass dish on Damiano's desk. She dropped the cellophane wrapping in the ashtray near her chair.

"Never . . . never," Celestina cried over and over.

"Celestina," her father said. "Let's think about this."

"But what will they say? No wake . . . no funeral . . . no grave? No, I can't. I don't care what she says. Angie's my husband."

"Of course he is, *cara*."

Teresa stood up. "Angelo's dead. He's nobody's husband anymore." She walked to the door. Damiano followed her. Celestina was close behind. He caught up with her outside.

"Wait, *signora*," he said. "I'll talk to her."

"I think I'm being fair," Teresa said. "After all, what am I asking for? Do I want anything for myself?"

"You're right," he said. Damiano looked back at his daughter. Her makeup was smeared in lines down her cheeks. Her hair stuck out from her head in greasy knots where she had pulled at it. The perfect widow, Teresa thought, like in the old country, and she pushed a stray piece of hair back behind her ear.

"Where do you want the body sent?" Damiano whispered.

Teresa took a walk around the neighborhood before she got on the El and went back home. She thought she would like it here, if things had been different. She thought about all the other places where she had never been, only a train ride away. When Nicky could walk again, she told herself, they would go places, take the train and see things.

Downtown on Sullivan Street, she went into Nucciarone's funeral home and told the undertaker to expect her husband's body. She told him she wanted the best for Angelo and she told him where to send the bill. The undertaker told her how sorry he was, how death was always so terrible and unexpected, and when he took her in the freight elevator to the room downstairs, she chose the bronze casket, the one lined in white velvet.

He complimented her on her choice. He smiled at her and held her hand. The body would be ready tomorrow afternoon, he said, and he left to call the newspapers.

The next afternoon, the people waited outside the funeral parlor. There was no more room on the sidewalk and they stood in the street. The men laughed and ground out cigarettes underneath their polished black shoes. The women whispered, heads covered. They waited for the widow and her son to arrive, to go in first. The children held their mother's hands, restless, wanting to go in, to get it over with, to go to the park, to get ice cream, to do all the things they were promised after they had visited the dead.

JoJo Santulli drove Teresa and Nicky to the funeral home in his uncle's car. Dante was in the car, too, sitting in the front next to JoJo, and he opened the door for Teresa and helped her carry Nicky into the funeral parlor. Teresa and Dante held Nicky between them. His feet dragged along the ground. Everyone followed behind and held their breath.

"*Poverino,*" someone said.

"And now this," someone else said.

The wake was in the back room, the big room, and the procession moved slowly along the narrow hall, Nicky and Teresa and Dante in front, following the undertaker in his long black coat, striped trousers, and top hat.

Over the coffin was an American flag in red and white and blue carnations. "He was a hero in the war," Teresa told the florist when she ordered it. There was a bleeding heart of red roses that said "Beloved Wife," with red satin ribbons streaming from its center, and a ship of white roses from Nicky. Underneath the ship was a sea of carnations dyed blue.

Angelo Sabatini lay inside the coffin in a double-breasted pin-striped suit, a small diamond stickpin in his tie, and the white velvet lining tucked under so that everyone could see that the coffin was bronze. He was still young when he died and he had died suddenly. "The perfect combination," old man Nucciarone told Teresa when he saw the body. "I'll make him look so good, no one will believe he's dead. Trust me," he said, and he patted her hand.

Nicky came into the room where his father was laid out. His mother and Dante were on either side of him, his arms over their shoulders, their arms across his back. Nicky had seen his father only that one time, when he came to Spring Street and showed him how to tie that knot. He stretched out his neck to look, saw the open casket, and smelled the flowers, and then he started to scream and cry.

The crowd behind pushed forward and Teresa lost hold of him. She shouted to God and to Dante, who reached out to grab him in an embrace before he fell.

But Nicky didn't fall. He put one foot in front of the other and he walked. He looked straight ahead and walked up the aisle to the coffin. Teresa shouted out and the crowd fell back. She moved toward Nicky, toward the coffin, but Dante held her. He dropped to his knees and pulled her down next to him.

The crowd began to mumble. The undertaker jumped on a chair in the back. "A miracle," he shouted. "God has performed a miracle . . . here . . . in this funeral parlor on Sullivan Street."

Teresa tried to get up. She still thought Nicky would fall. She wanted to protect him, to save him. "No," Dante said in her ear.

The undertaker had stepped down from the chair. He moved to the front of the room to direct the mourners. He pointed them to the velvet kneeler in front of the coffin, holding their hands in his for a moment as they passed by on their way to pray before the body. "A miracle," he told them as they moved through the aisles. He smiled, thought about expanding . . . selling relics. He kissed his fingers and touched the feet of the statue of the Madonna that stood on a pedestal in a corner of the room.

Nicky knelt at his father's casket. "I knew it," he said to the body. "I knew you'd come back and I'd walk again."

Donna Rubina Fiore from Bedford Street called out and made the sign of the cross on her forehead, her lips, her heart. She told the people near her that she had cast this spell. She had made Nicky Sabatini walk. The undertaker implied that the funeral parlor was blessed. "Ask yourself," he said. "Why has God chosen this place?"

When Nicky got up from the casket, everyone clapped and cheered. The men came and slapped him on the back, the women covered him with kisses. The children gave him gum and marbles and sucking candies they had hidden in their pockets. Jumbo gave him half a Hershey bar, the mark of his fingers imprinted in the chocolate. He had stolen it from Sam & Al's candy store only that morning.

Teresa took places and that night she collected the envelopes the undertaker had provided. They were stuffed with money. Everyone was hoping for some of her blessing, her luck, to rub off on them. The number runners didn't get home until midnight that night and every night of Angelo Sabatini's wake. Everyone played the date of the miracle, the time of the miracle, the street number of the funeral parlor. Everyone went to sleep determined to remember their dreams. Every night of the wake the mourners dug deep into their pockets and filled the envelopes with money, a token of their sorrow and respect and hope for a score.

He left her alone in life, they said about Angelo Sabatini, but he worked a miracle for her in death.

Teresa insisted that Nicky sit in the first chair, the chair of honor, and greet all the people who filed past the coffin. They kissed his hands and pressed them against their foreheads.

Nicky took Salvatore on the side and told him it was creepy and he would be glad when it was over. Salvatore told him to enjoy it. He had been touched by God, Salvatore told him. Even Magdalena had said it and she knew these things. It was a once in a lifetime.

The night before the funeral, Teresa made Nicky sit at the kitchen table and then she went to all the windows and pulled down the shades. She locked the door and hooked the chain, and then she took out the white envelopes that she had collected every night at the wake and put them on the table. She gave half of the envelopes to Nicky, and the two of them unfolded the money from inside the envelopes and put it into piles, stacks of ones, fives, tens, and twenties. There was even a hundred-dollar bill from the undertaker and Nicky held it up and turned it over in his hands until his mother slapped his face and told him to put it down. "It's only money," she said. "First comes honor."

There were hardly any ones. She told him he could keep the few there were. Then she made him stand up. To look at him, she said. She made him walk around the table, to see his legs work. "Tomorrow's the funeral," she told him. "Tomorrow, in the morning before church, we go say goodbye to your father. You stay in the room with me when they close the box. You watch with me."

"Why?" Nicky asked her.

"To make sure they don't take nothing. You think they care? They strip you naked before they close the box if nobody's looking."

"You're gonna bury him with the cuff links?"

"Why not? How's he gonna look when he gets where he's going with no cuff links? Like a pauper?"

"What about the ring?"

"Which ring?"

"The one he gave me, that time he came. Remember? I showed you and you said I'd lose it and you put it away. Well, you must of given it back to him because he's wearing it. I saw it on his hand. It's a big ring, square, all gold. It's got shapes on it, like a tongue . . ."

Nicky's mother pushed the side of his head with her hand. "What are you talking about? A tongue . . . How can you talk to me like that?"

"What? Whadda you want from me? It looks like a tongue. He said he got it in Hong Kong, in a crap game. The guy didn't want to give it to him but he had no money, all he had was the ring."

"So?"

"So can I have it? Papa gave it to me."

"Why not? Remind me tomorrow when they close the casket and I'll get it for you. You're his only son. You deserve something."

She pulled him down on her lap and put her mouth against his ear. "Poor Nicola," she said softly. "Your father's dead."

"What do you think it's like to die?"

"It's like going to sleep."

"Where do you think Papa is now?"

She turned her face away at this question. With devils burning his feet, she hoped to herself . . . with monsters poking sticks into the openings in his body. She shrugged her shoulders, tightened her arms around Nicky. "I don't know," she told him, "but how bad could it be? Nobody ever comes back." She petted his head and kissed his temples. "You're not too sad, are you, Nicola?"

"Nah, we all gotta go," he told her.

He squirmed in her lap. "What?" she said. "What is it? Tell me."

Nicky fingered the dollar bills she had given him. He touched the piles of money on the kitchen table one by one. "Look at all this, Ma."

"What?"

"All this money. We're making out like bandits."

"So?"

"So, can't we keep him an extra day?"

Teresa grabbed his ears and pushed him off her lap. She knocked him to the floor. She picked the money off the table and threw it at him.

"What should I expect?" she said to no one. "His father's son." Nicky watched her. Then he smiled and came and stood behind her. He put his arms around her waist and buried his face in her neck like a lover. She covered his hands with hers.

And Teresa walked in the procession for Our Lady of Mount Carmel, even though Nicky could walk, even though the miracle had already happened. She walked barefoot carrying a lighted candle all the way up to 115th Street because she had promised. She prayed in the Cathedral of Our Lady of Mount Carmel to protect her son, the way years ago and far from New York, Magdalena had prayed in a village church to the Black Madonna to grant her wish, the same Black Madonna that looked over Antoinette's kitchen, that lay hidden in Teresa's top dresser drawer. Always, there was the Black Madonna.

MAGDALENA

1936

Amadeo Pavese was married a year when his wife gave birth to twin sons. She died delivering the second, who was stillborn. Amadeo Pavese named the first baby Salvatore and made the priest christen him before he said the prayers for the dead.

The midwife spoke with Amadeo about the infant Salvatore. What did he know about babies? she asked him. Amadeo covered his face with his hands.

"The baby needs a *nutrice*," the midwife said, "mother's milk. He needs a *bambinaia* to wrap him in strips of cloth so his legs grow straight, to swaddle him in blankets so he feels secure." She crossed her arms in front of her chest and held herself. The priest put a hand on Amadeo's shoulder.

"But who?" Amadeo said. The priest put his hands behind his back and walked the length of the room.

"Teresa Sabatini," the midwife said. She had thought only a moment. "She's around the corner on Spring Street. You can see into her windows from yours. Here," and she pulled Amadeo over and pointed with a finger.

Amadeo looked up. The priest nodded. "A good choice," he said, "a good woman. I just baptized her son. She named him Nicola."

The midwife took Amadeo's hand. *"Povero tu,"* she said. "This terrible thing. Ah, who can understand God?" She shot a look of anger at the priest. He stepped forward and frowned, raised a hand in benediction. "A good woman, Mrs. Sabatini . . ." he said.

"Perfect," the midwife said. "Her baby is just months old. I delivered him myself. Her husband's always away at sea. Her house is clean. She's filled with milk. I was there only yesterday." She patted Amadeo's hand. "I'll talk to her."

"When?"

"Now, I'm going over there now."

The undertaker came to the house to get the bodies. He covered the windows in the front room with a black curtain and cleared a space for the coffin. He brought two lamps and twenty folding chairs.

The coffin was polished red mahogany and the mother and child lay inside together, the baby in the white christening dress that had been brought from the village of Castelfondo in Lucania, the mother in her wedding gown, the baby in her arms.

The wake went on for six days and was talked about for years after. It was the pain of life laid out in a box for everyone to see. Everyone who looked into that coffin felt lucky, made the sign of the cross and promises to God.

Antoinette Mangiacarne went to the funeral parlor every day, and every day when she came home she would knock on Teresa Sabatini's door and tell her about the flowers and the people and the coffin where Amadeo's wife lay with her son in her arms. She called Teresa a saint for nursing the orphan.

"He's not an orphan," Teresa told her.

"Ah, no, but without a mother is like an orphan, as unfortunate as an orphan. How is he?" she asked. "I hear he's frail." Antoinette looked around, hoping to catch a glimpse of the infant, but Teresa had the babies tight together in the cradle in her bedroom, blankets up to their noses, away from Antoinette's eyes.

"He's beautiful," Teresa said, "a treasure, like my Nicky. They could be brothers."

Antoinette shook her head. "Delicate babies are sweet, easy to take care of—not like my Jumbo. She laughed. "What a handful!" And Antoinette excused herself, promising to come again.

Teresa closed the door after her before she went to the back to look at the sleeping boys. She had agreed to nurse the baby because there was no one else and the priest had promised her grace. She had more than enough milk and while she thought she had no more love or attention to give, that Nicky had taken it all, she was surprised by her own feelings when the infant clung to her. Nicky was almost five months old, already alert and moving. This one was newly born, and to him, Teresa was the world.

Six days is too long," the undertaker said, worried about the Health Department. The bodies were starting to turn black. He had seen the discoloration after the third day. "There's a reason we do things," he told Amadeo. "I'm an undertaker, not a miracle worker." The funeral Mass had been postponed twice. The priest was getting edgy, looking for sin. "Enough is enough," the undertaker said. "Believe me, I know. You don't want them talking that you're crazy. Grief-stricken is bad enough."

There was a white hearse on the seventh day, like a wedding coach, and the neighborhood held its collective breath when they saw it parked outside the church. A teddy bear of blue flowers and a wreath of white orchids covered the top of the coffin and after the priest said the prayers at the grave and the people had all gone home, Amadeo Pavese stayed with the gravediggers until the coffin was deep in the ground and covered with dirt. Every Sunday he went back. On Christmas he brought a fir tree strung with lights, and at Easter, a basket of colored eggs and a yellow stuffed bunny.

After the funeral Amadeo came home to the empty house and sat at the table to write a letter to his Uncle Carmelo and his Aunt Guinetta in Castelfondo telling them about the death of his wife and child. He sent the letter along with the money he sent every month the way his father had done. Amadeo Pavese never forgot the family in Castelfondo. When his business did well, he sent more money, and in return he received photographs of the carved and varnished door of the house in Castelfondo, the indoor toilet with the porcelain seat, Zia Guinetta in front of the house, her hand on the brass doorknob. Pictures arrived of the daughter, Maria, in her Communion dress, and of Mammone, the most important mother, in a hat of silk flowers.

Amadeo had once brought over Zio Carmelo's son Tommaso to work in the business when he was first starting, but Tommaso had gone back home two months later, appearing in Castelfondo with a cardboard suitcase full of new clothes, ten words of English, two of which were "For chrissakes," and the attitude of a man who has seen the world. He never worked again. The sort of work available in Castelfondo, he explained to his father, was beneath him. How could he possibly go into the fields after having been to America?

Having been to America became his career. Having been to America had made him a man of stature. Tommaso loved America and he loved his cousin Amadeo, whose money his father sent him to collect at the post office every month on the fifth. The only thing better than being a rich man, Tommaso told the men in the café, was to be a rich man's relative.

Zio Carmelo sent long and detailed letters from Castelfondo, addressing Amadeo as *figlio mio*. When Amadeo was married, he sent an elaborate gift from a shop in Matera.

When Amadeo was married was the first time Zia Guinetta worried. "After all," she said, "Amadeo will have a family of his own now. Suppose he forgets us?" But Zio Carmelo waved his hand at her.

"The girl is from Lucania. She knows about family, how one helps the other," he said, and for sure, month after month, the money was there at the post office when Tommaso went to pick it up.

"I told you there was nothing to worry about," Zio Carmelo said one evening while Zia Guinetta massaged his feet, but when the news of the deaths of Amadeo's wife and son arrived, Zio Carmelo suffered a bout of indigestion. He blamed the garlic his wife crushed on his bread in the mornings, the tomatoes she used for her sauce. He blamed her, but in fact, it was fear. He felt a pain in his heart for his nephew, but the pain in his stomach was for all of them in Castelfondo: Guinetta, Maria, Tommaso, Mammone. They were stuck away in the mountains of Lucania. Who would remember them if Amadeo Pavese forgot?

When Amadeo lost his wife and his infant son, he closed his heart. There were women who passed by the stoop of his house purposely to talk to him, women who came to his store and lingered too long, but he had no interest. The only woman he saw was Teresa Sabatini, because she took care of his son. If Zia Guinetta had known this, if she could have seen across the ocean to New York, she would have slept better, but instead she worried. There was not a lot to think about in the village of Castelfondo.

The eclipse . . . I knew when the year began with an eclipse of the sun that 1936 would be unlucky." Everyone knew this, but Zia Guinetta knew it more than most, because she was a witch. She had learned the arts from her mother on Christmas Eve, the only day of the year when the powers can be transferred. It was said that she had captured Zio Carmelo with more than her physical charms. She had made him love her and marry her despite his mother, who had scratched her face until she drew blood when she heard about their courtship.

Zia Guinetta had been the housekeeper of a local priest who took her in when she was orphaned as a young girl. She had cooked his food and cleaned his house and aborted his babies, until the day she saw Zio Carmelo coming home from the fields. She was there every day after that, waiting for him where the path turned and led up to the village.

She would let her hair loose when she saw the top of his hat. She offered him sausages she had made, bread she had baked, cakes filled with almonds, jam made of figs. In each of these, she put bits of her skin and hair and monthly blood until he became so obsessed with her that he couldn't eat or sleep. His mother consulted doctors from as far away as Potenza, but no one could help.

Zia Guinetta came to Zio Carmelo's door but his mother pushed her out into the street. She tore the buttons off Zia Guinetta's dress. Zia Guinetta stood there and shrugged her shoulders. "He'll eat from my hand," she told Zio Carmelo's mother, "or he'll die. His insides will dry up like fruit left in the sun."

Zio Carmelo's mother slapped Zia Guinetta's face and pulled the gold hoop from her ear, but Zia Guinetta didn't move. "Without me, he'll die," she said. "There's nothing you can do." Zio Carmelo's mother sat down on the stoop of her house, covered her face with her hands, and cried until she lost her eyesight, while Zia Guinetta went inside and fed Zio Carmelo bits of sausage and bread and almond cake from her fingers. She covered his tongue with her jam made of figs. Zio Carmelo's mother died before they married and the newlyweds took over her house. An orphan from the village of Tolve came to live with the priest.

Suppose," Zia Guinetta told her husband, while he pulled apart yesterday's bread to soak in his coffee, "Amadeo takes a second wife, an American, who says to him," and here Zia Guinetta changed her voice, making it high and shrill, " 'Why should you send all this money to family in Italy? Who are they after all?' What would happen then?" She shuddered. "I tell you, Carmelo, what would happen. You would have to go back into the fields on Don Carlito's estate, if he would have you, and why should he? You're not a young man anymore."

Zio Carmelo coughed until his chest hurt. He gasped for breath. "I know, I know. It would be terrible," he told Zia Guinetta. He, Carmelo Laurenzano, a man who had always held his head high, would be forced to sit in the piazza, staring across at the café, longing for a glass of anisette with a black coffee bean at the bottom that he could no longer afford. His back would be bent. And this would be only the beginning of his troubles. His daughter was coming close to marriageable age. With the family's prospects reduced, what kind of husband could she get? A simpleton, an old man with twisted legs? Zio Carmelo held his head in his hands. "Think, Guinetta," he said.

"I have been thinking," she said, coming around behind him, kneading his shoulders with her hands. "Write Amadeo a letter. Invite him here. Tell him to leave his troubles and come to Castelfondo." Zia Guinetta put her face close to Zio Carmelo's. She stroked his cheek with the back of her hand. "Maybe a pretty girl will catch his eye. He needs a wife, no? A mother for his son? What better thing could we do for him? He'd be bound to us then, tied to Castelfondo."

Zio Carmelo turned in his chair. He took her face in his hands and kissed her forehead. He called her his treasure. She brought him pen and paper and sat down next to him, pulling her chair close to his.

Zio Carmelo wrote a letter to his nephew expressing his sorrow, his devotion, his love, and his invitation to Castelfondo. He read aloud to Zia Guinetta as he wrote. He had been to school and wrote documents and letters for the whole village. Zia Guinetta had never been to school and depended on her husband for these things. She leaned over him, her hand on his arm as he wrote.

F*iglio carissimo,*" Zio Carmelo wrote, and here Zia Guinetta took the pen and marked X's for the kisses she wanted to send to Amadeo. Zio Carmelo told her they went at the end, but she insisted he leave them where she put them. Her eyes narrowed and she bit her lip in approval when he wrote: *"All of Castelfondo shares your sorrow."* Zio Carmelo blotted the ink with the green blotter he had bought from the postmaster, waved his arm over the paper, and went on: *"Castelfondo grieves for the loss of your wife and infant son and wishes you would come back to the embraces of your family and country-men."*

Zia Guinetta made Zio Carmelo give her the envelope to seal and she put a pinch of red powder between the pages before she licked the glue with her tongue and closed the letter inside. Zia Guinetta couldn't read or write but she knew about important things.

Zia Guinetta grew herbs in her kitchen garden and made medicines that she stored in earthenware jars. She experimented with love potions and aphrodisiacs, but for these the residents of Castelfondo came to her back door after dark. For the medicines she took no money, but she always accepted gifts for the magic. She had a great reputation, concocting each potion separate from the others, because, she said, the fever of love was different every time.

Although he considered himself a modern man, Zio Carmelo was glad for the red powder. He called to Tommaso to go and mail the letter. "Amadeo shouldn't mourn too long," he told his wife. "It's bad for a man's health." Zia Guinetta agreed.

Amadeo Pavese's life was sad but his business was good. He had a fruit and vegetable stand that got bigger every year, until he had a store that took up half a block. His connections with the neighborhood powers filled the shelves with imported olive oil and canned tomatoes, and he thought about buying a Cadillac but he was afraid of tempting fate. He had had his share, everyone agreed, but who knew how much misfortune was enough?

The flower signifying death was barely removed from Amadeo Pavese's door, the last shovelful of dirt thrown on the coffin where his wife lay inside with her baby son in her arms, when the letter arrived from Castelfondo. Amadeo had only just put the black armband around his sleeve.

In Castelfondo, even though the money from America continued to arrive on the fifth of every month, even though the amount had increased from before, Zio Carmelo worried. For the first time, Zia Guinetta's medicines didn't help. He lost weight, his face got small, and his nose looked big. Next to his wife in bed at night, he rolled from side to side. "The *nutrice,*" he said. "He mentions her in every letter. I hope we're not too late."

Amadeo Pavese bought a dark green Chrysler and thought he might make the trip to Italy someday. He worked six days a week. His son Salvatore was with Teresa Sabatini, whom he paid in fruits and vegetables and a weekly envelope filled with cash. On Sunday she brought Salvatore to his father's house, along with her son Nicola, and they played on the dark red carpet in the living room. If the weather was fine, they ate lunch in the backyard under the grape arbor or else in the big kitchen on the bottom floor of the house. Amadeo cooked. He liked Teresa. She wasn't bad to look at, tall and slim, strong, the way he liked women, and her skin . . . it was beautiful, smooth and clear. He was sure that if he could touch it, it would feel soft and velvety, like the skin of his baby son, whose neck he nuzzled when Teresa put him in his arms.

He found himself watching her. Every Sunday he was aware of something else about her. When she caressed Salvatore, he noticed her hands. When she took off her coat, he saw the straightness of her shoulders. He began to hope she would reveal herself, but Teresa was stoic. She listened when he talked about his business, his son, about what he hoped for the future. She was smart, he decided. She didn't gossip. She was clean. She was good to his son.

They were in the garden, after lunch, the Sunday before Easter.

Teresa was stirring sugar into his coffee and he stopped her hand. "It's almost a year," he said. Teresa looked up. Another woman, he thought, would have looked down. "Salvatore loves you," he continued.

Teresa made a sound with her tongue. "I'm the only woman he knows."

"And you're the only woman I know," Amadeo said. He was careful, tentative. She took the spoon from the coffee. He let go of her hand.

"I'm married," she told him. "There's enough talk as there is."

"Your husband's never here. He's like a ghost."

"I have to think about my son and you have to do the same."

"I always think about my son, and I think about you, and your son. Be honest, Teresa. We're a family, all of us. A family that fate put together."

It was hot in the garden, unusually hot for the Sunday before Easter. Teresa had put the babies down to nap after their lunch. She had taken off her hat. Amadeo could see that the heavy knot of hair at the nape of her neck was coming loose, about to unwind. He could see the rounded ends of her hairpins. Her hair was close to falling, he knew, past her shoulders, down her back.

Teresa opened the top button of the dark wool dress she had sewn to wear on Sundays. She fanned herself with her linen napkin. "It's so hot out here, even under the grapevines."

"Let's go inside," Amadeo said, "where it's cool and dark."

The black armband was still around Amadeo's sleeve when he wrote to Zio Carmelo that he was thinking of coming to Castelfondo for a visit.

It's months and months now that I don't sleep," Zio Carmelo said to his wife that day the telegram arrived. Zia Guinetta poured coffee into his bowl. She had put the telegram under his spoon.

Zio Carmelo crossed himself before he touched the yellow envelope. "It could be something terrible," he said. "This could be our end." Zia Guinetta turned away to stir her pot of beans. She smiled but he couldn't see.

Zio Carmelo wiped his face with his handkerchief. He gathered up the crumbs on the table and threw them on the floor for the rooster. He got up and walked outside to pee against the tree. When he came back in, he opened the telegram. Zia Guinetta had not moved.

"I told you. I knew it," Zio Carmelo shouted at her back. "You never listen. You worry for nothing."

"What?" she said, never turning.

"Look at this. Amadeo is coming to Castelfondo at the end of the month." Zio Carmelo kissed the yellow paper. He went over to Zia Guinetta and kissed away the drops of sweat that had formed on her upper lip as she bent over the steaming pot.

Zia Guinetta wiped her hands on her apron. "There are important things to do," she said. "The bride . . . Don't forget about the bride."

"Of course not. What am I? Stupid? But you have to tell me, who? Which girl? Who would make the best wife for Amadeo? Think hard. I'll do the rest. She has to be beautiful, young, clever, grateful, docile . . ."

"A docile girl won't leave just like that for America with a strange man. And Americans don't like docile women."

"How do you know what American men like?"

"Tommaso. Tommaso knows everything about America."

"Guinetta? Our Maria . . . What about our Maria?"

"Pig. Your own daughter to your sister's son? Are you crazy? Pig," Zia Guinetta said again and she didn't speak to him that whole day.

Now when Zio Carmelo walked through the town, when he sat at the coffee bar in the piazza until noon, he looked carefully at his compatriots, remembering their sisters and daughters and grand-daughters, conjuring up their faces, their figures. One of them, he thought, would be the right girl for Amadeo.

He said nothing to anyone until the day he crossed paths with Giacomo Caparetti and remembered that he had a beautiful daughter. She had been hidden in the house since her brother's funeral, but the year was almost up. Magdalena Caparetti had smooth white skin, Zio Carmelo remembered, and strange wonderful eyes, bright, as though a lamp were held behind them.

"Magdalena Caparetti," Zio Carmelo told his wife that night, wiping up the oil on his plate with a crust of bread.

"Ah . . . a beautiful girl," Zia Guinetta said. "Those eyes . . . but she's very young."

"So? He needs a young wife. The one he had was his age and look what happened, she dies, just like that." Zio Carmelo snapped his fingers.

Zia Guinetta shook her head "I don't know . . . the blood . . . her mother."

"Her mother?"

"*Uffa,* don't you remember nothing? Marietta Caparetti . . . that goat of a friar from Naples?"

"*Porco Dio,* I remember." Zio Carmelo smacked his forehead with his hand. "So what happened to her?"

Zia Guinetta shrugged. "Who knows? She's gone."

"And the daughter, like the mother? What do you say?"

Zia Guinetta shrugged again. And then she smiled. "Spirit is a good thing in a woman," Zia Guinetta said. She put her hand against the front of Zio Carmelo's pants and whispered in his ear. He remembered how she would take him into the countryside late at night and the things they would do, things that he could never say to anyone, that the men in the café would not believe could be done, except in the pictures on the back of the playing cards that Rienzo Portare had brought back from Rome. There had not been blood on Zia Guinetta's wedding sheets.

"Talk to the father tomorrow," Zia Guinetta said.

"And Amadeo? What if he doesn't want a wife?"

"It's not important what he wants. He needs a wife. He needs a mother for his son. Why not a girl from here? He'll be grateful to us forever."

Zio Carmelo nodded. "He needs us now," he said. "My poor nephew, my sister Filomena's only son, God rest her soul." Zia Guinetta patted her husband's shoulder. Things would work out. There were ways.

My nephew is coming from America," Zio Carmelo announced in the café. He passed the telegram around and each man looked at it as though he could read and made a face to show he was impressed.

"A wealthy man, my nephew, my sister Filomena's only son, God give her peace. A businessman . . . He has a big business, very big. Every year it gets bigger." Zio Carmelo ordered an anisette with a coffee bean and sat down at one of the tables near the door. "When my nephew comes, there'll be a big feast, a real celebration. Everyone's invited."

This announcement sparked some interest and a few men clapped their hands together. "Bravo, Carmelo," they said.

"Fireworks," Zio Carmelo said. "Streamers everywhere . . . the band from Matera. Giovanni," he called out to the bar owner. "A drink for my friends."

Zio Carmelo went to see Giacomo Caparetti in the afternoon. The village was shuttered against the heat. By the time Zio Carmelo reached Giacomo Caparetti's house, his shoes and clothes were covered with dust. He knocked but no one answered. He could hear snores from behind the closed door.

Zio Carmelo had chosen this time to give the meeting great weight and also to catch Giacomo Caparetti by surprise. Through the crack in the door, Zio Carmelo could see him lying on his bed, his pants over a chair. He knocked again, louder, put his face to the crack, and called out to him in a loud whisper.

"What? Who's there?" Giacomo Caparetti said. He sat up in his bed and looked around.

"Open the door . . . Giacomo. It's me, Carmelo Laurenzano." Zio Carmelo pounded on the door with his fist. He stepped back when he heard shuffling inside. "*Paesano* . . ." he said when the door opened. He stretched out his arms.

Giacomo Caparetti invited Zio Carmelo in and offered him a chair at the table. He took out a bottle of wine and two flyspecked glasses. Standing across from Zio Carmelo, he poured the wine and touched his glass to Zio Carmelo's. "*Salute,*" he said and drank. Before he sat down, he poured another. The stubble of his beard was gray.

"Let me get right to it, Giacomo. You're wondering why I'm here, am I right? Why I've interrupted your sleep. What could be so important, you're asking yourself." Zio Carmelo took out his handkerchief and wiped his face. "This heat," he said. "Every year the same."

Giacomo Caparetti shrugged his shoulders and drank his wine. He watched Zio Carmelo closely.

"Your daughter . . ."

Giacomo Caparetti squinted. His eyes were small and shiny from sleep and suspicion. "Magdalena?" he said.

"Yes, your beautiful Magdalena, your beautiful daughter, lovely like her mother."

Giacomo Caparetti stood up. His wine spilled. "Not like her mother, never. Mother, what kind of mother? *Puttana* . . ."

"Wait . . . Wait . . . Giacomo . . . God forgive me if I meant anything." Zio Carmelo crossed himself.

"What is it? What do you want?"

Zio Carmelo sighed loudly. He picked up the wine bottle. "May I? . . ." he said, and poured himself some wine. He righted Giacomo Caparetti's glass and filled that, too. He mopped up the spilled wine with his handkerchief. "Listen, Giacomo, my nephew is coming from America, my very fine, very rich nephew. He lost his wife. He has an infant son. I'm here to propose a match . . . my nephew . . . your Magdalena."

Giacomo Caparetti put both hands on the edge of the table and leaned over. "Who knows from your nephew?" he shouted at Zio Carmelo. "My Magdalena's beautiful. She can have anyone, anything. A husband from Matera . . . Potenza . . . maybe Naples . . . a prince from Avellino! What does she want with your nephew?"

"Please, Giacomo, sit down." Zio Carmelo put a hand on Giacomo Caparetti's arm but he pulled away. Zio Carmelo stood up and pushed back his chair. "If you don't sit, Giacomo, then I stand."

Giacomo Caparetti sat down slowly, his eyes on Zio Carmelo. He took the stub of an old cigar from his pocket and lit it. He still looked angry.

"Don't I know your Magdalena can have anyone?" Zio Carmelo told him. "Why do you think I'm here? Why do you think of all the girls in Castelfondo, I want Magdalena for my nephew? The women in the village follow me like wolves since they heard about my nephew. I can't say the things they offer me for an introduction. Your heart would stop. You would never close your eyes at night. If I was a different kind of man . . . but no, I tell them. I won't be bribed. My mind is made up. The only woman for my nephew is Magdalena Caparetti."

Giacomo Caparetti was silent. Zio Carmelo took a breath. He leaned over, put a hand on Giacomo Caparetti's arm. "Magdalena is beautiful," he said to him, "but for a woman, beauty is a sword with two edges. It can lead to trouble." Zio Carmelo sat back in his chair. "Men desire her. Women envy her. You know, my friend, what can happen." And here Zio Carmelo bowed his head, lowered his eyes. "The rose has thorns," he said, looking up artfully from under his half-closed lids, hoping that Giacomo Caparetti was thinking of his missing wife.

Giacomo Caparetti's eyes were wet. He wiped his face with the back of his hand. "My daughter's a good girl," he said.

"I know that, Giacomo. Would I want her for my nephew if I didn't know that? Think about it. Magdalena would go to America. And for you, Giacomo, a dream come true. She'll come back to you dressed in silk, diamonds around her neck the size of the Madonna's tears . . . a father's dream. I would give this . . ." Zio Carmelo held out his right arm. He sliced it below the elbow with his hand, then he poured them both another glass of wine.

"But the dowry . . . ?"

"Pffft . . . small . . . almost nothing . . . a token. You can give it directly to me and save any embarrassment."

"She's all I have," he said.

"I know. Don't I know? Don't I have a daughter? But she'll have a good life. And she'll take care of you. You can forget worrying. My nephew sends money every month. He's a good boy."

"But he's a stranger, an American . . ."

"Giacomo, I can't believe what I'm hearing. A stranger? He's my blood. My poor sister Filomena's only son. You remember Filomena? Ah, God should give her peace." Zio Carmelo drained his glass.

Giacomo Caparetti filled it, turned the empty bottle on its side and went to get another. "She's only fourteen," he said over his shoulder.

Zio Carmelo sucked in his breath. Zia Guinetta was right. She was young. He was quiet for a moment, pushing the thought out of his head. "Not so young," he said, when Giacomo Caparetti came back to the table. "Magdalena's a big girl. And you know, Giacomo, my wife, Guinetta, is the ear of Castelfondo. Malicious tongues are wagging."

Giacomo Caparetti started to cry. His tears splashed onto his hands and arms, onto the table, into his wineglass. Zio Carmelo would have offered his handkerchief if it had been clean. Instead, he patted his hand. "You'll talk to her then? My nephew will be here in five weeks."

"What do I do?" Giacomo Caparetti swayed in his chair. "How will I . . . ?"

"I'll take care of everything," Zio Carmelo said. "There should be a dinner . . . a few other things. This is all separate from the dowry, of course."

"There isn't much," Giacomo Caparetti said.

"Don't worry. What there is, there is." Zio Carmelo poured them both more wine.

"I can get it for you now," Giacomo Caparetti said. He stood up.

"No, no, you don't have to. What's the rush?" Zio Carmelo held up his hand. Giacomo Caparetti sat back down. "Of course, if I had it," Zio Carmelo said, "I could get started with the arrangements right away."

"I'll get it then."

"It's not really necessary."

"Yes, yes, wait here. Drink up. I'll be a minute."

Zio Carmelo poured himself more wine. He tried not to think about the size of Magdalena's dowry as he listened to the movements in the back room. Giacomo Caparetti returned with a black sock knotted at the top and handed it to Zio Carmelo. "Like I said, there isn't much, but that's all of it."

Zio Carmelo slapped Giacomo Caparetti on the back. "You should be proud, Giacomo. How many fathers have no dowry at all put aside for their daughters?" Giacomo Caparetti wiped tears from his eyes. Zio Carmelo wondered where they all came from.

"Thank you, Don Carmelo," Giacomo Caparetti said, and reached for Zio Carmelo's hand to kiss it.

"No, no," Zio Carmelo said. He stood up and put an arm around Giacomo Caparetti's shoulders. "Please, Giacomo," he said, "we're almost family." He kissed him on both cheeks. "You just take care of Magdalena. I'll take care of everything else."

Zio Carmelo was out the door when Giacomo Caparetti called to him. "Your nephew . . ." he said, ". . . he's handsome?"

Zio Carmelo turned around. He threw up his hands. "How handsome does a rich man have to be?"

Zio Carmelo took his time going home. He stopped at the piazza and waited for the coffee bar to open and the men to gather. He covered his pocket with his hand, feeling the bulge of the black sock with Magdalena Caparetti's dowry inside. Zio Carmelo played a few games of cards. He told the men that Magdalena Caparetti would marry his nephew, who was coming to Castelfondo at the end of the month. He bought them all drinks and he invited them all to the wedding. "It will be three days of celebration," he said, and the men all nodded their heads and picked up their cards.

In New York, Amadeo made his arrangements to travel to Italy, to leave his business, and most important, to take care of his baby son. He talked with Teresa about taking Salvatore with him but she wouldn't hear of it. She called him crazy. "How long can you be?" she said. "A month? Two? Why upset him? Someone else's milk, someone else's arms. He's too young. And he'll miss Nicky. They're like brothers. Look at them."

Amadeo sat in her parlor on the couch under the shelf of dolls that Teresa Sabatini's husband sent to her from all over the world and looked at Salvatore sitting on the floor with Nicky, mother's milk glistening on his chin.

"But won't he miss me?"

"Yes, yes, of course, but no matter what, you're still only a man. You can try but you can't know. Trust me. Look at Nicky. Isn't his father away? Isn't he fine? Go," she said. "Enjoy yourself."

It was not what Amadeo wanted to hear. He looked around the room. He held a hand out to Salvatore, who caught hold of his fingers. "What if we all went?" he said. "A vacation . . . the four of us. You never had a vacation, have you? You work so hard, taking care of the two boys. We could all go together."

Teresa laughed, low, in the back of her throat. "Where are the brains you were born with?" she said. "How could I come back here after that?" She shook her head. "God Himself couldn't save me."

The day before he left, Amadeo came to see his son at the building on Spring Street, in Teresa's apartment on the fifth floor, He brought an envelope bulging with ten-dollar bills, the address of his aunt and uncle in Castelfondo, and a letter for the lawyer on Bedford Street, Vincente Violotti, who would take care of whatever she needed while he was gone. Amadeo promised he would write often and not be gone long.

Teresa held Salvatore in one arm and her son Nicky in the other.

The boys were wearing matching white suits she had knitted by hand. She stood on the landing at the top of the stairs to watch Amadeo leave and had the two boys wave their fat fists goodbye long after the outside door to the building on Spring Street had banged shut. He had kissed her for the last time.

The day Amadeo was scheduled to arrive in Castelfondo, Zio Carmelo went down to the café. He had hired Terragrossa, the owner of the only automobile in Castelfondo, to meet Amadeo's bus at the crossroads. He had given a gift of money to the mayor in return for a promise to keep the peasants out of the fields and in the piazza, so it would be filled with people when Amadeo entered the town.

At home, Zia Guinetta had the dowry safe in her cupboard, and when Zio Carmelo left, when the house was empty, she sat down to count it.

Zio Carmelo had spent some, and kept some back. Zia Guinetta suspected this. She didn't know that he had thought about keeping all of the money secret from her, a private cache of drinking and gambling money, with a few pennies left over for the widow who sold votive candles to light in front of the Black Madonna of Viggiano.

Castelfondo waited for Amadeo Pavese from New York. The goats made more noise, the babies cried louder, the peasants grumbled. Zia Guinetta made up Amadeo's bed in her daughter Maria's wedding sheets, the tiny initials embroidered on the hem by the girl's own hands for the day she would marry. Maria complained about the sheets, but Zia Guinetta had no good sheets of her own, not having been a proper bride with a trousseau of linens. "If things work out," she told Maria, threatening to slap her, "you can wipe your behind with these sheets. Pay a little now, more will come later."

In the piazza, everyone talked about Amadeo Pavese. Everyone was curious to see the nephew from America. Tommaso tried to get attention by saying that he could answer their questions. Who knew Amadeo better than he? But today no one listened to Tommaso. They wanted to see for themselves.

"Would the nephew come from Naples?" they asked each other. "Through Matera? Potenza? Had his ship landed at Bari? And would Terragrossa, waiting at the crossroads, know who he was?"

They laughed at Terragrossa the next day when he sat in the café and bragged that he knew Amadeo Pavese the first second he saw him. "Who else got off at that godforsaken place?" they taunted.

Terragrossa pushed his hand through the air. "If the Pope and his army got off the bus, I would have known Amadeo Pavese. His shoes were made of leather, not cardboard, like yours," he said, pointing to Silvio Racioppi, "and his hair was black and smooth with pomade. Ah, I said to myself, this is an American."

Terragrossa had run up to carry Amadeo's suitcase. He had insisted, pulled it from his hand. He ran to open the door of the car. He was confused when Amadeo resisted his attentions until he remembered that Americans were democrats. Terragrossa had smiled at his own intelligence.

"A long journey?" he said.

Amadeo nodded. He looked out at the countryside. He thought of the desert, the face of the moon. There were no trees, nothing. The town was set into the hill, bleached white, medieval. He could have been born here, he realized. He could have had another life. Part of the town had fallen into the ravine at the last earthquake, Terragrossa told him.

"My uncle lives in town?"

"In a palace," Terragrossa said, "two stories." He held up two fingers.

"You can take me to a hotel in town."

"Hotel? What hotel? There's a widow who rents rooms but you couldn't stay there. The tax collector, the pig doctor, stays there. There's lice in the sheets. Your uncle gave me instructions. 'You bring him straight here,' he told me. 'Do you know how many years I've waited to see him?' He had tears in his eyes when he said it." Amadeo thought he saw a tear in Terragrossa's eye and offered him his handkerchief. Terragrossa fingered the material and tucked it into his shirt pocket.

"There's things you should know," he told Amadeo.

"Tell me."

Terragrossa lowered his voice and covered his mouth with his hand. "This place is filled with *streghe* and you should be careful. They poison the bread and the sausage and the wine. They put things in the food, terrible things from their bodies, and they take over your soul. There was a man, Cosimo Carbone, who threw himself off this cliff, right here," and Terragrossa pulled the car off the road and stopped it at the edge of the cliff so that Amadeo could see where it had happened. He shook his head and looked back over his shoulder at Amadeo. "They'll go wild for a man like you."

He turned the car up the road that led to the village and drove into the center of town. A bright red banner with BEN TORNATI written in gold letters was strung across the piazza. The mayor had commissioned the banner for the soldiers returning triumphant from the war in Abyssinia, even though there had been only one volunteer from Castelfondo. The mayor had been glad to rent the banner to Zio Carmelo for the day. He had added a small fee for hanging it across the piazza. The red-and-gold banner hung in contrast to the black ones that flapped above every doorway. They marked death, and were left there until the wind and the weather tore them down.

Four musicians waited in the square, not from Matera as Zio Carmelo had promised, but peasants from the village. They played goatskin bagpipes and the children covered their ears. Zio Carmelo got mad when anyone asked about the brass band. "At the wedding," he told them, annoyed. "You people always want everything right away."

When Amadeo got out of the car, the bagpipes played "God Bless America." Zio Carmelo came up to embrace him. "Look," he said. "The whole town is here to welcome you. They should be sleeping. They should be in the fields." Amadeo stood in the noon sun; he tipped his hat and thanked them all. He smiled and they smiled back except for some of the peasants who were disgruntled at missing a day of work for nothing, as far as they could see. Zio Carmelo had promised a spectacle. To save face, Zio Carmelo had to buy drinks in the café for the men and sweets for the women and children.

So the men drank and the women and children sucked on candies and the bagpipes played "God Bless America" over and over. Amadeo was made to sit in a chair under a makeshift canopy and the mayor made a vague speech of welcome in which he mentioned the glory of Rome and Zio Carmelo brought the residents one by one to meet Amadeo. The most important people of the town came first, the mayor, the doctor, the head of the carabinieri. They shook Amadeo's hand and kissed his cheeks. Amadeo would not let anyone kiss his hand although the peasants tried. The young girls hid behind their mothers, who offered Amadeo bits of sausage and bread and cakes on small plates. Terragrossa bulged his eyes at Amadeo from behind the women's backs and pointed to the food and sawed his hand across his throat in warning.

Magdalena Caparetti was there, leaning against a wall. Her father had brought her. He had not told her about the betrothal, but only that the rich and handsome nephew of Carmelo Laurenzano was coming from America and there would be a celebration in the piazza. She was very glad to end the year of mourning for her brother. She had brushed her hair into a long braid and put on the necklace her mother had left for her. "He's fat," she told her father when she saw Amadeo.

Giacomo Caparetti pinched her arm. "Of course he's fat. In America, everyone's fat. They have plenty to eat, not like here, where everybody starves." Her father thought to introduce her but he didn't know how, so he went over to Zio Carmelo and pulled at his sleeve. Zio Carmelo turned angrily until he saw who it was. "Giacomo . . . *Paesano* . . ." He embraced him. "What do you think?" he said. "A fine man, eh?"

Giacomo Caparetti nodded. "Should I bring Magdalena to meet him?"

"Of course, why not?"

"I haven't told her anything."

"So what? There's always time. Patience gets you through this life. Fate decides the rest. Bring her here. Guinetta will introduce her."

Zia Guinetta took Magdalena by the hand and brought her to meet Amadeo, who was sitting under the makeshift canopy drinking the local wine. He smiled at her and shook her hand, and she went back to stand against the wall.

"Beautiful, no?" Zia Guinetta put her face down to Amadeo's ear.

Amadeo laughed. He had been traveling for days and days. His head was light from the wine. His stomach felt strange from the food. "Zia," he said, "she must be twelve years old."

"No, no, much older. It's the mountain air. Women here always seem young. Look at me," she said, and she moved her hands down her body suggestively.

As it got dark, everyone started drifting home. Amadeo was asleep in his chair and Zio Carmelo had to shake him awake. He and Zia Guinetta walked up the street to their house with Amadeo between them. They paused in front of the door, to give Amadeo time to appreciate the varnish and the brass doorknob that he had seen only in photographs.

Inside, the first thing they showed him, before they even showed him his bed, was the toilet bowl with the porcelain seat. They wanted him to understand, to know that they were a family he could be proud of.

"But Zio," Amadeo said. "There's no water. How can you use it?"

Zio Carmelo stood in the doorway with his arms folded across his chest. "What does that matter?" he said. "It's the only one like it in the province. It's famous."

Amadeo agreed it was magnificent.

In the mornings, Zia Guinetta made Amadeo a bowl of coffee

and milk with an egg beaten into it. She put the jam on his bread herself. She cooked pasta for his lunch and turned down the bed for his afternoon nap. They had given him the back room and set up their cots in the kitchen. Amadeo had protested but Zia Guinetta wouldn't listen. They preferred sleeping in the kitchen, she said.

"Ha," Zio Carmelo said to her. "At least now that he's here we eat decent. No bread and oil . . . not with him here. We eat pasta . . . with meat in the sauce."

"Shhh." She put a finger to her lips and pointed to the back room where Amadeo slept. "You want to look like a peasant in front of your nephew? Go cut holes in the elbows of your sweater then. Just the kind of man he will trust to find him a bride, a *cafone* who eats bread and oil."

"But if we can eat like this now, why don't we always eat like this?"

"Because we have to be careful. I save for bad times . . . the next earthquake . . . the next war. Who knows? If it was up to you, we'd have nothing."

Zio Carmelo put a hand under her dress. She turned and hit him with the wooden spoon. He pulled her into his lap and bit the tip of her ear. Tommaso called from outside and Zia Guinetta pulled away.

Zia Guinetta doted on Tommaso. He was, after all, her only son, and if he spent his days in the piazza telling stories, she didn't mind, but was proud that people listened to him. And they did. Someone was always willing to buy him an espresso or a grappa to have him tell his stories of New York. Everyone who could had already left this place, for Rome, for Naples, for New York. Those fated to stay were glad to listen to Tommaso. He told them that the streets were paved with gold, but there was nothing like the simple life of Castelfondo. Hadn't he returned? And they would nod, all too happy to believe that they were the lucky ones.

Once in a while Tommaso was hired to go into another village or to Matera to attend a funeral and present himself as the rich nephew of the deceased who had made a fortune in America. Tommaso would wear the suit he had bought in New York and carry the cardboard suitcase. Terragrossa would drive him to his destination and Tommaso would pay him when he returned.

Zio Carmelo folded his hands in his lap and thought about slipping out to see the widow while the others slept. Zio Carmelo put a kilo of dried pasta, rigatoni, the widow's favorite, into his sack and made his plan.

In the afternoon, when he and Zia Guinetta lay side by side in their underclothes and he heard her snores, he pulled on his shirt and pants, picked up his sack, and left the house. Even the flies were asleep. He made his way out of the town, past the shuttered houses, to follow the path to the fields and the stone shed where the widow lived. It was a place the peasants had built to keep their tools in but it had been abandoned when part of a wall fell down. The widow had fixed the wall and moved in. When the tax collector came by once a year, she would take down the wall and hide in the fields. Everyone else left her alone.

Zio Carmelo came to the stone shed and opened the door. He called out her name. "Mafalda," he said into the darkness, the taste of it sweet in his mouth. It was cool inside and she straddled him across the big bed she had gotten with the money he had given her. "We're not animals after all," Zio Carmelo had said to her, pressing the money into her hand after he had taken her on the dirt floor, in the hay. He gave her money for linen for the bed and set up a goatskin to catch the rainwater so she could wash, but she never washed, and she only slept in the bed when he came to her. After a while, he forgot about her washing, and the smell of her, the memory of the smell of her, made his heart bang in his chest.

They never spoke. He asked her nothing. She took the kilo of rigatoni and hid it in a corner. He licked her body and bit circles into her shoulders. He burrowed into her from behind. He felt like a young man, young enough to work in Don Carlito's fields.

He sighed at the quiet. He thought about Guinetta finding out and sweat broke out on his forehead. But Guinetta slept like the dead, he told himself, and she was so set on the scheme to marry off Amadeo, to tie him to them and to Castelfondo, that she was blind to everything else, even his visits to the widow. He twisted his hands in Mafalda's black hair. Amadeo never stopped making his life easy, he thought.

At first he had worried all the time that Zia Guinetta would find out, that she would cast a spell, and his prick, which he loved, that waved like a flag for him every afternoon and night would never stand up again.

After the first time with the widow, he had stopped eating for two days, sure that Zia Guinetta knew and would get her revenge with poison, but when he finally ate and didn't die, he visited the widow again. One more time, he told himself, and then one more time after that. When he realized he would keep seeing her, that she was worth the risk, he gave her the money for the bed and the linen sheets. Every good thing in life had a price attached, he told himself, like the shellfish from Bari that carried the cholera.

Zia Guinetta was in her kitchen garden every night picking herbs. Zio Carmelo heard her early in the morning, before the sun came up, boiling them on the stove, grinding them into powders, and even though he was convinced the magic was for Amadeo, when her back was turned, he moved the plates around the table, exchanging the one meant for him with Maria's or Tommaso's.

He took Amadeo to the tailor to make him a corduroy suit and they went into the mountains to hunt for rabbits. Zia Guinetta made stews. Amadeo forgot about his business; he forgot his grief. He let them take care of him, feed him, plan his days. He sat in the coffee bar in the piazza and played cards. He waved to the peasants when they came back from the fields and he waited outside the post office for the mail to come.

There were never any letters for him and he would wonder about

---

it and ask Clemente the postmaster to check again. Clemente would flip through the envelopes a second time, wetting his thumb between each one, his lips moving silently, carefully, as he read the names and addresses. He would trace the ink with his finger. There were never more than three or four letters, but Clemente took a long time because Amadeo was an important person and postmaster was an important position. It was a perfect match, but still he would always get to the end, look up, and shake his head. *"Niente,"* he would say.

Amadeo mentioned this at home, but Zia Guinetta cleared his mind. "A small village . . . stuck up in the mountains. You think it's America? Here time stands still."

"But if something happens?"

"Uffa! Bad news is the only kind that travels. Bad news always arrives."

So Amadeo listened to Zia Guinetta, trusted her, and drank his anisette with a black coffee bean the way Zio Carmelo ordered it for him and sometimes he sat back, leaned his chair against the wall, and closed his eyes.

"He's enjoying himself," Zio Carmelo told Zia Guinetta.

"Good," she said. "But what are you doing? You're no closer to the match with Magdalena than the day he came. He'll leave one day and that will be the end of that. All you do is drag him around the countryside and sit him in the cafés." She spat carefully into the herbs she was grinding. "I can't do everything," she said, turning her back to him. "I've even been paying Clemente at the post office to give me the letters that come from New York." She went to a wooden box she kept in the corner and took out a packet tied with string. She threw it in his lap. "Every week they come."

Zio Carmelo took one out and looked at the envelope. "These are from the *nutrice,*" he said. "Teresa Sabatini. He's told us about her. Why don't you give him these letters?"

Zia Guinetta pulled the envelope from Zio Carmelo's hand. "I want him to forget New York. He might get homesick if he reads all these letters. And who is this woman? What is she to him? Do we know?" Zia Guinetta sat down and fanned herself with the envelope. "Ah, it's very complicated. Anything could be. Anything could happen."

"This woman takes care of his son. He told me."

"And you believe him."

"Why not?"

Zia Guinetta stood up and put her face close to Zio Carmelo's. "Because I know men," she said, and she pushed at Zio Carmelo's shoulder in disgust. He thought of the silence of the widow, how she moved over him, mute and adoring.

"Talk to him," Zia Guinetta said. "Mention the girl's name. Keep her in the conversation."

"And you think I don't?" he said to Zia Guinetta. "Every day I lay the seeds. I'm always saying things, throwing hints. 'Amadeo, how fine you look,' I told him when I took him to the tailor. 'You will have the women crazy.' I said. When I take him hunting I tell him if he had a wife from the village, she would make him a stew, the best he would ever eat. Every chance I get I tell him he's a young man, he needs a wife, more children. I tell him his baby son needs a mother. You think only you do anything? My mind never stops . . . all the time I'm thinking. It would be easier for me just to give it all up and go into the fields."

Zio Carmelo went out the door. "Patience, Guinetta," he called out to her from the street. "The rest is fate."

Zia Guinetta believed in fate but she believed more in power. She went into the corner of the kitchen where she kept a small black stone that she had fixed with a picture of the Black Madonna of Viggiano. A candle in a red glass burned in front of it. "I am more clever than any man," she told the image. "Why do my powers have to be dark and hidden?"

She was terrified when the Madonna spoke. "Why complain to me?" the Madonna said. "It's not enough that I find your lost children and cure your sick goats? What do I get? A festival once a year, some lira notes pinned to my robe, maybe a few American dollars. Don't I do enough?"

Zia Guinetta fell to her knees, stretched out her arms, and touched her forehead to the stone floor. She kept her face down, afraid to look up, and mumbled an apology into the floor, but she kept her ears open and listened carefully to the instructions the Madonna gave her. On the first night that there was no moon, she did what the Madonna had told her. She walked far out into the fields and sacrificed a black goat. She kept a sliver of the goat's thighbone, polished it until it shone, and wore it on a black cord around her neck. No one was allowed to touch it, not even Zio Carmelo.

Zia Guinetta kept reminding Zio Carmelo about the betrothal, about the wedding. The men in the coffee bar were starting to get restless, asking questions about the *festa*, when it would take place. It got so Zio Carmelo was not at all his usual self, but nervous and restless.

He entreated Amadeo to stay at home. He would insist on going along with him for walks so as to keep him out of the town. He found some English books at the doctor's house, Victorian novels with cracked spines and water-stained covers, and encouraged Amadeo to read them, "to preserve his English."

Giacomo Caparetti was pestering him, wanting to know what to do, when to tell Magdalena, how to tell Magdalena. Zia Guinetta was at him day and night, her voice a hoarse whisper. "When? When?" she said. She badgered him so much that he would arrive at the widow's and lie across the bed, the sheets stiff from bleach and sun, he himself limp and useless. He bought candles from the widow to appease her and sold them to Giacomo Caparetti to light before the Black Madonna in the church.

Giacomo Caparetti did everything he was told. He was determined now that his daughter should marry the American. He had handed over all his savings for her dowry. There was no choice. He kept Magdalena in the house. He was afraid if he let her go out, she might meet a boy and something would happen. He worried that something had already happened. When he left in the morning, because he was gone all day, he tied her to the bedpost.

"Why are you doing this?" Magdalena asked him. "You've gone crazy. Ever since that American came here, since his arrival in the piazza, you've been a madman, tying me like an animal." She started to cry. "You can't do this. I'll go to the *professore*," she said. "The doctor, the father. I'll tell the head of the carabinieri. He doesn't like you as it is. But he likes me, that one. I've seen him watching me. God knows what he'd do if he found me like this."

Magdalena narrowed her eyes, arched her back, and cried until Giacomo Caparetti worried that he was destroying her spirit and her beauty and ruining her chance of marrying the American and living in New York.

"Stop crying," he said finally. "You're marrying that American, Carmelo Laurenzano's nephew. It's all arranged. Now do you understand? I'm only being careful. I'm protecting you."

"What? What?" Magdalena wiped her eyes with the hem of her dress. "The American?" she said. "The fat old American?"

"Stupid," her father said. "You don't get fat for nothing. I told you that before. Here we scrape for everything. But you, you'll be in America, silk dresses, a car, paint on your face, too, for sure."

"I'm not marrying a fat old man."

"He's not old."

"He's fat, then."

"He's healthy. You know why? He's rich. He eats meat every day. When he drinks coffee, he dunks cake in it. Listen to me. If you stay here, you'll marry some *cretino*, some moron. Don't I want the best for you? Aren't you everything I have?" and Giacomo Caparetti started to cry, which made Magdalena cry, and they held each other and howled into the air. They threw back their heads like the wolves that came to the edge of the village in winter. They screamed and they shouted and when they were tired, when their throats were scratched and raw, Giacomo Caparetti kissed Magdalena's face.

"No," he said. "You don't marry the American. You stay with me. To hell with the dowry. I'll find you a husband, a doctor, a lawyer, no, a prince. You don't worry," and he kissed her hair, her forehead, her nose. "My poor baby," he said. "Your mother left you. How could I send you away?"

"The dowry . . ." Magdalena said. "You gave away the dowry?"

"I'll get it back."

"You gave away the dowry?"

Giacomo Caparetti hit his head against the wall. "Carmelo convinced me it was a good match." He hit his head again. "He said you'd wear diamonds the size of the Madonna's tears."

Magdalena put a hand on her father's shoulder. "I will, too," she told him. "Diamonds the size of hen's eggs. I'll live in New York. I'll be *la signora di New York*," she sang, and she danced in a circle as far as the rope her father had used to tie her to the bedpost would let her.

Her father continued to bang his head against the wall. "But you said he's fat, that he's old."

"He's not so old. And if he's a little fat, so what? It's all that meat and cake. I'll get fat, too." She put her hands on her hips. "Look at me," she said. "How will I look wide like this"—and she stretched out her arms, her hands open as though holding her flesh—"my hips out to here."

"Covered in silk," her father said.

"Don't forget the diamonds."

"No, of course not."

"When is the wedding?"

"I don't know. Carmelo said to wait."

"There must be something we can do."

Giacomo Caparetti took out the votive candles Zio Carmelo had bought from the widow. "We can light these."

"I'll do it," Magdalena said. She took her father's hand. "The priest will open the church for me." She put a black scarf over her hair as though she were in mourning for her mother, who Magdalena sometimes pretended had died.

The church was closed when she got there and she went to the priest's house and knocked on the door. The housekeeper told her to go away. She blocked the door with her body and told Magdalena the priest was asleep but Magdalena pushed past her and when he saw who it was he put on his shoes. He touched the braid that hung down her back and called her his child. He took her arm on the walk to the church, his hand pressing against her breast.

Inside, Magdalena lit the candles in front of the Black Madonna of Viggiano and asked her to help her marry the American. She made promises she could keep only if she married the American. She wanted the Madonna to understand this.

She spoke in a whisper so the priest couldn't hear. When she knelt down, she raised her skirt and showed her legs to amuse him. He walked her to the end of town and kissed her very close to her mouth. The housekeeper was waiting for him, scowling and angry. That night he slept alone.

In the church, Magdalena had asked the Black Madonna to bless her marriage with the American and she had asked for a son. She had done this quickly and under her breath because the old priest was waiting. When she got home, she told her father that she had taken care of everything.

Giacomo Caparetti was relieved at first, then terrified. Magdalena's ambition, her fearless nature . . . not desirable characteristics in a woman, he thought, and she was still so young, only a girl. When his wife was pregnant for the second time, he had asked the Madonna for another son, this one strong and handsome, not like the first, small and sickly, gasping for breath. He had thought when Magdalena was born that his wish had been denied, but now he knew he had gotten the strong and handsome child he had asked for, only the child was a girl. The Madonna had played a trick. He had thanked her anyway.

Giacomo Caparetti put his head on the pillow that night and

had trouble sleeping until he heard a voice in his ear. He felt a touch on his shoulder. He squeezed his eyes shut, afraid to look. "Sleep, Giacomo," the voice said. "She's under my protection. You don't worry."

The village was filled with gossip. Zio Carmelo could hardly go near the piazza without everyone who stood there and sat there wanting to know when the wedding would be. Had he made the arrangements? Hired the band? Ordered the fireworks? the food? What was going on? They demanded to know. They had waited long enough. And where was this nephew? Never with the men anymore but always at home with the women. What kind of a man was this?

Among the women, there was some speculation as to his suitability as a husband. The noose of tales and promises wound more tightly around Zio Carmelo's neck. Someone called him a windbag, and wondered aloud if there would ever be a wedding.

In the home of his aunt and uncle, Amadeo was getting restless and bored, tired of hunting rabbits with Tommaso. He said he was thinking that he should go back to his business and his baby son. He had been here almost two months. Zia Guinetta patted Amadeo on the shoulder. "Ha, in Castelfondo time means nothing. Two months is the flick of an eye."

Zio Carmelo poked Zia Guinetta in her side. "Now what?" he said. "Now how will we keep him here?"

Zia Guinetta gave him her look, the one that silenced him and sent him out to the street and into the fields. She went to see Clemente and sighed when she handed him the extra coins, but she came back that morning with a telegram for Amadeo from Teresa Sabatini in New York that said that Salvatore was fine.

Stay as long as you like, the telegram said, but Amadeo was still restless. Zio Carmelo and Zia Guinetta talked and argued endlessly about how to bring Amadeo and Magdalena together, how to be sure the thunderbolt would hit its mark. Walks in the countryside, they decided. Long walks that would wind past Magdalena's house, and every time they came near, Zio Carmelo would spin another tale about the beauty that lived inside. "Is that her in the window?" he would say, poking Amadeo. "Could we be so lucky?" Zio Carmelo would shield his eyes from the sun. "Look! Look! Do you see?"

Once in a while something would move inside the house and Zio Carmelo would insist that the two of them had seen a vision, that they should keep it secret, because every boy and man in the village would be out here, would be consumed with jealousy. "This girl," Zio Carmelo told Amadeo, "this Magdalena, does not belong on earth, but in heaven with the angels. What else is there to say?"

One afternoon, Amadeo woke up and he couldn't get back to sleep. The heat in the back room was suffocating and the flies were buzzing and settling on the figs Zia Guinetta had strung outside the door. He got up and pulled on his pants and not to disturb his aunt and uncle went out the back way and walked into town.

When he reached the piazza, Natale, the bartender, was closing down for the afternoon. He saw Amadeo come into the square, take off his hat, and wipe his forehead with a large white handkerchief. Natale called to him to come over and he pulled a small table and two chairs into the shade of the awning. He took out a special bottle of homemade grappa and two glasses and invited Amadeo to sit down.

"So," Natale said, "where have you been? Getting ready for the wedding or are you getting cold feet?"

"Wedding?" Amadeo said. He scowled. His eyebrows met across his forehead. "I'm in mourning," he told Natale. "My wife and baby son are in each other's arms in a box under the earth in America." He drank his grappa and Natale poured another.

"But you're betrothed . . . to Magdalena Caparetti . . . the most beautiful girl in Castelfondo. Your uncle promised us fireworks, the brass band from Matera. The whole village is waiting to dance at your wedding."

"Natale, please. What wedding? I don't even know this girl you're talking about."

"Yes, you met her. I saw you. The day you arrived. Your aunt brought her over to you." He filled Amadeo's glass. "There are no secrets here. Everyone knows. The women are sewing dresses. The mayor is ready to declare a holiday. We only want to know when."

Amadeo laughed. He asked Natale if there was brandy. Natale had only one bottle that had been brought back from France during the Great War. No one had ever asked for brandy before. He opened the bottle and they drank it. The sun was almost down, the brandy almost finished, when Amadeo got up to go back to Zio Carmelo's. He had insisted to Natale that he wasn't marrying anyone, but Natale slapped him on the back. "You're not fooling me," he said.

By the time Amadeo stumbled home drunk, he believed Natale. He was convinced that he was marrying Magdalena Caparetti, the most beautiful girl in Castelfondo. The question was why he was the only one in Castelfondo who didn't know it.

He rang the bell outside Zio Carmelo's house. It was the one house in the village with a doorbell but no one ever used it.

"The devil," Zia Guinetta cried out, startled from sleep. "Who else would ring the doorbell?" Zio Carmelo opened the door, and Amadeo fell in. Zia Guinetta pulled him close to her to smell for a woman but there was only the stink of alcohol and she held him in her arms, his weight making her stumble. She helped him over to the bed and took off his shoes. She rubbed the leather with her hands, admiring it, wondering if the shoes would fit Tommaso, and if so, could she induce Amadeo to leave them when he went back to America. Amadeo was mumbling something and trying to sit up but Zio Carmelo held him down and made him drink a tea that Zia Guinetta had brewed. She whispered that it would make Amadeo sleep until tomorrow.

"What do you think happened?" Zio Carmelo asked his wife.

"What do I know?" she said. "But everyone's patience is wearing thin. It's time to give fate a shove."

The next morning, when Amadeo woke up, red-eyed and ill, Zia Guinetta made a paste from the herbs in her garden and rubbed his temples. She tied a wet rag tight around his head and brought him his coffee black.

"So," she said, sitting near him, "you don't feel so good. Where were you yesterday?"

"With Natale . . ."

"Oh, that gossip, worse than the barber . . ."

"And I hear, Zia, that there's going to be a wedding, a big wedding, with fireworks and a brass band, a *festa* as big as the *festa* for the Black Madonna."

"Eh . . ." Zia Guinetta said. She looked up when Zio Carmelo came in from the front room. "Those big mouths," he said. "Those horses' asses," he said, having overheard. "Those *chiacchieroni*. I'll kick their knees from under them. I'll beat them black and blue."

"Zio . . ."

"Never mind." Zio Carmelo sank down next to Amadeo on the bed. He took his hand, and pushed his head back down on the pillow. "Don't worry, *figlio mio* . . . It won't be ruined. I'll take care of everything." He stood up, paced back and forth, cursing the town, the province, Mussolini, the Abyssinians. "I should have gone to America when I had the chance," he said. "This is no place for honest men."

Amadeo watched his uncle pace the room. His head hurt when

he moved his eyes. "Tell me, Zio, what's this about a wedding?"

Zio Carmelo sat down again on the bed. He put his arm around Amadeo's shoulders, lifted him to a sitting position, and kissed his left temple. The smell of Zia Guinetta's herbs made him gasp. "Ah, now it's ruined."

"What's ruined?"

"The surprise . . . the wonderful surprise I'd planned. Finished . . . ruined . . ." and he raved and cursed and said he would cripple every man in the café with a shot to the ankles. He said if this was Sicily, they would pay with more than their legs.

"Zio, one more time I'm going to ask you . . ."

"Forgive me, figlio mio. I get too excited. If not for Guinetta's medicine, I would be dead long ago from a nervous condition. My Guinetta. Ah, there's nothing like love. I married her against my mother's wishes. Poor Mama. She died of a broken heart. I left my wedding bed to close her eyelids. The things I could tell you, but forget about me. What's important now is you."

Amadeo held his head. Zio Carmelo spoke in his ear. He kept his voice to a whisper. He told Amadeo that the most beautiful girl in Castelfondo, the one who lived in the house that they would pass by on their walks, that very same girl, was going to be his. "I've arranged the betrothal and I'll arrange the wedding feast," he said. Zio Carmelo told him how this girl, who loved him already, would be his wife, a mother to his infant son. She would give him more sons, Zio Carmelo said. Her own mother was gone, better this way, no apron strings to cut. Zio Carmelo burst into tears when he finished, tears of joy, he assured Amadeo, who had sat through it all without saying a word, except for an occasional moan from the pain behind his eyes.

Zio Carmelo covered his face with his hands, his fingers open like lattice, and he looked through them to Amadeo's face. "Then it's settled," he said suddenly, kissing him on the mouth with a loud noise. "Tomorrow. When do you want to see your bride? Not to-day. You look terrible. She'll run away if she sees you like this. Tomorrow, then, yes? Guinetta? He'll be fine by tomorrow?" Zia Guinetta sat in the corner. She crossed herself when Amadeo pulled himself out of the bed.

"Are you crazy?" he said to them. The sound of his own voice, his shouting, made him stagger. He could hardly hold up his head but his fury sent the cousins, Tommaso and Maria, to crouch together by the back wall. They whispered, heads touching. "How could you think I would come here for a visit and get married just like that . . . like some old greaseball . . . Forget it, Zio. When I want a wife, I'll find one. This is the twentieth century for chrissakes, not that anyone here knows it." He sat down on the edge of the bed.

Zio Carmelo stood over him. He squeezed his eyes, hoping for tears. "I was looking out for you," he said. "Sometimes a man doesn't know what's good for him. That's what family is for, to help him through life. You should be grateful, but no, Mr. Big Shot, instead you insult me." He turned his back on Amadeo. Zia Guinetta nodded her head. She thought it was going well.

Amadeo lay back down. "Well, I'm sorry, Zio, but forget it. I can look out for myself."

Zio Carmelo took this opportunity to sit next to Amadeo again and embrace him. "But, *figlio mio,*" he said, "you don't understand. It's all arranged. This is a small town." He pointed to his head. "Small-minded people."

"What's that got to do with me?"

"Don't you care about your uncle? How he holds up his head? I promised a *festa* . . . Everyone's waiting."

"Zio, this is my life."

"And the girl . . . this poor girl . . . what about her life? Ruined, that's what. She'll never find a husband. 'Abandoned by the American,' that's what they'll say . . . disgraced, an old maid. She may just as well drown herself in a well."

"I thought she was the most beautiful girl in Castelfondo."

"She is. She is. Would I lie? Would I get you anything but the best?"

"So?"

"So, nothing. Your head is made of wood. If you leave her, no one will want her. Her poor father trusted me and now look . . ."

"Zio . . ."

"Never mind. There's nothing to say."

"Right. Let's forget it."

"You have no choice. A man of honor fulfills his obligations."

"I do have a choice."

"No. No. No. The father might even try to kill you. Tell him, Guinetta. He won't listen to me."

Zia Guinetta came over to the bed and pulled on Zio Carmelo's arm. "Let him sleep," she said. "Let him be."

Zio Carmelo jumped up. "Sleep? I'll kill him. I won't wait for the father. I'll do it myself. Thick, like his mother . . ."

Amadeo shook his head. He pressed the heels of his hands to his temples. "Not now, Zio . . . Please, calm down. Later."

"Come, Carmelo," Zia Guinetta said, and she took him outside into the street. She let him rave until he was tired, until he was grumbling under his breath. "Let me talk to him," she said. "You go." She gave him a blanket and told him to go into the open air, take a walk, have his nap in the fields. He said he would go, only to please her, but the scent of the widow was already in his nostrils. He had done all he could with Amadeo.

Zia Guinetta made an exceptional dinner while Amadeo slept. She woke him when it was ready and set the table for just the two of them. She poured the wine into the crystal glasses the priest had given her when she married. She put out cookies filled with almonds and dates and her secrets. She led Amadeo to the table. She put a hand out to touch his cheek and then pulled out his chair. "For you," she said. When he sat down, she stood behind him, her hands on his shoulders. He was surprised at how long he had slept and how light-headed he still felt. "Now, we talk. You and me."

"Zia, you can talk from now to doomsday. Nothing's going to change."

"Ah, Amadeo . . . Don't be angry."

"I'm not. Let's just forget it."

Zia Guinetta poured more wine. She bent over and cut Amadeo's meat with her knife. "This is a lovely girl, a good girl. She'll take care of your son. She'll look out for you. And anyway, Amadeo, what's done is done. Sometimes you just have to accept what is. You leave this girl now, she's ruined. Her life is finished before it starts. You can live with that? Could God forgive you that?" Zia Guinetta shook her head. She crossed herself and kissed her fingers and touched them to Amadeo's lips.

Amadeo put down his fork. "What am I going to do with some peasant girl in New York? It would never work out. Zio made the deal. He'll have to get out of it. It's not my contract. Now, can we eat?"

"She's a good cook. You marry this girl, you'll eat good." Amadeo was opening his mouth to protest again when Zia Guinetta suddenly stood up. The knife she had cut his meat with was still in her hand and she waved it in his face. "You don't marry this girl, you disgrace us. Your uncle doesn't go to the piazza ever again. Your cousin Tommaso rots in the house. Maria never marries. If you don't do this thing, then we all come back with you to New York. We can't live here anymore." She threw the knife on the table and sat down. She leaned over, put her hand on Amadeo's arm. "Just think about it." Her voice was suddenly soft, seductive. "One meeting . . . just one afternoon."

"I'm leaving," he said.

"Caro mio," Zia Guinetta said. She handed him the biggest cookie on the plate. "What's one afternoon? What is it? You can't do that? . . . And then you go back to New York."

Amadeo bit into the cookie. Zia Guinetta smiled and he remembered what Terragrossa had told him on the long ride into Castelfondo. Amadeo felt the noose tighten around his neck. The cookie stuck in his throat.

In New York, on the stoop outside the building on Spring Street, Teresa sat in the sun with the two boys. The women asked her how much longer before Amadeo Pavese came back. Teresa waved her arms in the air. She raised her voice. "I think the earth's swallowed him," she said. "There was a letter when he first arrived, from Naples, and then nothing."

"*Peccato* . . ." the women said. "What could have happened? *Poverino,*" they said, chucking Salvatore under the chin, pinching his cheek. This made tears slide down his face, which made the women sigh. "First his mother and brother, and now . . ." They turned to Teresa. "If he never comes back? What will you do?" Teresa shrugged a shoulder. She tilted her head to the side and looked up to heaven. "I'll manage. I take care of Nicola, don't I? What's another?" and she kissed the tip of Salvatore's ear.

"You miss Amadeo?" Mary Ziganetti said, eyes narrowed. "All those Sundays, just the two of you . . ." The women on the stoop giggled.

"Amadeo Pavese pays me to look after his son," Teresa said, standing up. "It's the boy I love. You forget I'm married? One man is enough for a lifetime."

The women put their heads together when she left. "What a fate," Jumbo's mother Antoinette said. "One way or the other men are forever abandoning her."

Rumors flew that Amadeo had been killed, bewitched, fallen into a ravine, kidnapped by brigands. They were not all wrong.

Zia Guinetta laid her plans. The next few days found her on her knees in front of the Black Madonna. She spread out herbs and flowers to dry in the sun. Late at night, she left the house and came back at dawn with blood on her hands. She wore amulets against the wolves and the evil spirits of the unbaptized babies that roamed the countryside when the sun set. She visited Magdalena and told her about Amadeo's reluctance.

Magdalena cried and Zia Guinetta put her arms around the girl. "Trust me," she said. "Let me teach you. Give me what I ask and do what I say. Tell no one."

Magdalena nodded, her head on Zia Guinetta's shoulder. "Whatever you want," she said. Zia Guinetta could feel Magdalena's lips forming the words. She took Magdalena's hand and closed it around the polished leg bone that she wore around her neck. Zia Guinetta kissed the top of the girl's head. "Everything will be yours," she told her.

Things were happening in Castelfondo. Amadeo came down with a strange fever and was delirious for three days. Terragrossa's car wouldn't start. He lay under it in the hot sun and cursed the men who made it. He raised the hood and looked at the engine until his shirt was soaked with sweat. He went home in the evenings talking to himself, his face and hands streaked with dirt.

Amadeo couldn't eat. Zia Guinetta cooked him delicate dishes and clear soups. She boiled greens and strained the liquid. She held him upright in his bed and fed it to him with a small spoon. Tommaso told the men in the piazza that Amadeo was ill, but that his mother would make him well, and the men brought the news home.

When Amadeo was better, still weak but strong enough to leave his bed, Zia Guinetta set up the meeting with Magdalena. She promised Giacomo Caparetti that the two would not be alone, not for a moment, and the morning of the tryst, the first thing she did was put a chair for herself in the corner near the stove.

She put the table and two chairs near the door so there would be light, but not so near the door that anyone passing could hear what was going on inside. She woke Amadeo up and gave him tea with a red leaf in it. He took the tea but he wouldn't put on the corduroy suit the tailor in town had made for him. Zia Guinetta shrugged her shoulders. "Never mind," she said. "Tommaso's wanted a suit like this for a long time." She brushed off the dust that had collected on the shoulders of the suit and put it back on the hook near the door. She sat Amadeo at the table. *"Poverino,"* she said, "weak as a kitten, but you'll see, after today, you'll be well again."

Zia Guinetta opened the top half of the double door and leaned out to watch for Magdalena and her father. Amadeo was just finishing the tea when Zia Guinetta let out a long, fervent sigh. "Here, here she comes." Zia Guinetta pulled Amadeo's arm, never taking her eyes off the street. "Quick," she said. "Take a look. See? Did I tell you? Have you ever seen a girl beautiful like this one?" She pointed down the twisted street.

"I'd have to have the eyes of a hawk to see that far away, Zia." He tried to lean farther out the door but she pushed him away.

"Shh . . . You don't want to look anxious." She waved a hand at him and sighed. "Where did she get such beauty? God . . . the devil . . . her mother . . . those same eyes, light behind them . . . Quick, sit down. They're almost here." Zia Guinetta went and sat in the chair in the corner.

Amadeo wondered again how he had gotten himself into this swindle but he was stuck and he knew it. He had agreed to meet the girl. He was so tired. He had been so ill. He would meet the girl and explain to her. He would give her money to add to her dowry, to make up for the misfortune of her engagement, and everyone would be satisfied. He was talking to himself when Magdalena Caparetti came into the room. Zia Guinetta hissed at him from her chair in the corner by the stove and he stood up. He shook hands with her father, who was short and a little crooked and wore a felt hat that a dog had chewed. Magdalena looked straight at Amadeo when Zia Guinetta introduced them and he could see that she was very young and that her eyes were extraordinary.

She did not put out her hand to him. He was not supposed to touch her, and he let his hands fall to his sides. The father left and Zia Guinetta motioned for them to sit down. Magdalena Caparetti sat in the chair opposite Amadeo. She put her hands on the table in front of her and laced her fingers. Amadeo could see the dirt under her nails. He could not take his eyes off her. She stared back at him.

Zia Guinetta served them coffee and cakes she had baked that morning. Before she went back to her chair in the corner, she put a cake on Amadeo's plate and broke it in half with her fingers. "Eat," she said, her hand on the back of his neck. She made a sign to Magdalena. Take nothing, it said.

"So, you're Magdalena," Amadeo said. He ate a piece of cake and she smiled at him. Amadeo was finished. She knew it. He was hers. She pushed her hair out of her eyes. Her father had told her to braid it but she had left it loose. Zia Guinetta had told her not to listen to her father. Magdalena's hair was dark and wild and covered her shoulders. There was a berry stain on her cheek. Without thinking, Amadeo leaned over to wipe it off. Magdalena didn't move.

Zia Guinetta rocked in her chair in the corner. She wondered if this match was such a good idea after all. It was obvious to her that the girl was an occasion of sin. What had the Creator been thinking? And then there was the mother. There's nothing to do about blood, she thought. But could they have tempted Amadeo with an ordinary girl? It was for all of them, this match. She crossed herself.

"Do you know what's going on?" Amadeo said to the girl sitting across from him. "Do you know what they're proposing, your father, my uncle?" Zia Guinetta shifted in her chair. She leaned forward, but Amadeo made a movement with his hand as if to hold her back. He never took his eyes from Magdalena's.

Magdalena straightened her back. "You will take me to America," she said, "to New York."

"And what do you think about that? You're a young girl. How old are you? Fourteen? Fifteen? I could be your father. I have a son in America, a baby. New York is a big city, nothing like here. Everyone speaks English. You won't have your father, your friends, no one, nothing that you're used to."

Magdalena's eyes filled up with tears. "You don't like me," she said. "You hate me." She covered her face with her hands and she started to cry.

"Hate you?" he said. "That's ridiculous. How could I hate you?"

"You don't want me, then. You think I'm ugly." Magdalena Caparetti sobbed into her hands.

"Ugly? You're beautiful. Why wouldn't I want you? Any man in his right mind would want you. You're a beautiful young girl. Why are you crying like this? Please . . ." Amadeo looked over at his aunt, but Zia Guinetta's eyes were closed. She was fingering her rosary. Her lips moved without a sound.

Amadeo shook his head as if to clear it. "Where am I?" he said. "Sitting here in some ancient betrothal ritual trying to make sense with a teenage girl." He stared across the table. Magdalena sat very still. She wouldn't take her hands from her face but she had stopped crying. "You're just a little girl and this is a terrible idea," he said. "Believe me . . ."

Magdalena uncovered her face and put a hand up to his lips to silence him. "Not such a little girl," she said.

In her chair in the dark corner near the stove, Zia Guinetta moved her fingers along the beads of her rosary and smiled to herself. "Everyone has a story, no?" she heard Magdalena say to Amadeo. "I'll tell you mine. Then you decide."

Zia Guinetta nodded in the corner. She watched Amadeo watching Magdalena. She watched how he sat, leaning forward, how he listed into her words like a sinking ship. The button on Magdalena's blouse was open, whether through carelessness or design, who could know? But Zia Guinetta could see Amadeo losing strength. She could see him falling. Magdalena's beauty was as potent as Zia Guinetta's magic. The combination was deadly. His food had been filled with that magic. It had made him ill and it had made him well. The scent of female power filled the kitchen.

"My mother . . ." Magdalena began, and Amadeo listened. His eyes never left her face. "My mother was very beautiful," Magdalena said. "She was married and already had me when a friar came to Castelfondo from Naples. She went to work in his kitchen. He had wine from France that was sealed in bottles. He had a room where sausage and cheese hung on ropes from the ceiling. He had traveled. He would tell my mother about the places he had been."

Magdalena stretched her arms above her head and pulled her hair into a knot. Her hair was red where the light from the open door caught the color.

"She went to live with him," Magdalena said. "And then she disappeared."

"Disappeared?"

"They say she had a son and the friar sent her away."

"Where did she go?"

Magdalena rested her elbows on the table. She opened her hands, shrugged her shoulders.

"I'm sorry," Amadeo said. "And your father?"

"It would be better for him if I went away." In the corner, Zia Guinetta sat very still.

Amadeo opened his hands. Magdalena put her hands inside his and she held his wrists. "You see, there's nothing for me here. All I have here is the reputation of my mother." She tightened her grip on him. Her nails cut into the skin on the underside of his wrists. "The Madonna sent you to me," she said, "to fulfill my destiny, don't you see? There's nothing else to do."

She stood up and came toward him. He saw points of gold in her eyes. He saw her lips part and then she spun around, away from him. His skin burned where the hem of her dress brushed his arm. He thought he would never leave this spot, never get up from this chair. He suspected he would die.

Zia Guinetta thanked the Black Madonna from her corner by the stove. She and Carmelo and Maria and Tommaso would never worry again.

"Whatever you want," Amadeo said to her.

She touched her fingers to her lips, then her heart. She smiled at him and turned away. He could see the muscles in her back where her blouse was cut low. He watched her walk through the door into the street and he didn't move until Zia Guinetta came over and spoke in his ear.

"Well?" she said.

"Tell me what you need." Amadeo ran his hands through his hair. He pressed his fingers into the bone above his eyes. "I have things to do . . . go to Matera . . . Dammit, Terragrossa's car won't start. How do I get there?" He slammed his fist on the table. He felt his strength coming back.

"Never mind," Zia Guinetta said. "Tomorrow morning Terragrossa's car will start. Eat something. Take your nap."

"But I have to go to town. I have to send a telegram to New York . . . my son." Amadeo shook his head as if to clear it, to find his past.

"Rest for now," Zia Guinetta said, her hand stroking the back of his neck. "I'll take care of everything."

"What happened, Zia?" he said. I feel it here . . . and here. He put a hand to his head, moved it to his belly. "Was it God or the Devil?"

Zia Guinetta clicked her tongue. "Fate," she said. "It's always fate." But under her breath, she praised her Madonna.

The wedding was everything Zio Carmelo had promised. Amadeo turned his pockets inside out and complained about nothing except that Magdalena was hidden in her father's house for the weeks before the ceremony.

Zia Guinetta fed Amadeo bits of meat and raw eggs and milk from the goat and when the day of the wedding arrived, he had to admit that she had saved his life. She pinched his cheek between her thumb and forefinger. "So handsome," she said. "Any girl would be lucky."

The wedding celebration lasted three days. There were fireworks after the vows, and the brass band did came from Matera. The musicians wore red uniforms with big gold buttons in two lines down the front of their coats.

Zio Carmelo had ordered paper lanterns in different colors strung across the piazza so the party could go on through the night. Silk banners decorated the balconies. Goats were roasted on spits, and the wedding cake, filled with almonds and honey, was so high that Magdalena had to stand on a stool to cut it.

The children got sick from all the sweets, the men got drunk from all the wine. The priest held the bride after the ceremony and kissed her for too long a time on the mouth.

Magdalena looked like a Madonna. Everyone said so. Five seamstresses had worked for two weeks to finish her dress. They had grumbled at such short notice but Zia Guinetta had put her hand in Amadeo's pocket and the seamstresses were sorry when the dress was finished.

Everyone talked about the embroidery on the bodice, the train that was as long as the church aisle. There were whispers that virtue was not rewarded, that the Devil's power was clear in the forces at work between men and women, but no one could say that it was not the most extravagant wedding Castelfondo had ever seen.

It was such a celebration that Zia Guinetta worried that it was too grand, grander than the festival for the Black Madonna. "She might take offense, get jealous," Zia Guinetta said. "She's a woman, after all," and so she dug into Amadeo's pockets and the papier-mâché statue in the church was replaced with a plaster statue that Zia Guinetta swore cried tears on the anniversary of the wedding. Zia Guinetta would wipe the tears with a lace handkerchief that she never washed but kept in a velvet-lined wooden box under her bed. The priest and the mayor talked about sending the handkerchief to Rome but Zia Guinetta would not give it up, not even for the Pope.

Zio Carmelo wrote all this in a letter to Amadeo and when Amadeo showed it to Magdalena she was not surprised.

The couple left in Terragrossa's car, which had miraculously started just as Zia Guinetta had said. The car was decorated with bits of colored cloth and ribbons and pieces of tin and mirror that caught the sun. Giacomo Caparetti would not let go of his daughter and cried until his eyelids swelled shut and Terragrossa said if they didn't leave soon they would miss the bus.

On the way to Naples, Magdalena told the people on the bus that they had just been married and she gave them pieces of wedding cake that she had wrapped in an embroidered cloth. She uncorked a gallon of wine and by the time they reached the city, it seemed as though they had had another wedding.

Magdalena held Amadeo's arm when they walked in Naples. She had never been outside of Castelfondo, never seen a city. In the hotel, she ran the water in the bathtub until it overflowed. She flushed the toilet over and over to watch the swirl of water go down. To where? she wanted to know. She stood at the balcony and looked out at the sea for hours. Amadeo made her a bath with bubbles.

She's a child, he thought, but when he lay with her at night, he wondered where she had really come from and how she had come to be his. She knew things. How? he asked himself. It frightened him, and when she saw this in his face, she laid her head on his shoulder and took his hand.

"Who are you?" he said.

"I'm yours," Magdalena told him. "And you'll never be sorry."

So," the women said to Teresa Sabatini on the stoop outside the building on Spring Street. "What do you hear from Italy?"

"He's coming back soon."

They all nodded. "Well, it's about time."

"And he's gotten married."

All of them gasped. "No," from the first step. "It can't be," from the second, and then, "So soon!"

"Wait," Teresa said. "Stay right there," and she went upstairs to check on Nicky and Salvatore, who were sleeping under the open window so she could hear their cry from outside on the stoop. She put a hand on their foreheads and pulled the blanket up under their chins. From behind the sugar bowl she took the yellow envelope with the telegram that had come from Italy. Downstairs, she smoothed her skirt under her and sat down on the top step. She handed over the telegram. The women passed it around.

"It doesn't say much."

"Only that he's taken a wife."

"A young one, I bet."

"And maybe big like this," someone said, and she leaned back and held out her arms in a circle in front of her. The others laughed.

"Too bad," Jumbo's mother Antoinette said, putting the telegram back in its envelope, handing it up to Teresa, who sat on the step above her. "He would have been a good catch for you. You've practically raised his son."

"What are you talking about?" Teresa folded the envelope into a small square and stuffed it down the front of her dress. "I have a husband."

"Oh, that's right. It's hard to remember," Antoinette said. "Who sees him?"

"And I have my own son."

Antoinette smiled. "That's right, too," she said, bouncing Jumbo on her knee. His body shook and trembled and everyone there could see that he was the biggest baby boy.

Amadeo took Magdalena everywhere in Naples. They went to dinner and to the theater. He bought her clothes to wear and rings for her fingers and her ears. She was a witch, he told her, and he was caught under her spell. She laughed at him deep in her throat.

"We have to go back," he said one morning. "My son . . . the business. I didn't know I would be gone so long."

"There's something . . . before we go," she said.

"What? Anything."

"I want to see my mother. She's here, in Naples."

"Magdalena," he said. "You don't know that."

"She's here. I have proof. Wait." And she dug through her things to find a postcard of the Bay of Naples. The ink on the card was faded.

"So she sent you a postcard. How long ago? She might have been passing through. She might have had a friend send it. And even if she was here, how could you find her? Do you know how big Naples is?"

"You could find her for me. You promised me anything. You said that. I want to see my mother." She curled herself into the curve of his arm. She made a mustache under his nose with the ends of her hair. She left a trail of kisses down the center of his body.

"Magdalena," he said. She covered his mouth with her hand. "You'll find her. I know you will . . . for me."

Amadeo said he would try. She was a child, he reminded herself. She wanted her mother. When he was away from her, his head would clear and he would wonder how it had all come to be, but he could never understand. He would see her and he would forget everything that had gone before, except for Zia Guinetta's face and the way she had held Magdalena before they left in Terragrossa's car. How Zia Guinetta had whispered in her ear and touched the amulet from around her neck to Magdalena's lips. Amadeo didn't ask. The way of women. What could he know?

He ordered a coffee in a bar near the waterfront and thought about Magdalena's mother. A country girl with a small child arriving in Naples. A good-looking young country girl with no family and no money. He paid his check and asked the waiter the best place to find a woman in Naples. *"Una casa di tolleranza,"* the waiter said. "There's plenty, but forget the houses. I get you a woman."

"No," Amadeo told him. "I want a house, a good one."

"But this woman is beautiful, young. She comes to your hotel room, no questions. She does whatever you want."

"My wife is in my hotel room."

"Ah." The waiter shut one eye. "I understand."

Amadeo made a face he hoped was sly and held out a folded bank note. "Where do I go?"

The waiter took the bill and put it in his pocket. He smiled. "I know some places, not that I've been there. Eh, what would I be doing in a place like that? I'm a waiter. Life's not easy but you have to thank God. I always tell my children . . ."

Amadeo stood up. "Are the houses near here?"

"Yes, yes, very near," the waiter said, and he took the pad from his pocket and drew the directions to an area on the outskirts of the city.

Amadeo stood on the street across from the brothels. Outside the houses there were colored lights to show that they were open for business.

He went into the first one. There was a young girl on the couch in the front room. Her hair was in pigtails with yellow ribbons tied on the ends.

"I want to speak to the *signora*," he said. She smiled when she heard his accent and he saw she was missing a tooth. She was as young as Magdalena.

He thought about Magdalena then, about sending her back to her father. He could give her money and put her on the bus to Castelfondo. He had thought about this when he was sitting in the coffee bar near the waterfront. He always thought about this when he was away from her. What would happen to her in New York? She was so young. What was he doing anyway?

The girl in the pigtails had gotten up and was knocking on a door. She looked at him seductively as she waited, her hip against the door so that when it opened she almost fell inside. The woman who opened the door shouted at her and the young girl raised her hands to cover her head as if the woman would hit her.

"*Signora,*" Amadeo said, and his voice and his accent made the woman stop and look up. She was bony, and, Amadeo thought, very ugly, with a long nose and the mottled, yellowish skin of an opium smoker. He gave her a gracious smile.

She sent the girl away, up the stairs, and she came over to him. "So early, *signore,*" she said.

"The light was on."

"Yes, from last night. Saturday. "We are always busy on Satur-day." She yawned. He saw long stained teeth.

"Should I come back?"

"No, no. Sit." And she led him to the red couch where the young girl had been lying when he came in. Amadeo sat down. He knocked off the embroidered doily that covered the armrest with his elbow. The fabric underneath was stained and worn. The woman picked up the doily and pinned it back in place. "The girls make them when it's slow," she said. "Sweet, don't you think?"

Amadeo nodded. She did not seem so ugly now. She put a hand on his knee and moved closer to him and he remembered why he was here. *"Signora,"* he said. "I'm looking for a woman."

"You've come to the right place," she said. "Just tell me what you want, how you want it."

Amadeo leaned closer. "The woman I want came to Naples ten years ago. She had a baby with her, a boy, I think. She came from the mountains, from Lucania."

The woman sat back. *"Uffa,"* she said. "Naples is a big city. Girls are always coming here. They all have babies. They all come from the mountains. Ten years is a long time. Do you know anything else? The name of the village? You have a picture?"

"Castelfondo," he said. "Near Viggiano in Lucania. She was beautiful, strange eyes, anyone would remember them, bright, as though a lamp were held behind them."

"Lucania," the woman said. "I know Lucania." She smiled with one side of her mouth. "So who is this? Your wife? Your sister?"

"No."

"Who then?"

"Does that matter?"

"You want me to help you, you have to help me. Everything is important. Who are you? Why do you want to find her? Maybe you're up to no good. How do I know?" She paused, traced an eyebrow with a delicate finger. "So, now, tell me. What is this woman to you?"

"I've just married a young girl whose mother ran off to Naples years ago and she wants to find her. She wants to see her again before we leave for New York."

"Fortunata . . . this girl is lucky. Do you know how many *cafoni* come here and promise to take my girls off to America? Then the girls cry when they're left. You're an American. You could have any girl in this place."

"I don't want a girl, *signora*. I want to find my wife's mother. That's all."

"Of course, I understand. Didn't I have a mother? What is a girl without a mother? But who's to say that this mother wants to see her daughter? Or that she's still in Naples? That she's even alive? Not to discourage you, but things go on here. You wouldn't believe the things God allows. . . ." And here she kissed the medal of the Madonna that hung around her neck. "I pray to her every day to keep my girls safe." She held out the medal for Amadeo to see. It was the image of the Black Madonna. The woman tucked the medal back into the front of her dress.

"Can you help me?"

The woman lay back. "It won't be easy. I can't promise you anything."

Amadeo stood up. "Maybe I should go somewhere else."

"Please, sit down. Did I tell you no? You Americans. So nervous. Of course, I can help you. I just have to be careful. Your poor wife. You have to understand this won't be easy. I'll need some money." She paused. "Five hundred lire."

"That's a lot of money, *signora*."

She shrugged. "Nothing's free," she told him, "and nothing's easy. Women who run away don't like to be found or they wouldn't be gone in the first place."

Amadeo counted out the lire. The woman's eyes followed his movements. "How do I know you'll do what you say?" he asked her.

"You don't," she said. "It's the way of the world, *vero?*" She took the money neatly from his hand. She licked her thumb and counted it carefully. Then she stood up. "*Signore . . . ?*"

"Pavese."

"Signore Pavese." She bowed. "*Piacere.*" She held out her right hand, the money was clutched in her left. "You come back in a few days. You ask for Signora Carnevale."

Amadeo bowed and he turned to go. Signora Carnevale held

him back. "Liana!" she called, and the young girl who had let Amadeo in came down the stairs. "See the gentleman out," Signora Carnevale told her. "A few days," she said to Amadeo's back.

Out in the street, Amadeo questioned what he had done—giving five hundred lire to an old painted whore in the first brothel he had come to. He might have gone to the police. Maybe Magdalena's mother had come to the city and gotten a job as a maid, maybe she'd married, but these were fairy tales, he knew. She'd had a baby with her, no money, no experience. He stopped for an anisette before he went back to the hotel. He told the bartender to put a coffee bean in the glass.

Magdalena wanted to know where he had been. She said she was lost without him. She closed the curtains and wrapped her arms and legs around him. He told her that he had been looking for her mother. He forgot all his thoughts about sending her back to Castelfondo. He forgot everything except that she was with him now.

"Forever," she told him.

After a week, Amadeo went back to see Signora Carnevale. The cabdriver knew the place. "A good clean house, nothing to worry about," he said when Amadeo tipped him.

This time the young girl did not answer the door. It was later in the day. There were sounds coming from upstairs and two men waiting on the couch. The girl who let him in put an arm around his waist. Amadeo told her he was there to see Signora Carnevale, and she knocked on a side door and opened it.

"Come in," Signora Carnevale said when she saw him. "Would you like a drink? A cup of tea?"

"Did you find out anything?"

"I need more money . . . three, four hundred. Five hundred would be better. Then I wouldn't have to bother you again." She crossed her legs, pulled the silk kimono over her knees. "It's expensive to make inquiries." She twisted the curl at her temple around her finger while he counted out the money.

"I'll be back only once more," Amadeo told her, "in one week."

When Signora Carnevale heard the outer door slam, she leafed through the bills with a wet thumb. One week was enough time for what she had to do. She counted the bills again. Five hundred lire . . . if it hadn't been for the arthritis in her knees or if she had been ten years younger, she would have had him for herself.

At the hotel, Magdalena was waiting for him. She went out every day and filled the room with things she had bought: plaster saints, ceramic bowls, sugar-covered almonds. Today she had bought cosmetics, and she sat at the dressing table, drawing the line of her mouth with a red lipstick.

Her skin was pale from the weeks in the city. Amadeo thought she was more beautiful than ever. She looked fragile, but this was only visual. Every day, he could feel her more confident, more sure. In the late afternoons she would cover him with her body, pull him into her, lure him with the excitement she had built up during the day, the excitement she had absorbed from the city, from her new life. Amadeo would see the colors of the sunset through the window. She had stopped drawing the curtains.

She would laugh at him, make him get up, take her out for dinner. She would sit close to him, her hips and shoulders against his, and she would touch him under the table. She would flirt with the waiter and leave the top of her dress undone.

Back in the hotel, she would take off her clothes standing by the window, looking out. He would watch the curve of her back as she pulled her dress over her head, and wait for her to come to him. He would never be finished with her, she told him, never have enough of her. He believed what she said.

The week passed, and again Amadeo stood at the door of the *casa di tolleranza* and rang the bell. Liana answered it without a smile and led him to the side room. Signora Carnevale was sitting in a chair, her legs crossed. She swung her foot, her backless slipper slapping against her heel. She adjusted the bracelets that ran up her arm to her elbow. "I think I've found her," she said.

"Are you sure?"

Signora Carnevale looked smug. "I think so. A big city, Naples, but small if you know where to look." She clicked her tongue against the roof of her mouth and looked distracted. "She's from Lucania. There might have been a baby. The beautiful eyes? I don't know the details, but I hear there was an incident . . ."

"When can we see her?" Amadeo was getting impatient.

"Be calm. You are too nervous," Signora Carnevale said. "If you're not careful, this young wife of yours will kill you off before your time. Don't think she wouldn't be happy to do it." Signora Carnevale laughed. "I know life and I know young girls."

"This woman . . ." Amadeo said.

Signora Carnevale settled back. "If you want a meeting, I'll have to arrange it, won't I?"

"Tell me where she is. I'll go see her myself."

"It would be better to have me do it," she said.

"For a small fee?"

"What price can you put on a mother? We each have only one."

Amadeo was beginning to enjoy himself, caught in the web. From the moment he arrived in Italy, he had been caught. Pointless to struggle. Bow to the greater power. He took the glass of sambuca Signora Carnevale held out to him. At the bottom of the glass were three coffee beans. "I'm listening," he said.

"I'll go to see her. I'll talk to her, explain things. Who can know how she'll react? After all, this is a woman who left her family, her village, everything. Why should she want to see her daughter now?"

"Do it then, but soon. I can't stay much longer." Amadeo put his hand in his pocket.

Signora Carnevale kept her eyes steady but her hands fluttered in her lap like pale yellow birds. "One thousand," she said.

The next time Amadeo went to see Signora Carnevale, her door was open. She was sitting in a chair, her feet up, doing a needlepoint pillow of Adam and Eve in the Garden. "I love this story," she said. She held up the pillow to show him where the snake would go.

"Well?" he said.

"Your prayers are answered, *signore*. The woman has agreed to a meeting, and like I thought, she was very reluctant." Signora Carnevale sighed. "Fairy tales, that every mother loves her child. What does a child do for a mother? Make her fat? Take away her dreams? I had a child once, a boy. He's gone now. Good for him, I say."

"When can we see her?"

"She doesn't want to see you, only the girl. Tomorrow afternoon, at the Church of San Gennaro. There's a café across from the cathedral. She'll be there at three o'clock. She said she would be wearing a red felt hat with a black veil."

I've found your mother," Amadeo told Magdalena that evening when she came back from shopping.

"Ha, I knew you would. You can do anything." She dropped the packages on the floor and put her arms around him. "Where is she? When can I see her?"

"Tomorrow afternoon."

"Where?"

"She'll be waiting for you in a coffee bar near the cathedral."

"Ah, Amadeo," she said, "the Madonna did send you to me. You're my miracle."

She made him afraid with the things she said. He worried again about taking her to New York, that it wasn't fair to her, that she would never be happy there. "Maybe," he said to her, "after you see your mother, you should think about going back."

"Back where?"

"To Castelfondo . . . to your father."

"You're crazy. I'll never go back there."

"I'll give you money for a dowry. You'll get a husband, a young, handsome one this time. You'll have a good life."

Magdalena's eyes darkened, the points of gold disappeared. "How can you say this? You still don't know," she said, "that I'll leave you only when I'm dead and maybe not even then?"

"I'm sorry," he said.

She waved away his words and started opening the packages she had bought. "What should I wear?" she said. "This . . . or this . . . Which one?" She held the dresses up.

"Put them on," he said. "And let me watch you."

They took a taxi to the cathedral. There was a coffee bar across the street, tables in the street filled with people. Magdalena pulled at Amadeo's sleeve. "We'll never find her. There's so many people, so many women." She yanked at her dress like a little girl and leaned against him.

"Wait, let's look carefully, one table at a time."

"There's too many. Too many people. Never, we'll never find her. Maybe she isn't even here." Magdalena bit her lip. There was lipstick on her teeth, Amadeo saw, and he took his handkerchief and wiped it off. He wiped the lipstick off her lips, too, and she slapped his hand. He caught hers and kissed the inside of her palm, but his thoughts, his eyes, were on the people sitting at the tables in the street outside the coffee bar. He moved closer. He looked harder, and in a far corner, under the canopy that jutted out from the building, a woman in a red felt hat sat alone. He watched her take out a cigarette from a case on the table in front of her and when she turned her face to light it, Amadeo saw that the top half of her face was covered with a black veil.

"There," he said to Magdalena, "in the corner." Magdalena stood up on her toes and leaned over his shoulder to look.

"Come with me."

"No, she only agreed to meet you."

"What do I say to her? Now I feel stupid. Tell me, what do I say? Come with me. She won't mind." Magdalena held his arm.

He took her hand away. "I'll be inside the cathedral. When you finish, come and look for me."

Magdalena put her head down, like a child, and he came close to her and touched her face. "This is the last thing you will ever have to do alone, I promise you." She turned and walked away from him, angry, he thought, and he let her go. He watched while she went over to the table and when he saw her sit down, he left and walked up the steps to the cathedral. He sat in a back pew to wait. It was dark, cool. There was no image of the Black Madonna here. She was in the mountains taking care of her people. He hoped she was with Magdalena in the coffee bar across the street.

The woman in the red felt hat raised her face. "It's you," she said when Magdalena came near the table and then she smiled, her mouth wide and red below the black veil, which ended at the tip of her nose. The veil was thick, hemmed in black grosgrain ribbon, but still Magdalena could see the disfigured eye hidden underneath. The woman gestured for Magdalena to sit down. She wore black gloves with black pearl buttons at the cuff. Magdalena pulled out the chair across from the woman and sat, her back straight. She folded her hands on the table in front of her. Her tongue was swollen in her mouth. The woman laughed at her.

"So, you wanted to meet your mama. Here I am. Do you recognize me?"

"I was very young . . ."

"Well, what do you want from me? What can I tell you?"

Magdalena narrowed her eyes. She leaned forward. "Why you left us . . . me . . . what you're doing . . . how you are . . ." She reached out her hand to touch the woman's cheek but the woman pulled back and Magdalena's hand grazed the black veil. "What happened to your eye?" Magdalena was crying. "How, how could you leave me? How could you do that? For what? Why?"

The woman stubbed out her cigarette and reached for another.

"Desire . . . ," she said, "fate. It's always fate." She lit her cigarette, blew smoke rings at Magdalena, and laughed at her again, this time deep in her throat. "What did you expect?"

"That you would be glad to see me, that we could be together. I'm married, to an American. I'm going to New York. You could come. Amadeo wouldn't mind. I know it." Magdalena touched the black-gloved hand that rested on the table. She traced the black pearl with a finger. "Your eye . . . In America, they could fix it. You would be beautiful again."

"You little fool," the woman said. She flung her cigarette into the street and grabbed both Magdalena's arms. "I'm not your mother. A whore in a brothel paid me to come here, to masquerade as your mother. The money was good. 'Easy,' the *signora* said. Since this," and here she touched her face near her left eye, "I don't work much anymore." The woman looked away. "I don't even know your name," she said and she pulled at Magdalena's arms for emphasis. And she waited, for tears, for cries, but she was surprised.

Magdalena took back her arms, folded them across her chest, and leaned back. Her eyes were dry. "So, you're not my mother."

"No, I told you that."

"But you could be, couldn't you?"

The woman smiled at Magdalena, a crooked smile. Whatever had happened to her eye had also affected the left side of her face. It was a face without symmetry. "You're a clever girl, and a lucky one. Going to America with a rich husband."

"How do you know he's rich?"

"Who do you think paid the *signora?*"

"So you think I'm lucky?"

"I think fate is smiling on you."

Magdalena spoke slowly, carefully. "What's your name?"

"It doesn't matter. I am not going to tell you but I am going to give you something." From around her neck the woman took a black silk cord. It was very long and had been hidden underneath her clothes. From the cord hung a piece of bone, polished black.

She put it into Magdalena's hand. "I also come from Lucania," she said. "If I had had a daughter I would not have left her, and I would have given her this."

Magdalena closed her hand around the polished piece of bone. "Will I have a son?" she asked the woman, who stood up and re-arranged her hat. The woman stepped back and fixed her veil so that it stood out stiff from her face. She smiled at Magdalena. "Yes . . . and no," she said.

Magdalena found Amadeo in the cathedral and touched his shoulder. She said nothing and he asked her nothing. They went back to the hotel and she slept until dusk, when she dressed and he took her out to dinner. She drank too much wine and when he asked her about her mother she held up her wrist to show him a gold bracelet she had bought for herself in one of the jewelry shops near the cathedral. "She gave it to me this afternoon, my mother." She touched it with her fingers. Amadeo said it was beautiful. He watched her eyes. She didn't cry. She shook her wrist and watched the bracelet move. "The friar gave it to her when she left. She said she's kept it all these years for me."

"Ah . . ."

"The baby died."

"Well . . ."

"She said she was so happy for me. Maybe, she said, she would come to visit us in New York."

"Magdalena . . ."

"She wished me, us, a good life." Magdalena poured herself more wine. She emptied the glass and poured another. "She kept kissing me. She held my hands, and kissed every finger, one by one, like this," and she took Amadeo's hands to show him, kissing each of his fingers, one by one.

"So," Amadeo said. "You're happy now that you've seen her."

"Oh yes. She told me how she had to leave Castelfondo. It was terrible for her, she said. She wanted to take me with her but she couldn't. The memory made her cry." Magdalena lifted her glass. Amadeo paid the check and they walked back to the hotel along the waterfront. He held her under the arm and she leaned against him.

That night Amadeo woke up and saw Magdalena on the balcony overlooking the sea. She turned when he sat up in bed and called her name. She stood there facing him, her arms folded in front of her. Then she walked across the room and got into the bed next to him. "I told you," he said. "Today was the last time you will ever have to do anything alone. I promise you," he said to her.

Amadeo meant to hold her in his arms like a child but she wouldn't let him. The polished black bone that the woman had given her in the café hung from her neck. Magdalena held her hand over it. She knew, now, she had the power. She wasn't afraid.

"Are you sorry you found her?" Amadeo said. "Was it a mistake?"

"No," she said. "It was fate, like us, no?" She put her head on his shoulder. She put her mouth on his collarbone.

"Tomorrow," he said in her ear, "I'm going to buy you a bracelet."

"But I have this one."

"Another one, a more beautiful bracelet than this one." He touched her wrist. "So you'll remember me forever."

She pulled away. "You're still thinking again to send me back?"

"Never," he said.

"We go to New York?"

"On the first ship."

"You swear?"

"To the Black Madonna."

Antoinette

1968

To his mother, Jumbo was always special. He was, after all, her miracle, the son the Madonna had sent her after five girls, and not just an ordinary son, but a huge son, a giant of a son. Even the sight of his shadow caused a line of sweat to form between her breasts.

Jumbo grew up to fulfill the prophecy of his birth. He was forever Jumbo, the biggest baby ever born on Spring Street, and Spring Street was where he stayed: in his mother's house, at his mother's table, or in the kitchen of one of his five sisters. Filomena, Raffaella, Albina, Angelina, and Rosina had each in their turn, in the order of their birth, married and moved from their mother's apartment to another one in the same building. They were scattered, one on every floor, the eldest across from the ancestral home, and through their open doors they would recognize their brother's footsteps and call to him as he climbed the stairs. He would stop to eat with one and then the other until he reached his mother's house, where he'd eat again. The Last Supper, his mother, Antoinette, called it.

The neighborhood had changed since Jumbo was a boy, since Nicky had fallen three stories from the rope in the alley, since Magdalena had arrived from Castelfondo to be Salvatore's stepmother, but not much. Dante was still there in front of the building, but now, instead of standing, he sat in an old kitchen chair, stuffing poking through the upholstered vinyl of the seat cushion, and he ate in Antonina's restaurant since his mother had died, big sandwiches of capicollo and roasted peppers on bread from Dapolito's on Prince Street for lunch and four-course meals in the evening: *antipasto, primo, secundo,* and *dolce.* Some thought Antonina was sweet on Dante; there were rumors that he would rub up against her in the coat-check room when she took his coat in winter and his straw hat in summer but it could have been only talk. Antonina had thrown her drunken husband out into the street years ago and a woman alone, in business for herself, was suspected of every imaginable sin of the flesh, even down to a grope among the hangers during lunch hour.

Sam & Al's candy store was gone, and so was Barbato's Pork Store, where Jumbo's mother and Nicky's mother would run up their bills and check through the plate-glass window to see who was inside before they entered, the pork store being narrow with a row of chairs along the wall, and not a place to meet your enemy.

It was hard to believe that Nicky's mother still inspired dread in Jumbo's heart. But his own mother and his five doting sisters had kept the fear alive, always stuffing some medal or relic into one of his pockets to protect him from the ill luck they were sure Nicky's mother wished upon him. Sometimes Jumbo's mother Antoinette felt that in spite of all her efforts to protect the love of her life, her reason for breathing, Nicky's mother had managed to do Jumbo harm, had held him back from his destiny. Here he was, a grown man, with no wife and no children.

Antoinette had hoped for a better job for her son than bartender in Benvenuto's across the street. She had relentlessly badgered Filomena's husband, who worked for the Metropolitan Life Insurance Company on East Sixteenth Street, to get Jumbo a job, a nice clean job where he could wear a suit and tie and write with a pen at a desk. But these were the least of her worries.

There was the night Jumbo didn't come home and his sisters held their collective breaths along with the food they had set aside for him. Antoinette crossed herself and braced for the worst of news, which came quickly, as news always did in the neighborhood, everyone on top of one another and always interested in his neighbor's fate, fingers crossed that it was worse than their own. Word on the street was that Jumbo was into Fat Eddie Fingers for his life and to save it he had run away.

Not just Jumbo's mother and sisters and Fat Eddie Fingers knew Jumbo was gone. Everyone knew. Jumbo took up a lot of room. When he wasn't around, you noticed. Everyone on Spring Street and Sullivan Street and Thompson Street noticed. Jumbo was missing and they all knew why.

But unlike Nicky's mother Teresa, Jumbo's mother knew there were more important things than saving face, and she called together her gaggle of girl children and went off to Fat Eddie Fingers's café on King Street to beg for Jumbo's life. Fat Eddie Fingers had never had so many women in his café at once; it made him nervous. Some insisted it was the first time any women had set foot in his café.

It was commonly known that Fat Eddie didn't like women, not even his own mother, who had abandoned him for a country boy twenty years her junior and run off with him to a farm in Upstate New York when Eddie was only ten. The next-door neighbor, Mrs. Petrocelli, had fed Eddie and washed his clothes but it wasn't enough to change Eddie's mind about women in general and mothers in particular.

All that soft flesh stewed in perfume, all those females, and every one of them crying like a professional mourner had turned the tide, had convinced Fat Eddie Fingers to spare Jumbo's life.

The only thing Fat Eddie Fingers really wanted was his money, the vig on which was going up all the time. A dead man couldn't pay any vig, let alone principal, not to mention the inconvenience of making a body the size of Jumbo's disappear. A deal was struck.

Jumbo would work the bar in Benvenuto's restaurant, where Fat
Eddie Fingers was an undisclosed partner. With double shifts six
days a week and every paycheck signed back to Luca Benvenuto,
who would cash the checks and hand the money over to Fat Eddie
Fingers, Jumbo could be out of debt before he died of natural
causes. For the check-cashing privilege, Jumbo had to pay Luca
Benvenuto twenty percent. Once Antoinette knew her son was out
of mortal danger, she appealed to Fat Eddie Fingers's business side
and negotiated for Jumbo's tips. A man's got to eat, Antoinette told
him.

Jumbo looked on the bright side. Eddie could have put him behind the wheel of a truck or on the docks lugging cargo. But here
he was, walking to work, talking to people with clean hands, and
best of all he wasn't dead. He hadn't even lost any weight. He
hadn't been gone that long. On a really good day, he thought of
himself as being back "in the nightlife" like when he and Nicky
and Salvatore had worked the Savannah Club. That was Fat Eddie
Fingers's joint, too. It was the year they turned eighteen.

They had just finished high school, except for Jumbo, who had
dropped out in his second year at Textile, when he told them he
was going to work on Third Street, a block of nightclubs that fea-
tured high-yellow strippers with names like Hortense and Peaches.

"When?" Nicky had said.

"Next week. I start off as a bouncer. Then if I do good, Eddie
says I get to be a waiter. You know the kind of dough they pull
down in that joint?" Jumbo smacked his lips. He took two hand-
fuls of peanuts from his pocket and started to chew.

"Yeah," Nicky said. "So how'd this happen?"

"My uncle."

"What uncle?"

"Well, I call him my uncle but he's not really. He goes out with
my sister Rosina. He's connected. My mother don't like to talk
about it. She makes believe he's an insurance salesman like Frankie,

my sister Filomena's husband, until she needs something. Last week she heard about a Sasso olive oil shipment that got lost on Pier Forty-two and she asked him to get her two gallons. Forget that. What are you two gonna do?"

Nicky hit Salvatore on the back. "Salvatore's got a future," he said, ". . . tomatoes . . . broccoli . . ."

"The old man wants me to go to college," Salvatore said.

Jumbo shuddered. "More school?"

"Well, it sounds better than slicing salami . . ."

"It all sounds like crap to me," Nicky said. He shifted his cigarette from one side of his mouth to the other.

"Maybe I could take you with me," Jumbo said. "Lemme ask my uncle."

"I'm in," Nicky said. "You, Salvatore?"

"I don't know."

"If I ask, though, you gotta come," Jumbo said. "Don't make me look bad 'cause I got a future with these guys."

"C'mon." Nicky poked Salvatore. "Whatta you gonna do in college? This is a real opportunity." He turned to Jumbo. "He's in and so am I. Go talk."

Amadeo Pavese did not believe it when Salvatore told him he was going to be a waiter in Fat Eddie Fingers's club on Third Street with strippers who took the subway down from Harlem and worked the room when they were finished dancing on the stage.

"That's it?" he said to Salvatore. "You're going to serve drinks in some bust-out joint full of five-foot-ten hookers and drunken johns?"

"I don't want to go to college."

"Come in the store. It's yours."

"I don't want to come in the store."

Amadeo blew through puffed-out cheeks, shook his clasped hands in disbelief, and left the room.

Teresa hit Nicky with a wooden spoon when he told her. She cut open his head and waited until the blood had stained his shirt before she tried to bandage the wound. Nicky told Salvatore and Jumbo that the Neapolitans had twelve different words for a smack to the head and he knew them all. His mother blocked the door when he said he was going to the hospital. "The last time you came back a cripple," she told him.

Nicky sat back down. "We're all going to work there. Me and Jumbo and Salvatore. Jumbo's uncle said he'd vouch for us."

"Jumbo, Jumbo . . . from the day he was born he's been a knife in my side."

"It's always Jumbo," Nicky said, raising his voice. "What about Salvatore? How come you never have anything to say about him?" Teresa let go of the rag she had been pressing against Nicky's head and the blood started to pour out again. It ran down his ear and along the side of his face. "Ma . . . Don't be like that. I'm gonna make good money. You'll see. You'll be glad."

She sat down and drummed her fingers on the table. "I'll be glad when I'm in my grave," she said.

Magdalena put her arms around Salvatore and held him against her. She held the lobe of his ear between her thumb and first finger. "You do what you want," she whispered. "It's a free country, America."

From the first moment Magdalena had taken Salvatore in her arms, when he was just a baby, she had been his. From that first moment, she had wanted to give him everything.

When Magdalena arrived in New York, Amadeo had taken her to Teresa Sabatini's apartment on the fifth floor of the building on Spring Street to pick up Salvatore. Teresa had him ready but Magdalena had to almost pull him from her arms. He had been dressed in blue from head to toe, a knitted cap down over his ears.

"This is Magdalena," Amadeo had said.

"Piacere." Teresa did not hold out her hand.

"Where's Nicky?" Amadeo asked.

"Asleep. I didn't want him to see his brother leave."

"They're not brothers, Teresa," Amadeo said. His voice was low.

Teresa shrugged. "Blood . . . milk . . . who can say?" She looked over at Magdalena, who was taking off Salvatore's hat. "He gets cold easy. Better you leave his hat," Teresa said. Salvatore cried and squirmed in Magdalena's arms. "And he doesn't like to be held that way. He's fussy about the way he likes to be held."

"Please, *signora,* you show me how," Magdalena said. She brought Salvatore to Teresa and put him back in her arms. Teresa put him over her shoulder and held him close, his head in the hollow of her shoulder. Magdalena put the knitted cap on Salvatore's head and pulled it down over his ears.

Amadeo took the valise Teresa had packed with Salvatore's things and Teresa handed him to Magdalena. He was asleep.

"You'll come to see him?" Magdalena said. Teresa said yes but she never did, and Amadeo told Magdalena to leave it alone.

Antoinette was not happy, either. She blamed not the boyfriend of Rosina, who spoke for Jumbo with Fat Eddie Fingers, but Nicky, whose mother would not leave Jumbo's destiny alone. There was no other reason she could see why everyone else but Jumbo had graduated high school, why Jumbo played five dollars on the numbers every week, why he wanted to waste himself in nightclubs rather than, say, a nice steady job with the Metropolitan Life Insurance Company like Filomena's husband Frankie. Frankie had explained to her that Jumbo needed a diploma, that the Metropolitan Life Insurance Company was very strict about these things, but Antoinette didn't want to hear it. And it was no consolation to her that Nicky, too, was working in the strip joint on Third Street because Antoinette was convinced that Nicky would leave unscathed, but Jumbo? Something bad would happen to Jumbo and only to him because Nicky's mother would see to it with her evil eye and her widow's ways.

Nicky's mother had never taken off the black she had put on when her husband died, and she wore the black scarf on her head as though she were back in the villages of Lucania. Her handkerchiefs had black borders and her ear loops were black, not gold. She had a certain respect among the women who sat on the stoop for her devotion to the old ways. She had hidden the radio for two years after her husband's funeral and for the first six months had not gone outside, but sent Nicky on his new legs to do her shopping.

Antoinette was modern. She had bought a black dress and stockings for her husband's wake and funeral; the hat with a small silk net veil she had borrowed from a cousin, but the outfit had disappeared after the cemetery and lunch at Antonina's Restaurant on Thompson Street. By the next afternoon, she was on the stoop in a multicolored flowered housedress with two front pockets. In all fairness, the women who liked her said, at Antoinette's weight, it was hard to manage in anything but a housedress.

Salvatore, Nicky, and Jumbo went to work in the Savannah Club. It was the beginning of their lives as young men. They worked for tips and made more money than they could spend, serving fifty-dollar bottles of cheap white wine mixed with seltzer water and labeled French champagne. They rinsed out the bottles at night and refilled them in the morning, twisting gold foil around the corks, regluing the labels when they came loose.

After the show, the strippers sat with the men in school ties and business suits, their one hand delicately touching a cheek, the other under the table. When the men asked, the strippers would order champagne.

Jumbo worked the door while Nicky and Salvatore served bottle after bottle, shaking them first, so the cork would pop like Dom Pérignon, and turning the bottles upside down into the silver-plated ice bucket when they were still three-quarters full. They would smile, but never at the girls, who cut them into the action, and at the end of every night sat with them at a table in the back. With the jukebox turned up loud they would smoke reefer and count their tips. They left work with a wad of bills folded in half, fifties on the outside, making a bulge in their pants pocket. Sometimes they went down to the crap game in the basement, where Fat Eddie Fingers tried to take back the bulge in their pants, and sometimes they went uptown to Harlem with the dancing girls who loved them and taught them what to do in rooms with velvet paper on the walls.

They had sharkskin suits custom-made and while they got their hair cut, pretty girls in white coats painted clear polish on their fingernails. The three of them took an apartment together on West Tenth Street for the closet space and because they couldn't live home. They left the neighborhood far behind, they thought, for their new lives in the Village.

They were on their own except for Jumbo, who moved back home in three weeks. He missed his mother, he said, the way she pressed his shirts, her meatballs with pignoli nuts and raisins, the lasagne packed with sausage and mozzarella, and he missed his five sisters, who still bought him satin hearts filled with chocolates on Valentine's Day.

Salvatore felt bad when Jumbo left the apartment. They had been fourteen when they cut their hands and mixed their blood to declare their allegiance. They had waited for St. Joseph's Day, and had sliced a pocketknife across the center of their palms. Now they were bound for life, Salvatore said. Magdalena had told him about St. Joseph's Day, the day of the year when men could become brothers.

Nicky put a hand on Salvatore's arm when he brooded. "C'mon. Let's face it," Nicky said. "It's better with him gone. He took up an awful lot of room."

They were in the Savannah Club when Nicky had the rings made. They had gone down to shoot craps in the basement after work and they were losing. Salvatore and Jumbo were cleaned out but Nicky was hot. There was a pile of money on the floor. Only Fat Eddie Fingers was calm. He waited for the seven. Salvatore saw him moving his lips in a silent prayer, and sure enough, Nicky threw a seven.

Nicky stood up. "That's it," he said. "Tonight I worked for nothing."

Eddie grabbed his wrist. "You was doing so good," he said. "Why you gonna stop now?"

"Good? I'm broke," Nicky said.

Fat Eddie moved his head to the side. He took Nicky's arm. "What about this?" He pointed to the ring on Nicky's fourth finger.

"My inheritance," Nicky said.

"I like it. It interests me."

"Me too," Nicky said. He was looking up at Fat Eddie. Everyone else was looking down.

"You sure you're not in?" Fat Eddie still had his hand on Nicky's wrist.

Nicky shook his head. Salvatore held his breath. Jumbo thought he might wet his pants. Fat Eddie let go and picked up the dice. "Okay," he said. "But I expect to see you down here tomorrow."

Jesus," Jumbo said when they got outside. "That took balls. I would've given him the goddamn ring."

"Get outta here. It's the only thing I ever got from my old man."

Nicky thought a minute. "Unless you count the knot." If Jumbo heard, he didn't let on.

"Let's see it," Salvatore said. He turned the ring over in his hand. "Where's it from?"

"My father won it in a crap game in Hong Kong. He said he'd explain it to me when I grew up, but he dropped dead first."

Jumbo took the ring from Salvatore and held it up to the light over the poster of Peaches that was in a glass box outside the club. The ring was square on top with carvings that went down both sides. It was heavy in his hand and the gold it was made from had a reddish tinge.

"Something, huh?" Nicky said. "I showed it once to a friend of mine in Chinatown. He told me about these clubs he'd heard the old wise guys talk about where they kept girls from all over the world. The members wore these rings so they could recognize each other. He was surprised I had it, because they were secret societies. But who knows? It could all be bullshit."

"Wow," Jumbo said. "Your father belonged to a secret Chinese sex club?"

"What do I know? He told me he won it in a crap game." Nicky put an arm over the glass box and pointed to the poster of Peaches. "We're a secret society," he said. "We should all have rings."

They agreed that was a good idea, but they were drunk and it was forgotten until weeks later, when they were at Chi Chi Baines's whorehouse on 125th Street drinking shots of Seagram's and Nicky took out two blue velvet boxes. He handed one to Salvatore and one to Jumbo.

"Rings," he said. "Just like mine."

They woke up twenty-four hours later in the rooms Chi Chi rented above the bar. She had taken all their money, so she had her boyfriend Charles give them a ride downtown.

But one morning when they were corking the champagne bottles—except for Jumbo, who was home sick with palpitations—Salvatore told Nicky that the life was getting to him.

"You're crazy," Nicky said. "It don't get much better than this. We got money . . . We got respect . . . We got broads . . ." He counted on his fingers.

"Yeah, but do you want to be robbing johns ten years from now?"

"In ten years, we could have our own joint . . ."

"Stop dreaming. You still gotta have Fat Eddie," Salvatore told him. "There's always gonna be a Fat Eddie Fingers."

Salvatore had just come into work, was putting his suit jacket on the hanger, had changed into the short-sleeve white shirt and black pants he wore every night, when the busboy told him that Magdalena was on the phone. That it was important.

After the club closed, when Salvatore was sitting at the bar in the Bon Soir with Nicky and Jumbo, he ordered a vodka martini and lit a cigarette. "They're gonna shut down the Savannah Club," he told them.

"What?"

"You heard me. They're gonna close it down. They're gonna arrest everybody in it."

"Where'd you hear this?" Nicky said.

"Magdalena . . . My old man got the word."

"Close it down for what?" Nicky said. "The club's legitimate."

"The undisclosed owners ain't. The SLA is gonna pull the license."

"No disrespect, Salvatore, but I don't believe it. Fat Eddie Fingers's got every cop in the precinct on the payroll. That club's as

safe as Fort Knox. How do you know your old man isn't just saying it to get you out?"

"If he says it's gonna happen, it will, and we better not be there."

"Salvatore's right," Nicky said. "It ain't worth the risk."

"You guys are real pussies," Jumbo said, but when they shut
down the Savannah Club three months later, Jumbo was called as a
witness and spent the next two winters with relatives in the back-
woods of Georgia.

Teresa made the sign of the cross when Nicky went into the army.
Magdalena put Salvatore on the train for Syracuse University in
Upstate New York and Antoinette went to the woman on Bedford
Street for an amulet to save her son from the government and bring
him back safely from the wilds of Georgia.

It was the end of their life together as young men and the first
time Jumbo had to run away.

167

Nicky came to see his mother often. She was in the same apartment and would not move, not that he had anywhere to move her. He lived alone on West Twenty-third Street in a studio apartment that suited him fine. His ex-wife Gina had taken the house in Queens. She told him he might as well live in the city near his mother; he was way up her ass anyway. One of the things Nicky had never liked about Gina was her mouth. It was something about her he didn't miss. Nicky didn't want to think that he hadn't moved back into the neighborhood because of what Gina had said to him about his mother. He convinced himself that he liked Twenty-third Street. He could come and go as he pleased and nobody knew his business. They for sure weren't going to hear about him from Teresa. You could have squeezed her like a tomato and she still would never talk. Teresa should have married a Mafioso, the women on the stoop said behind her back, instead of that seaman. She would have been a good wife for a Mafioso. She never talked and she never got lonely and she always wore black.

Whenever Nicky came into the hallway of the building on Spring Street, he felt like he was home. The walls were painted the yellow of puke, the bottom half a dark red like dried blood, to hide the scuffs and smears of so many people, the kids who would run their hands along the wall and bounce balls down the steps and drag bicycles and carts made of boxes and a broken roller skate. Nicky remembered Anna the Blonde and her six boys, who would come down the stairs in a circle of arms and legs punching and kicking except when it was raining, and then one of them would take the big umbrella from behind the door and walk to the diner on Varick Street where she worked and pick her up so she wouldn't get wet. Whoever the lucky son was, he would hold the umbrella up high over Anna the Blonde's head, being careful to protect her shoulders, and when she got home another one would take her wet shoes and stuff them with newspaper while she put her feet up on the round hassock in front of her chair in the living room.

Anna the Blonde would leave on Friday night and not show up again until Sunday but her boys were devoted. "I'm not devoted?" Nicky would say when Teresa mentioned Anna the Blonde. He would take his mother's hand when he said this. It was all she would allow him to do. She would kill for him, he knew, but she had stopped holding him when he grew taller than she was.

Nicky pushed open the first door and then the second. There were mailboxes where before there had been simply a communal mail slot cut into the tile wall of the entrance hall, but now the residents waited for Social Security checks with the ardor of lovers and it never would have done to let those checks sit out in the open. These days, Nicky's mother was always telling him, Who can you trust?

He climbed the stairs, glad to see most of the doors open, even though as a cop he knew it wasn't smart anymore. He would tell his mother every scam he came across but she would only wave her hand at him. "Nicola," she'd tell him, "I never trust nobody. Why you worrying now?"

He knocked on the door to her apartment, which was held ajar by a string from the doorknob to a nail in the wall inside and she heard him and called *"Chi è?"* from the parlor, getting up from the chair she had placed by the window so she could watch the street.

"Stay, Ma, it's me, Nicky." He saw her through the cut in the wall dividing the kitchen and the living room. She sat back down on the kitchen chair that stayed permanently by the window. He put his fingers into the holy-water font inside her door and felt that it was dry. He went into the kitchen and filled a glass with tap water, which he poured into the half seashell. From habit, he crossed himself before he stepped inside to visit with his mother. She turned when he walked into the living room and she gave him her hand. He kissed her cheek, the skin dry and paper-thin, and he sat down on the couch, but she got up and made him come into the kitchen with her, where she put up coffee and took a box of cookies out of the tin cabinet next to the refrigerator.

"How are you, Ma? You feel good?"

"Who feels good at my age? Nothing works right anymore. . . . And those Mangiacarnes. The building's full of them. All the sisters and their husbands and their dirty rotten kids. After what her son did, you think the family'd be embarrassed, that they'd move somewhere else. Go away."

"Ma, what are you talking about?"

"Oh, you forgot already? That you were crippled because that big horse pushed you out the window?"

"You never would have had your miracle if that rope didn't break. And it wasn't Jumbo's fault. He didn't push me. We were playing Tarzan."

"He didn't help you neither." She fussed around the kitchen, setting a cup and saucer down in front of him and he grabbed both her hands and kissed them. She softened then and came near him, put her hands on his head, bent to kiss his forehead.

"So now, tell me. What's new in the neighborhood? What's going on?"

"What's to tell? Jumbo ran away, the boys were after him. This time I think they were gonna kill him . . . gambling, all the time gambling with no money. He owes his life. Poor Antoinette."

"So you're feeling sorry for Jumbo's mother?"

"Whatta you crazy? Look . . . Look the things I gotta do to keep them away." She pointed out the kitchen window, which faced the alley. On the clothesline from the window hung a dark brown army blanket. Nicky's mother nodded her head toward the window. "Rosina's across the alley. I gotta put that there so I don't have to see her or her sisters' or her mother's face every day they sit in the kitchen like they got nothing to do. Instead of cleaning their houses, maybe cook something for their miserable husbands . . ."

"That's insulting, Ma, no? You leave that blanket there all the time?"

"All the time, even though it's wool and when it rains it smells . . . I could care less about insulting them . . . if they don't know now . . ."

She walked him down the narrow hallway when he was ready to leave. She put her fingers into the holy-water font and was surprised to see it was full. Nicky told her he had filled it . . . with water that had come from Rome, that the Pope had blessed.

"Where's the bottle?"

"Whatta you want the bottle for?"

"The bottle had holy water in it, the bottle's holy, too. What'd you do? Throw it out?" She took the brown paper bag she had given him to put in the garbage pail downstairs and began to rummage through it. Nicky took the bag away and closed it back up.

"Wait," he said. "I got it. Don't worry. Just give me a minute." Nicky slipped into the bathroom, which was off the entrance hall, a long narrow room with a claw-foot tub and a toilet bowl at one end with a water tank above it and a flush chain. He rummaged in his pocket and found a small bottle of French perfume he had bought for his woman of the week. He flushed the toilet and emptied the small bottle into the swirling water. An ounce of Joy perfume. He'd paid plenty for it—he'd given up swag when he made detective—but the old lady would kill him if she thought he had put tap water in her holy-water font. He put the bottle stopper back on and wiped it with the hand towel hanging on a plastic hook glued to the wall. His woman would have to wait. His mother was more important and any woman who got involved with him now would have to know that from the beginning.

Maybe if Gina had had a child of her own she would have been able to deal with Teresa, who this second was banging on the door. "You got it? Whatta you doing in there?"

Nicky opened the door and handed his mother the bottle. "Here, Ma, I found it. It was in my pocket."

"Grazie, Madonna," she said, opening the empty bottle. She sniffed it and jerked her head back, her lips tight, her eyes closed.

"The Pope," Nicky told her. "He blesses water, it smells like perfume."

The next time he came, he saw the bottle on the night table by his mother's bed, her rosary beads wrapped around it.

All their mothers had painted plaster saints on tabletops and shelves and hanging on the walls. Votive candles flickered in dark red and blue glass. Nicky's mother had hollow crucifixes in every room with long, tapered candles inside, ready for the rites of the dead. There were strands of blessed palm from Palm Sunday wrapped around the crucifixes. All of this was sacred. Nicky was convinced that the reason for all the saints and holy cards and medals and strands of dusty palm was that there was no way to get rid of them.

You couldn't throw them out. "They're blessed," his mother would scream. You couldn't give them away; everyone had their own. So they slowly accumulated until they became part of the decor.

Nicky came into the street and the first person he saw was Dante, who came right over to him and put his arms around him. Dante touched Nicky's legs. He always said they belonged to him, too. "You always come around," he said. "Not like some of them, like your old friend Salvatore."

"Yeah," Nicky said. "Well, there's the old lady I gotta see and my precinct's right here."

"You did good, Nicky, you're a good kid." Dante put a hand on his shoulder. "But you were a sonofabitch small. I remember," he said, and he laughed. He stood straight for an old man. He showed Nicky the cane they gave him at St. Vincent's Hospital. "I don't know why. I don't go no place but I guess it's good to have." He kept it hooked over the back of the kitchen chair he sat on outside the building, and at night when he put the chair under the stairs, he put the cane there too.

"Did you hear about Jumbo?" Dante said.

"My mother started to tell me something."

"He's working in Benvenuto's. Did you know that?"

"No. I'll stop in and see him."

"Yeah, you should. It's slow in the afternoon. You can catch up. What a shame. He had the world by the balls, working uptown in Jilly's."

"What happened?"

"He got in over his head. You know Jumbo. If he had half the money he made, he'd be on Easy Street, but what can I tell you? We all end up in the ground anyway . . . pushing up daisies. Not that I ever seen a daisy growing in Calvary. I got a spot waiting for me, right on top of my mother, but I ain't planning on going just yet. Gives me the creeps. When I hit the number, I'm gonna get one of them drawers."

"Jumbo's in Benvenuto's now?"

"He's always in there. It was that or push up daisies. Myself, I think Fat Eddie made a bad deal. But what the hell, Eddie can afford it. Jumbo fucks up this time, Fat Eddie's gotta take care of him. Fat Eddie said this was Jumbo's last chance. That's what I heard anyhows. You hear a lot just standing around. I could write a book." Dante pinched Nicky's cheek as if he were still a small boy.

Nicky took the old man's hand. The skin was translucent, the veins thick and raised. "Maybe I'll stop in Benvenuto's. C'mon. I'll buy you a drink."

"Nah, thanks. I can't stay inside. I get too nervous. I get, what do you call it? . . . Claustrophonic? At night I go upstairs the last minute and I close my eyes and get in bed. The morning's not so bad but the night gives me the willies. I don't like the dark, makes me think about that place I mentioned before and bars are dark inside, even in the day, especially Benvenuto's." Dante raised his eyebrows and pointed across the street with his chin. "Too dark to count your change."

"I'll see you soon," Nicky said.

Dante shook his head. "I'm here," he said. "If you don't see me, go look in Calvary, unless I hit the number before then. Then you gotta go find me in the drawer."

Benvenuto's Bar and Restaurant had an entrance on the corner into the bar and one on the side for the restaurant. Nicky crossed the street and went into the bar. It was long and narrow and as dark as Dante's worst nightmare. Jumbo was at the far corner, his elbows on the bar, his head resting on his hands watching a baseball game on TV. Nicky knocked with his knuckles on the bar and Jumbo looked up, wary, suspicious. It was too dark to see and he walked down the length of the bar in what seemed to Nicky like slow motion. Jumbo was a big guy who liked to stay put. That much hadn't changed. Nicky leaned back farther into the shadows and waited until Jumbo was close enough to touch.

"Oh God, it's you," Jumbo said. He took hold of Nicky's arm and pulled him halfway over the bar. He put his hands on Nicky's shoulders, wrapped him in his arms. "I thought that bastard Jimmy Ticks was back from the grave. Remember how he was always rapping his knuckles on everything?"

"Disappointed?"

"Are you kidding? That was the only wake I can remember where everybody smiled for three days." Jumbo grabbed Nicky's head and held it. He kissed him on the mouth. "You rotten sonofabitch. Make good and we never see you."

"I'm here all the time. I come see the old lady."

"Well, you know, I was keeping late hours, working nights uptown. My sister was talking about you the other day."

"Which one?"

"Filomena, Raffaella, Albina, Angelina, Rosina . . . Who knows? They're all the same. They're all ballbusters, drive me crazy, but look at you . . . how d'ya stay so slim?" Jumbo ran his hand down Nicky's shirt. "Your tie lays flat. Me, I gotta get them made custom or they stick out like a handle. You still drinking Jack Daniel's?" Jumbo asked him. "Lemme buy you a drink." He set up two glasses with ice and reached behind the bar.

Nicky watched Jumbo pour the drinks. He saw the ring on Jumbo's pinky finger. Nicky reached out and touched it. "Still got it, huh?" he said.

Jumbo looked up. "What are you kidding? It's the only piece of gold I got left. I hocked everything, but not this. I ain't gonna forget them times, Nicky . . . Me, you, and Salvatore, that's once in a lifetime." He turned the ring. "Salvatore's still got his. I seen it on him last time he was down here. Salvatore, big-time lawyer . . . something, huh?"

Nicky picked up his glass. He shook it so the ice rattled. "Salvatore was always smart . . . and stand-up, like his old man. Good to everybody. Remember Amadeo? My mother thought he was God."

"And then there was Magdalena. . . ."

"Whatta you mean?"

"Nothing," Jumbo said, "but she wasn't exactly your everyday Italian mama, was she? She always had people talking. Taking over the grocery when Sally's father died. We used to make fun of Salvatore selling vegetables. Now it's a gourmade store. Magdalena was one smart cookie." Jumbo put a hand on Nicky's shoulder.

"And look at you, homicide detective, first class . . . not bad. Only me, I'm stuck behind this goddamn bar."

"I told you to come with me."

Jumbo waved the comment away. "Forget about it. I could never be a cop," Jumbo said. "I don't like running. I don't like guns. You gotta worry about being on the take. What's the point? I didn't expect to end up in Benvenuto's Bar and Restaurant, but listen, I'm not complaining. I got no carfare. I walk across the street to work. The only thing is Eddie takes my paycheck for the next forty years. I'm a fucking serf."

Nicky laughed and finished his drink and put a twenty on the bar but Jumbo gave it back and poured him another. Nicky put the bill in the tip cup. Jumbo leaned over on both his elbows. "You know, Nicky. I'm real glad you came by because you're just the guy I want to see."

"What? What is it?"

"I got a situation. It's personal and I don't know how to handle it."

"What?"

"I don't wanna talk here. It's a matter of the heart. It deserves some respect."

"You tell me where and when, Jumbo, and I'll be there."

"It's really important to me. The most important thing ever happened to me. I still can't believe it." Jumbo closed his eyes and screwed up his face. "I met a girl, a good girl, a nice one."

"I thought you always liked the bad ones."

Jumbo hit Nicky in the shoulder. "Shit, you remember all that stuff we did?"

"When I wasn't passed out, yeah. But this is great news. So what's the problem?"

"Ha, it's one problem after the other. But like I said, I wanna tell you in private. It's a very complicated thing."

"Okay."

"Do you think we could get together? Me, you, Salvatore? Like old times? Bat a few around?"

"Sure, no problem." Nicky gave Jumbo his card. There was a pair of golden handcuffs embossed under his name. He had paid for the cards himself. He thought it added a touch of class to a dirty job. "I'll talk to Salvatore and we'll set it up."

When Nicky left, Jumbo looked around the room, squinting into the dark. Then he took the twenty out of the tip cup and put it in his back pocket.

After the Savannah Club, Nicky had joined the army and then the police force. Jumbo had gone from one job to another, all of them on the fringes of legality, and Salvatore had left for college and then law school. He had married one of those long blond girls with a mouthful of long white teeth. One of those girls who looked like they rode horses. He lived in Connecticut in one of those towns on the train line. He told Nicky that his wife hated the city. She'd meet him midtown to go for dinner and a Broadway show but that was it. She described the neighborhood and Magdalena with the same word: interesting. And she avoided both like the plague.

Nicky felt like that was fine with Salvatore. He had always been possessive about Magdalena. It wasn't just a mother-son thing. After all, Magdalena wasn't really Salvatore's mother. It was as if she held him hostage, as though Salvatore was bound to her in some other way that Nicky didn't like to think about.

He walked up Sixth Avenue to Pavese's and stood in front of the half-block of plate-glass windows filled with cakes and breads and wheels of cheese, the store that Magdalena had put together after Amadeo died. Amadeo would have been crazy to see his store like this, Nicky thought, to see what his wife had done, the girl he had brought back from the mountains of southern Italy.

Salvatore had always said that the old man didn't know what he had, not really. He was blind to what was under his nose. "He never saw how smart Magdalena was, how she maneuvered our lives, her and that Black Madonna she keeps in the top of the house."

"Black Madonna? What are you talking about?" Nicky had said. They had been breaking up the apartment and Salvatore had looked away, down at the suitcase he was packing. He closed it, concentrating on lining up the top to the bottom, fastening the clips.

"Nothing," he said. "Something she brought from the old country, a stone with an image glued to it, a Madonna with a black face." He wouldn't say anything else and Nicky had let it drop.

Pavese's was beautiful inside. In the center were piles of fruits and vegetables. Against the walls were counters of cheese, meats, fish on mountains of ice.

Nicky knew her immediately. It was her eyes, points of gold in them, he had heard the women say, strange eyes, bright, as though a lamp were held behind them. Magdalena was still a beautiful woman, and there was still something odd about her, exotic, ethereal.

Nicky had always been secretly in love with her. They all had been, he was sure. He remembered how Jumbo's hands would shake when she touched him, but they had never confided in each other. It was too much to think about. She was Salvatore's mother, but when she came onto the stoop in her thin cotton dresses with the sleeves rolled up on her arms, Nicky had almost felt pain. He remembered her in summer when she would sit on the stoop with her knees apart and open the top buttons of her dress and wipe the sweat from her neck and the cleft of her breasts with a man's white handkerchief. She would go under the open fire hydrant in the street holding her dress high up on her legs.

She was standing now toward the back of the store talking with a vendor. She was smiling, handing him something, a paper, a check. Nicky watched her. She had never married again, never been seen with a man. That wasn't unusual. His mother had been young enough when his father died and no one thought about her remarrying, but Magdalena they had suspected, watched her closely, waited for her true nature to reveal itself, the truth of her heart to surface, because she wasn't like any other woman. She wasn't like them.

She worked in the store after Amadeo died, and she was there, always, for Salvatore. When Salvatore asked her how she did it, she would lift her chin and mock him. "Luck," she said, "and magic."

Nicky waited until she was alone. "Magdalena," he said. He stood in front of her, took off his hat. She looked up at him, her eyes narrowed, the brows together, but just for a minute.

"Nicola . . ." She reached out to him, palms up, and he put his hands in hers. Come inside," she said, motioning to him, clearing a path with her hands.

She led him into a room behind the store. It was a kitchen. A table in the center was piled high with papers.

"My office." She cleared the papers from the table and put down a bowl of fruit. "Sit down," she told Nicky. "I make you coffee." She brought out a tray of pastries, put it down and frowned. "Maybe you want to eat something," she said. "Tell me, what do you want?" She petted his shoulder. He was ten years old again. He was eighteen. She poured his coffee and sat down in the chair across from him. She bit into a cannoli. "Tell me. What are you doing? How are you?"

Nicky told her he was a homicide detective in the First Precinct.

"You married?"

"Divorced."

"Stupid woman," she said, and stirred sugar into his coffee without asking.

"How's Salvatore?"

"*Un' uomo importante,*" she said. "The lawyer, I call him. His father should be here to see."

Nicky finished his coffee. Magdalena peeled a mangosteen. The thick purple skin stained her hands. She handed him a section. It was white, slippery. The juice ran down her fingers. There was a naturalness to her. There always had been. She caught him watching her and he was embarrassed.

"I need to get ahold of him," he said.

"Nothing's wrong?"

"No, I just want to see him. It's been too long. I was down on Spring Street with Jumbo and we thought it was time to get together."

"The world turns upside down," she said, "and nothing changes." She put her fingers to her throat. There was an amulet, he saw, black, polished, an uneven shape. It was on a velvet ribbon around her neck and she stroked it absentmindedly as she talked. He thought to ask her about it but he didn't. There were so many questions around Magdalena.

She got up, went to a bulletin board that was over her desk. "He's just moved. I have the number up here somewhere . . . Ah . . ." She pulled down a slip of lined white paper. "Here," she said. "Let me copy it for you."

Nicky bent down and kissed her hand when she gave him the paper. "*Ciao,* Nicola," she said before he closed the door.

Nicky met Salvatore in the Munsen diner because it was one of their old haunts. "Oh, my God, it's good to see you," Salvatore said. He took Nicky's head in his hands and kissed him on both sides of his face. He slid into the booth and leaned over the table. "So how the hell are you?" He reached out, touched Nicky's cheek. "What's going on? Things are good?"

"Yeah, pretty good."

"How's Gina?"

"Gone."

"I'm sorry."

"Don't be."

"I told you not to marry an Italian girl. The rest of the women in the world think we're great."

"I should have done like you but where was I gonna find her? What's her name? Susan?"

"Lindsey."

"Mercy, Salvatore. That don't even sound like a girl's name."

"I think she was named after her father. You'd like her. And you know what? Three kids and she looks the same as when I met her."

"Magdalena looks the same as when we were kids."

"Magdalena . . ." Salvatore stopped smiling and took a drag on his cigarette. "Magdalena's got some kind of deal going. I don't know if it's with God or the Devil or . . ." He reached over, covered Nicky's fist with his hand. "Forget that. What's going on?"

"I saw Jumbo last week. He's working in Benvenuto's paying off a debt to Fat Eddie Fingers."

Salvatore shook his head. "Nicky, I love you. I love Jumbo. We go back a long time, but you know, things change. I have a whole other life. Jumbo's got to understand I can't get involved with penny-ante wise guys who shoot you in the leg if they don't get their money. When I left the Savannah Club I made up my mind that I was going to follow the rules and stay away from the local lords of Thompson Street."

"Sally, c'mon. Jumbo's not looking for anybody to bail him out. His mother and the Five Furies took care of that just fine. It has to do with his heart. It's personal. He was wondering out loud if the three of us could get together. Hey, we're brothers, you forgot?"

Salvatore laughed. "St. Joseph's Day. My father thought I was in a knife fight. Only Magdalena knew what happened. She's the one put me up to it."

"Funny, she never had any kids. She was so young."

"My father didn't want it. He lost my mother in childbirth. He didn't want to lose Magdalena. But you know what, if she had wanted a baby, she would have had one. Magdalena always got just what she wanted."

"You can't get away, Salvatore. You gotta take the good with the bad."

"You mean I have no choice?"

"You coming or what?"

"You tell me when . . ."

Nicky stopped back down the neighborhood to see Jumbo before he went to work in the First Precinct. His eyes adjusted to the dark of the barroom and he saw Jumbo, his bulk bent over the bar sink rinsing glasses. He looked up when Nicky came in. "Hey, Nicky, feast or famine."

"I came in to let you know I met Salvatore. He says anytime you want."

"Really. I'm impressed. Was he worried I wanted something?"

"Nah, Salvatore's not like that."

"You know, Nicky, I don't want to blow this all outta proportion, keeping you in suspense."

"Go ahead."

"I met a girl."

"For chrissakes, Jumbo. You told me that already. Whatta you getting senile?"

"But this ain't no ordinary broad. She's very classy . . . from Long Island. She's got a *college degree.* Can you believe it? A girl with a college degree interested in me? I can't hardly read the newspaper."

Nicky squinted. He had been the route with college girls. They liked tough guys, or what they imagined to be tough guys. Just being a cop had gotten him plenty of action, one of the reasons his marriage broke up. He could see where Jumbo would be appealing, the opposites-attract thing, and who knows, maybe this girl had a thing for oversize guys, although as he remembered, Jumbo was no swordsman. He sat down on the bar stool and reached for the dish of peanuts but it was empty. Jumbo came over and stood in front of him. He leaned over on the bar, his fingers laced, his beefy forearms almost touching.

"You wanna drink?"

"I'm actually on duty."

"C'mon, Nicky. There ain't been an unexplained homicide in this area since Tommy Rye disappeared. Does that count? When there's no corpi delectable?"

Nicky smiled. "I'm not organized crime, Jumbo. I'm homicide. So tell me about this girl."

"She's perfect, Nicky. A little fat, but hey, I'm no Cary Grant. She teaches school in the Bronx. Third grade. The kids love her. They make her birthday cards every day."

"So where'd you meet her?"

"She used to come in Jilly's with her girlfriends. You know how these career girls hang out together. They don't need no men. They got their own money. They got their own apartments. I seen a million of them, but Judy stayed late one night and we started talking. I bought her a drink. And then she started coming in without the girlfriends. You know how it is. . . . And I'm crazy about her. I feel like God's giving me a chance to make something outta my life. I feel like I got a purpose."

"But what's the problem? It sounds normal to me."

Jumbo sighed. He reached under the bar to fill the dish of peanuts. Luca Benvenuto complained to Fat Eddie Fingers that his peanut bill was cutting into the profits. How were the peanuts supposed to make the customers thirsty if the bartender ate them all? Jumbo dipped his fingers into the peanut dish and lowered his voice. "Nicky, she's a *mazzucriste*."

"C'mon, Jumbo . . . this is 1968. . . ."

"I wanna marry this girl. I love this girl."

"Jumbo, it's no big deal. Wake up, you're not the first one. Joe Tucillo married a Jewish girl."

"Yeah, and where is he? He ain't here, is he? He moved to Timbuktu."

"Well, face it, you gotta be sick in the head if you think you're gonna marry any educated girl and move her down here in one of these tenements with your mother. Christ, my ex-wife came from Mulberry Street and I had to buy her a house in Queens."

"That's too bad she left you, Nicky. Maybe you're not the one I should be talking to about marriage. If she left you, you can't know much."

"Maybe my mistake was marrying an Italian girl. You think they're gonna understand and they don't."

"Like what?"

"Like Gina couldn't stand my mother. I told her, 'My mother's a widow, she's been on her own since I was twelve. What does what I do for my mother have to do with you?'"

"That's the other thing, Nicky. My mother . . . she's convinced I'm hers forever now. I hear her all the time with my sisters. Promise me, she tells them. When I go, you take care of him. And she thinks nobody's good enough. Now I'm gonna come home with Judy Bernstein?" Jumbo was sweating. It was too dark for Nicky to see, but he could smell him. When Nicky arrested people, they'd smell like that. It was fear. And Nicky understood why. Antoinette Mangiacarne had Jumbo tied tight. And the apron strings were around his neck.

Some guys came in and sat at the other end of the bar. They called out for a drink. "Hold your horses. Can't you see I'm busy over here," Jumbo yelled down the bar. "Goddamn ballbusters," he said to Nicky.

"Jumbo, you're the bartender. They're customers. Go take care of them. What the hell are you doing?"

"Well, I'm not used to this, Nicky. You know you had time to get used to it. You went in the army. Now you're a cop. You're used to people telling you what to do. Me, I been an independent all my life. This shit is hard for me."

"Hey." Again from the end of the bar.

Nicky patted Jumbo's forearm. It reminded Nicky of a pork

roast. He thought about getting a sandwich in the grocery store next door. Jumbo was always an inspiration. "Go take care of your customers. If you're gonna get married, you're gonna need a job."

"My mother's right," Jumbo said, picking himself off the bar. "I'm cursed."

Judy Bernstein was the apple of her father's eye. Her mother would have wished for a daughter a little slimmer, with a better nose and a finer set of teeth. Braces took care of the teeth, but the nose, which Sylvia knew could be fixed just as easily, Judy refused to alter, and Harvey Bernstein agreed. He spent part of every day of Judy's life telling her that she was the most beautiful creature who walked the earth and smart, too. When she was born, Harvey told Sylvia he didn't want any more children. This one was perfect and all he would ever want, so why should they have another?

Sylvia was content. She hadn't liked being pregnant, she hadn't liked giving birth. She didn't particularly like little children. She didn't even like what you had to do to get one, and with this most of her girlfriends agreed, except for Ann Hirshfeld, who would deal the cards for their weekly bridge game and tell them they didn't know what they were missing.

Sylvia was content. God had sent her Harvey, who provided a good living and never complained. Sylvia didn't have to cook much or clean at all and Harvey was happy when she spent his money. She did hope for more for her daughter: a professional man, a real professional—a doctor, a lawyer, an accountant. Sylvia had been on the right track herself. Harvey had been in podiatry school when she married him, but bad times hit and he left to go into the family bra and girdle business.

The store was on Grand Street and the business was cash. Harvey expanded to include sleepwear and hosiery and took over three other stores on the block. The Bernsteins moved from a tenement apartment in the Bronx to a house on Long Island. It was a commute but Harvey liked the quiet of the train and then the buzz of Grand Street, familiar and comfortable. He would talk with the other shopkeepers selling lingerie and fabric and bedspreads and custom curtains and eiderdown quilts. The customers were attractive and well dressed, wearing hats with feathers and three-quarter-length gloves that they would take off to finger the lace on a strapless bra or stretch a corset with long elastic garters for stockings.

Harvey had a makeshift dressing room in the back so the ladies could try things on and he kept a young shop assistant to help them with the hooks and snaps so essential to ladies' underwear. He'd have his lunch every day in the dairy restaurant across the street where the old waiters with bad feet and body odor knew his order, the same every day: potato-leek soup with dill served in the thick china of coffee shops, the soup slopped into the cup so that it had flowed over the edge, the cup sitting in a puddle of soup in the saucer that Harvey would put to his lips if no one was looking.

The trend to abandoning undergarments worried Harvey. He had read where the young girls weren't even wearing panties, let alone girdles, but Sylvia said he was crazy. Where was a woman without her foundation garments? Anyway, they had put enough away for a rainy day. The only thing left for them to do was to marry off Judy, but to tell the truth, this worried Sylvia. When Judy turned thirty, Sylvia had arranged a quiet dinner for the three of them at Trader Vic's in the city. She didn't want to advertise Judy's age, to start her friends gossiping or not being responsive when a possible suitor, a young nephew or a friend's son, came into town. Sylvia didn't want Judy to be thought of as old . . . as in maid. She remembered the dreaded card in the game Judy would play with her father as a little girl, the ugly hag with the disgruntled face.

Sylvia wished Judy would dress up more, tweeze her eyebrows, shorten her skirts. Those glasses! Sylvia would fret to Harvey in bed after the lights were out. She would only let Harvey read in bed for fifteen minutes and then the light had to go out. "She's not a bad-looking girl," she would say in the dark. "What could it be?"

"Leave her alone. She's having fun. She's young yet."

"She's not so young, Harvey, God forgive me for saying it. She's past thirty. And she's not even dating. We never should have let her move to the city. Who's she gonna meet there?"

"Who's she gonna meet here?"

"Oh, stop it. If she was here she'd be at the club on weekends. There's always a stray man here and there. People would see her. They'd want to fix her up. Now she's just Sylvia and Harvey's daughter who moved to the city. Besides she seems too independent. No one wants a girl like that."

"Sylvia, she'll be fine."

"You think so, Harvey? She's got nobody. Not a brother, not a sister, just us, and when we die someday, God forbid, Judy's gonna be all alone." Sometimes when Sylvia said this, she would cry softly into her manicured hands. Her hairdo would quiver and Harvey would pat her hand and sometimes take her in his arms and sometimes even get a hard-on and make love to her, careful not to disturb her hairdo.

Antoinette Mangiacarne, sometimes known as Mama Jumbo, thrived on her only son. Even his missteps, somewhere deep in her heart, gave her pleasure because they tied him to her all the more tightly. She never hesitated for a minute to go to Fat Eddie's Club on King Street that time Jumbo had run away. For her son, she would have thrown herself in front of a moving train and pulled her daughters along after her. She believed when he was born that he was destined for great things but fate had intervened when Nicky's mother had targeted him for her grudge. Antoinette knew that if she had had an ally more powerful than Teresa Sabatini,

Jumbo would be a doctor by now, a lawyer, a business owner, a restaurateur, an executive in the Metropolitan Life Insurance Company.

But if it wasn't to be, her consolation was that she was here to protect him from real terror and physical harm. He had stayed healthy, thank God, with an appetite that never faltered through all the usual childhood sicknesses and the most terrible stomachaches and flu and fevers. Antoinette could not remember a time when Jumbo's weight dipped even a pound, when his pants had ever been loose at his waist. For this she was grateful and could put up with the evil eye that Nicky's mother had invoked. After all, if you didn't have your health, you had nothing. Antoinette knew this because she and her family had nothing but their health, and cheap rent on their tenement apartments.

Secretly Antoinette thought it was not a bad thing that had brought Jumbo back to the neighborhood bar in Benvenuto's. She had worried about him uptown at night. This way he was here. She could see him coming and going. She knew where he was every day and every night of the week because Fat Eddie Fingers had been clear about the hours Jumbo had to work if he wanted to continue breathing and Antoinette had solemnly sworn on the head of her dead husband that Jumbo would do exactly as Eddie asked. Antoinette finally felt that things were under control. Nicky's mother's curse might have been lifted or frittered away, its energy spent, or Jumbo just too vigorous and healthy to be influenced by its evil anymore. If Antoinette had known what was brewing, she might have lost her appetite, she might have needed more than two handkerchiefs in her apron pocket to collect her tears or contain her fury.

It had been a slow night at Jilly's, a Tuesday. Jumbo thought the group of girls who came in and sat at the bar looked snotty. Haughty would have been the word but Jumbo would not have used a word like haughty. They all ordered brandy alexanders except for one girl. She ordered scotch on the rocks, telling Jumbo her father had taught her that when you drink, it was the sugar that killed you. "Smart man," Jumbo said, and liked her right away. When all the girls got up to leave and she purposely waited for him to come down to her end of the bar, he took her drink off the check and smiled at her.

She had long brown hair and glasses, which Jumbo thought made her look smart. On her way out he noticed her big ass and the line of her panties underneath her knit dress and then and there he hoped he would see her again.

Jumbo never thought about girls except the ones you paid for or else left before dawn. To get serious meant responsibility and Jumbo knew his limits. Mouths to feed and rent to pay? He had never lived on his own. He hadn't even been able to make it with Nicky and Salvatore. That three weeks when he was eighteen had been the last time he had been out of his mother's house, except for that time he hid out in Georgia, which no one counted. Antoinette had cried when he moved back home. She had lovingly hand-washed every piece of dirty clothing he brought back with him, and his sisters Rosina and Albina had stayed home from work one whole day to press everything, even his boxer shorts and undershirts, and fold them neatly one on top of the other and place them back in the empty drawers that had waited for his return.

Her name was Judy, not Angelina or Cosima or Bernadina, and when she walked into Jilly's alone that Friday night, Jumbo swooned. He hadn't remembered her mouth being so full. She wore lipstick and a sweater that was cut low enough so he could see the top of her breasts and she sat alone at the bar and leaned over so that when he poured her scotch he could see down into her sweater. He imagined he could see her nipples pushing against the wool but of course he couldn't because Judy Bernstein's father was in lingerie and her bra was padded and double-layered with lace and Jumbo would have had to have X-ray vision to see even the hint of a nipple but he imagined where they were and that was good enough.

He took her to an after-hours joint down on Broadway and then to Ratner's for breakfast. "You're Jewish?" he asked her when he heard the name Bernstein.

"Why? That matters?"

"No, whatta you kidding? I meet all kinds of people in my business. You kidding or what?"

"I don't really observe."

"What?"

"Observe . . . the rules . . . like not eating pork."

"Pork?"

"Jews don't eat pork . . . or shellfish. Don't you know that?"

"Sure I know that. So you don't eat pork?"

"I do. I thought God would strike me dead the first time I had a ham sandwich but here I am."

"I'm glad, Judy."

"That I eat pork?"

"No, that God didn't strike you dead."

They went out for four months. Jumbo knew his way around the city. He took her to shows and restaurants and clubs and discos. They went out every weekend and twice during the week. He was going into debt but he wasn't worried. It was small potatoes compared to when he was gambling.

Antoinette was suspicious. He was staying out later and later and he had stopped giving her money for the house, which before he had forced her to take. "No," she always said when Jumbo pushed the rolled-up bills into her hand. "That horse's ass, that *s'facime* takes everything you make." Jumbo would slip the money into her pocketbook and she would find the bills at the bottom of her bag when she went shopping.

But lately, Jumbo had been apologizing. "I got some expenses,

Ma," he told her. "You know that fat bastard takes everything."

Antoinette smelled a rat. She tortured Rosina and Albina and Filomena and Angelina and Raffaella but they swore they knew nothing, had seen nothing. Antoinette noticed a smear of pink on Jumbo's shirt collar and had a mild fainting spell. She showed it to Rosina. "Ma, he's a man, for chrissakes. You want him to be a fag?"

"You think that's it? Just a one-time thing?"

"Well, I don't see no steady girl around here, do you?"

"No, you're right. It's nothing, right? A little fun. He's a man, after all."

"Didn't I just say that?"

"But suppose some girl tricks him, gets herself pregnant? Suppose it's not even his baby? She's a big whore. Gives it out to everybody and poor Jumbo gets stuck because he's a dope. Your father never told him anything. And how could I say those things? I'm his mother."

"Ma, please, Jumbo's thirty-two years old. He can take care of himself. You should be glad if he's with a woman. My Tony was thinking for real he might be a *riccone*."

"Why? Because he's not a pig like the jerks you and your sisters married?"

"Ma, please, I'm trying to make you feel better."

"You're not. I don't feel better. I feel sick to my stomach." Antoinette mixed a big glass of water and Brioschi. The bubbles soothed her stomach, the fizz tickled her nose, which she used to sniff for perfume and other aromas that would give her fears a name.

The Bernsteins were pleased when Judy told them she was seeing somebody and that was the reason she hadn't been home to visit. With her job and all, there wasn't time. Sylvia didn't pry. She didn't want to interfere but she poked Harvey every night when he turned off his light and rolled over. "D'ya think it's serious? It's been months. Did she say anything to you?"

"No, Sylvia."

"But she always talks to you. She's closer to you than she is to me. I'm her mother. She should tell me. But she hasn't, not a word. She should be asking me for advice. After all, there's ways to get a man. I hope she's being careful. You know, nobody buys the cow when they get the milk for free. It sounds old-fashioned, but it's true."

"Oh, Sylvia, please . . . She's thirty-five years old."

"Don't say that. She's near thirty. That's how you say it, near thirty."

"Sylvia, go to sleep."

"Oh, Harvey, do you remember when we first met?"

Judy wanted Jumbo to meet her parents. She said if he really liked her as much as he said, if he loved her the way he said when they spent the night in the hotel on Twenty-third Street where he knew the night clerk and he pulled her on top of him, being much too large to risk it the other way, then he should meet her parents. Unless he wasn't serious, she said, but using her just to have a good time.

Jumbo cried when she said this. He loved her. He had never loved anybody before her. He swore this, but he was nervous. He knew she came from a nice family. He was positive. She was so educated, so cultured. Maybe they should wait. Give her parents time to get used to the idea of an Italian son-in-law, a bartender, no less. He knew that Jewish mothers wanted doctors; they wanted lawyers, professors. They went for titles. He knew he was right.

"Stop it," Judy said, when he went on and on this way. "I'm telling them this weekend."

"Whatta you gonna tell them?"

"That I met a man. That I love him. That I'm happier than I've ever been and I want them to meet him."

"Ah, Judy, that's really how you feel?"

"Yes."

He kissed her hands, sucked each finger one by one. He wished he could eat her except that then she would be gone.

"So? You'll come?"

"Suppose they don't want to meet me? Suppose they say 'You're dead to us' and have a fake funeral. I heard about that. Vinny Maisano married a Jewish girl and her family did that. They never spoke to her again. It was like she was dead." Jumbo had tears in his eyes. "Can you imagine that? They made believe like she died."

"Jumbo, stop being dramatic. My parents wouldn't do that. They'll love you. If I love you, they'll love you. They'll have to."

Sylvia and Harvey could not have been happier when Judy announced she was taking the 11 A.M. train home to Lawrence on Sunday and that she had something to tell them. Sylvia was beside herself. She made Harvey bring Nova Scotia and bagels and cream cheese from the East Side for their brunch. She told Harvey that she knew the news would be about Judy's beau. Fiancé, she hinted to her friends on the golf course. Engaged, she mentioned to her bridge club. She didn't sleep Saturday night. Sunday morning she was up at six setting out the Lenox.

Harvey picked Judy up at the train station and drove straight home. Sylvia told him not to stop, but to come right back, which he did. She watched through the bay window as they got out of the car and came up the steps between the porch columns that reminded Sylvia of Tara and had convinced her to buy this house. Judy looked to Sylvia like she had put on some weight. This was the first disappointment. Didn't love take away your appetite? How could you snare a man carrying around twenty extra pounds? But Sylvia embraced her only child. She held her at arm's length and told her how wonderful she looked. Had she lost some weight?

They sat at the table with the fresh flower centerpiece and the cut-crystal glasses filled with freshly squeezed orange juice while Judy told them about Jumbo. The Nova Scotia caught on Sylvia's temporary cap when she heard he wasn't Jewish but she recovered. Italian wasn't the worst thing. They were family people. Italians and Jews had lived side by side in the Bronx. It could be worse.

When Judy mentioned that he was a bartender, the bagel caught on what Sylvia feared was a tumor in her throat but she waited calmly to hear the rest, that he owned his own restaurant, which had in it a very graceful bar, like the divine Romeo Salta's. Didn't the owner sometimes step behind the bar to serve drinks? Sylvia asked herself. Successful restaurateurs had to be hands-on. Her Uncle Seymour had owned a restaurant. He had always said it. No absentee owners in the restaurant business. But no, Judy was saying, Jumbo didn't own the bar and restaurant. He only worked there.

College . . . what college had he gone to? City College had its share of *wunderkinds,* her brother Saul, for example. CCNY was an excellent school. Who could afford Yale and besides they had quotas. Sylvia was sure there must be quotas for Italians the same as for Jews.

Sylvia relaxed. She coughed up her bagel and took a sip of coffee. He hadn't gone to college? Self-educated? Sylvia's words, not Judy's, who was telling them how wonderful and kind and generous and smart her boyfriend was, and you know what? Judy said finally, "I love him."

Harvey took Judy's hands in his and said he was so happy for her. Sylvia sat back in her chair and bit her tongue.

"Are you sure, dear? It's so important to have things in common."

"I'm sure . . . And I'm sure you'll love him, too. You'll have to."

"We will, won't we, Sylvia?" Harvey nodded his head, smeared cream cheese on his bagel. "Our Judy always had the best taste in friends."

Sylvia rolled her eyes and wiped her mouth with her full-size linen napkin. Sweat broke out on her forehead. For the first time in a long time, she was lost for words. "You'll have to bring him out, sweetheart. Let us see this guy of yours." She laughed. "You haven't even told us his name."

Judy laughed, too. "It's Alfonso but everyone calls him Jumbo."

Sylvia swallowed hard. Harvey carried the ball. "What an interesting name. How did he get it?"

"He thinks it's after that famous circus elephant. He was the biggest baby born on Spring Street, he tells me. The *Daily News* sent a photographer to take a picture of him and it was on the second page of the paper. Jumbo says the Italians love nicknames. Everyone has one."

"Well, Jumbo's certainly easier to remember than Alfso."

"Alfonso."

"Excuse me," Sylvia said.

"You okay, Mother?"

"Oh, I'm fine. You two go on. I'll be back in a minute."

Sylvia Bernstein went upstairs to the pink bathroom attached to the master bedroom and threw up her guts. She washed her face and reapplied her makeup. Harvey and Judy waited for her in the living room.

"Sylvia," Harvey said. "Are you okay?"

"Oh yes. It's the orange juice," she said. "I shouldn't drink it. Too much acid."

Judy hugged her mother when she came close enough. "Oh, I feel so happy now that I've told you. And you don't mind too much that he isn't Jewish?"

"We can talk about all that later," her father said.

Sylvia retired to bed with a lace handkerchief drenched in Chanel No. 5 tied over her eyes. "Look on the bright side, Sylvia," Harvey said. "Our baby's happy. She's found a man who loves her. What else can we hope for?"

"The bright side," Sylvia said. "He has arms and legs. He has a job. And Jewishness passes through the mother."

"See, you're doing good already."

Sylvia sat up in bed, she tore off the lace handkerchief. "He's an uneducated Italian bartender with no future and, we can only hope to God, no past."

"Sylvia, you were doing better before."

Salvatore had told Magdalena about his meeting with Nicky. "Jumbo wants to see me and Nicky, the three of us, get together. Says he's got a problem of the heart."

Magdalena thought this was funny. "Such a big man must have a big heart."

"I don't know. At first, I didn't want to be bothered. What do I know about Jumbo's heart? Or anyone's heart for that matter?"

Magdalena came and sat down next to Salvatore on the couch. She pulled her legs under her and leaned against him. "Come," she said. "You have a great gift with women. I could see it when you were just an infant." She put her arm around him, behind his back. "I fell in love with you the second I saw you."

Salvatore remembered how when he was a little boy and he was unhappy or scared, he would bury his face in Magdalena's hair and cry. She called his unhappiness *miseria* and she would hold him so close he couldn't breathe. She would dry his tears with her long black hair, like Mary Magdalena, she would tell him, holding his face in her hands.

Salvatore would look her in the eyes. He would stop crying. "She dried his feet," he told her.

"Don't believe everything you hear," Magdalena would say, and pull him closer.

So, how's Lindley?"

"Lindsey, Magdalena. It's Lindsey."

"What a name . . . there's no translation. It means nothing. It's not a saint. It's not a flower. Huh . . ." Magdalena was polite to Salvatore's wife but she did not take her seriously. She was too foreign, too pale, too benign. Magdalena thought Salvatore had forgone passion. She never believed that still waters ran deep. There were things you couldn't hide behind your eyes.

Magdalena's loyalty was only to Salvatore, the rest of the world was incidental. Since Amadeo's death, Salvatore was the only one she cared about, but she never bothered him. She never called him. He had to seek her out, and when he said this to her, she shrugged her shoulders. "You know I'm here for you, Salvatore, and only you. You don't have to hear my voice every day."

So," she said, getting up. Salvatore was glad when she got up. She unsettled him. Magdalena was still seductive, powerful. "Have your friends come here, Nicky and Jumbo. You can have the house to yourself. Zia Manfredi can cook for you and leave it in the kitchen. I'll bring you *antipasti* from the store, olives and prosciutto and provolone, and fruit. If I remember, your friend Jumbo likes to eat. Tell them both to come here. You can have privacy and hear about Jumbo's heart."

She kissed him good night and he watched her go upstairs, watched the straightness of her back and the roundness of her hips move away from him. She was still a young woman, his stepmother. She was beautiful.

He wondered if she was going up to the top of the house. He knew this was where she kept the Black Madonna that she had brought from Castelfondo more than thirty years before. Salvatore never went to that part of the house, had never gone, except one time when he was twelve and Magdalena had taught him the secrets.

"A pity," she had said to him one winter night during Advent, "that you weren't born a girl."

"Why?"

"I could teach you."

"Teach me anyway."

But Magdalena told him she was afraid. How could she teach a boy? He would grow into a man and then what? But then when he was twelve, she had covered his eyes with a handkerchief and led him up the stairs. It was Christmas Eve and she took him to the top of the house, under the eaves, and uncovered his eyes. She sat him in front of the shrine and fed him a special cake she had wrapped in the hem of her dress and warned him to be careful with what he would learn. Death magic, she called it. Love magic.

Afterward she made him kneel and she knelt behind him, her legs inside his, in front of the Black Madonna and she prayed for forgiveness for both of them. Salvatore had fallen asleep in her arms at the top of the house but woke up in his bed.

Salvatore loved Magdalena. She was his fantasy, his dream, the mother of fairy tales, the only mother he knew. In the neighborhood they whispered, they suspected, they believed in their hearts that Amadeo would be sorry for taking a child bride with a son who would grow up. They knew the stories, they knew the power of familiarity and the pull between men and women and they knew that Salvatore would grow out of his short pants and become a man. They held their breath for years and years but then Salvatore was out of the house and Amadeo was dead. Thank God for America, the women on the stoop said. In the old country, it would have turned out different.

So Nicky and Jumbo and Salvatore met in the house on Sullivan Street where Salvatore had grown up. Jumbo had to ask Luca Benvenuto for a couple of hours off. Jumbo shrugged when Luca agreed but docked Jumbo two hours' pay.

Salvatore opened the door when they rang the bell. Nicky was dripping wet even though Jumbo held a big black umbrella over him. "I passed by the bar to pick Jumbo up and he wasn't there," Nicky said. "So I had to wait downstairs and got caught in the rain. No way I could go up the house and get him. His mother goes crazy when she sees me."

"C'mon. It's not my mother that's the problem. Your mother started all the trouble. She's the one's got it in for me ever since I was a kid. Like it was my fault what I weigh."

They stepped inside. Jumbo stuck the umbrella in the stand near the door and Nicky wiped his shoes on the mat inside the entrance hall. "Wipe your feet," Nicky told Jumbo. "Where's your culture?"

"I know. I know. That's my problem. This girl . . . Judy . . . She's got culture up the ass. How's it gonna work?"

"Who's Judy?"

"You're rushing me. I'm confused, and you're rushing me."

Salvatore hugged Jumbo hello, surprised at the size of him. He was a behemoth, solid like a mountain. "You haven't changed," Salvatore said.

"Oh, but you have," Jumbo said. "Look at you. Mr. Big-Shot Lawyer. Although to tell the truth, I think I'm wearing a better shirt."

Salvatore laughed. "Brooks Brothers," he said.

"Emilio Garcia on Avenue C. Check out the monogram." Jumbo held out his arm and on the cuff in light blue thread were his initials. You couldn't see them unless you looked close, which was just how Jumbo liked it.

They went into the kitchen. It was below the street level but looked out onto the garden in back. "Christ, Salvatore, I forgot what this house was like. It's a fucking mansion. The three of you lived in this whole house. How come we was always hanging out in Nicky's? My apartment was one big whorehouse with them sisters of mine. But this is something else."

"Yeah," Salvatore said, "but there was nowhere to go, only the garden. From One Ninety-six, between the fire escapes and the back alleys, we had the run of the neighborhood."

"And please," Nicky said, "don't remind me about fire escapes."

Salvatore set out a bottle of vodka and three glasses with ice. Jumbo eyed the plates of *antipasti* Magdalena had made up from the store.

"So, brothers, here we are all together. Now tell us, Jumbo, what's going on."

"What about the food, Sally? What's all that food over there? It's for us or Magdalena's saving it for a party or something?"

"Christ, Jumbo," Nicky said. "How big could this problem be if all you're thinking about is sliced provolone? Man does not live by bread alone."

"You got bread?"

He told them then about Judy Bernstein.

Nicky shook his head. "Ahhh, Jumbo, you're in trouble. I'd be really worried if I were you."

"See. I knew it. I should be scared, right? I knew it. I'm not crazy. This is gonna be terrible."

"What are you talking about?" Salvatore said. "This is 1968. I didn't marry an Italian girl."

"Yeah, true," Nicky said, "and aside from the fact that you're wearing striped shirts, you're doing better than me in the marriage department. But we're not talking marriage here, we're talking Antoinette Mangiacarne."

"My mother wanted me to be a priest, Sally. She said she could only give me up to the church."

"No, Jumbo, your mother wanted you to be her husband."

"You take that back."

"Okay okay. We're getting off the track here."

"No, I think we're right on target. Jumbo's going out with a *mazzucriste* but his mother wouldn't be happy if he was with the Queen of England, so where does that leave him? Sounds like up shit's creek to me."

Salvatore leaned back and poured another drink. "Correct me if I'm wrong, but do you realize we're three grown men conspiring like we're twelve years old?"

"I wish we were twelve again. Those times were great," Jumbo said, "except when you was crippled, Nicky. That wasn't so good. That's when your mother started hating me."

"Forget my mother and your mother, what about her mother? You aren't exactly a great catch."

"Thanks for rubbing it in."

"Just tell her, Jumbo. Just tell Antoinette you're getting married. You do want to get married? Or am I rushing you again?"

"No, of course I wanna get married. I want a nice life. I want some kids."

"Does this girl know how much you weighed when you were born?" Nicky said. "Maybe she'll think twice."

Salvatore put a hand on Jumbo's shoulder. "Just tell your old lady, Jumbo. Who knows? She might be happy. She probably worries about who's gonna take care of you when she's dead."

"Believe me, she don't worry. I got all them sisters. I'm covered in the taking-care-of department." Jumbo speared slices of mortadella, provolone, salami, roasted peppers, and artichoke hearts and layered them on a loaf of bread. He didn't bother with the plates Salvatore had laid out.

"So, you think it'll work out."

"It'll be fine. Your mother loves you. She'll only want the best for you."

"And you guys, you'll walk in my wedding?"

Nicky put an arm around Jumbo. Salvatore did the same from the other side. Jumbo left his hands where they were, holding his sandwich, but he had tears in his eyes.

Jumbo met Judy uptown. They walked in Central Park, through the zoo, where Jumbo got sad at the lions and gorillas in small iron-barred cages inside houses that stank of rotted vegetables and animal shit. He didn't see the romance in zoos. And the smell got into the bag of peanuts and the candy bars he bought to eat along the way and took away some of his appetite. He wished he could bring Judy down the neighborhood but he had visions of his five sisters tearing out her beautiful brown hair strand by strand, breaking her glasses, and then he would have to hit them and he didn't think he could do that, not even for Judy.

"Did you tell your mother?" she asked, sticking a hand into his bag of peanuts. He didn't like that. He had told her he would buy her a bag but she had said no, she didn't want any, and here she was mooching his, but he loved her, so he held the bag closer to her and let her grab a handful.

"I didn't. I been working later and later and she's asleep when I get home."

"Well, I told Sylvia and Harvey." Just the names of Judy's parents made the short hairs at the back of Jumbo's head curl.

"And?"

"They're fine; they can't wait to meet you."

"Really?"

"Really. When can you come? It's got to be the weekend. We could take the train out and have lunch with them. What about this Sunday?"

Sunday was the day Antoinette cooked special for the whole family: Rosina, Filomena, Raffaella, Albina, Angelina, and their husbands and their kids all crammed into Antoinette's kitchen eating meatballs and sausages and *braciole,* drinking the homemade wine Frankie Watermelons sold from a horse and wagon he parked on Sullivan Street. They'd have romaine lettuce and tomatoes with red onions that Antoinette would soak in cold water to make them sweet, and then coffee and banana cream pie and Boston cream pie and éclairs and cream puffs from Dellarova's on Bleecker Street. The Mangiacarne family loved all kinds of cream cake with their espresso. The kids had theirs with milk.

"Jumbo, Jumbo, what about Sunday?"

Jumbo reminded himself that this was the girl he loved. "Sunday. Sure. Sunday's a good day for me." He handed Judy the bag of peanuts. His appetite was gone.

He left her off at her apartment on Seventy-third Street and Park Avenue. She asked him to come up and he did but he was too nervous to do anything but watch television. He never stayed over. She thought it was quaint and old-fashioned that he worried about her reputation. What would her neighbors think if they saw a man leaving her apartment, he told her, and who could miss him?

But the truth was, he liked to sleep home. He slept in the tiny second bedroom off the kitchen that faced the back alley and his mother peeked in every morning, even before she made coffee. He had slept in the living room as a young boy, on the pull-out couch, his sisters all piled together in this bedroom that was his now, his parents in the bedroom off the front. Jumbo got the bedroom when the last of his sisters married. The room was small but it was cool in the summer and quiet, and it had a door. Antoinette had always been proud that none of her children had ever had to sleep in a *brande* in the kitchen. It was one of her badges of honor. That and that they never went hungry. Hunger was not a problem in the neighborhood, but the sheer size of the Mangiacarnes spoke of the good life, of excess. Antoinette let the curtains turn to tatters and the linoleum crack and split but her table always groaned with the best that money could buy.

Her daughters had followed her example, which was why Nicky's mother brought down invective on their heads. One dirty woman in the building was tolerable but now they were six. Six Mangiacarnes, one messier than the next.

Teresa laughed when Nicky told her that Jumbo's mother believed she had the power to cast the *malocchio*. "Ha," she told him. "If I had the power, they would all be in kingdom come by now." She lowered her voice and spoke into Nicky's ear. "Magdalena has the power. But she's very clever. She keeps it only for herself."

"Magdalena doesn't believe in that, Ma. You forget when I couldn't walk, she sent you to the doctor?"

"I told you. She keeps it for herself. You think it was an accident Amadeo married her, a peasant girl young enough to be his daughter with his poor wife still warm in the grave? He was over there weeks and weeks. I never heard a word. I was taking care of Salvatore. I went to the priest. I thought Amadeo was dead and I would have two mouths to feed instead of one. And then he shows up, married."

The neighborhood had buzzed when Amadeo came back from Lucania with Magdalena. The women spent so much time on the stoops and in each other's houses that almost nothing got done. The dust mops stayed on the hooks in the wall and there was no line at the butcher's. They heard about Magdalena before they saw her. No one could remember who first told the story.

They watched the entrance to Amadeo's house from early in the morning. Amadeo went to his store and came home, and they greeted him and he greeted them back, but no one mentioned his bride (if he had even married her, who knows these things, the women on the stoop said).

Magdalena stayed inside the house. She would get down on the floor and put her cheek to the cold tiles. She would go from room to room and say the names out loud in English of the colors on the walls. She would stack and restack the dinner plates in the glass cupboards, and of course, she would play with the baby, who was getting very pale from staying inside.

To entice her to go out, Amadeo bought her a coach carriage, an English one that turned at the touch of a finger, and on the first day of the new moon she dressed herself and Salvatore, put him in the English coach carriage, and went for a walk. She walked for hours, up one block and down the next. She crossed Houston Street and went over to Bleecker. She walked all the way to Fourth Street Park and sat under the shadow of the arch with the nannies in their white uniforms watching their Fifth Avenue babies. She smiled when anyone looked at her, and before she went home, she passed by Amadeo's store, and when he came outside, she kissed him on the mouth in front of everyone in the street.

"Bold," someone said, on the stoop the next day, and the women fell into a circle, heads together, the younger ones filled with envy, the older ones shaking their heads, feigning shock. The feeling was that she was too young, too beautiful, too slim. Her hair was too black and there was too much red where the light caught it. Her eyes were too strange. They had gold in them, one of the younger women said.

Magdalena wore the polished goat's bone close to her skin, and when she bathed, she let the water run over it to move its power into her. She did the same with all her jewels, and Amadeo would find her in the bath adorned with all the pearls and rubies and diamonds he had given her. She put together a shrine to the Black Madonna at the top of the house, under the eaves, with the stone Zia Guinetta had pressed into her hand when she left Castelfondo, the stone with the face of the Black Madonna. In front of the shrine Magdalena put offerings of food and flowers. She burned candles. To the women on the stoop, she was inaccessible. Sometimes she was giddy like a young girl and then suddenly serious like an old woman. They never drew her into their circle. She didn't want to come. She was an outsider. They never went to her house for coffee and cake, or invited her into their houses, and at Easter they didn't taste her pies filled with sausage and cheese or bring her pieces of theirs wrapped in dish towels, the crust thick and rising to a dome.

They saw her garden of herbs from their fire escape windows and they smelled her cooking that wasn't food, and they talked among themselves, but they were always polite because she was Amadeo Pavese's wife and he was a *padrone* and they were always frightened of what they couldn't understand. It was a trait that went back hundreds of years, the way they shouted when all they meant to do was talk.

Nicky pinched his mother's cheek. "You do too have the power," he said. "You're the *strega*." And he kissed her on the mouth the way she loved but pretended that she didn't.

Over pastrami at Katz's Deli, Judy told Jumbo that it was set for Sunday. They ate at Ratner's once a week and at Katz's every Thursday. Jumbo wanted to show Judy how much he loved her. How better than loving her food? Besides, he believed that if he married her, he would spend the rest of his life eating pastrami and blintzes, and he wanted to practice.

When Jumbo told Antoinette he wouldn't be home for dinner Sunday, she didn't blink an eye. Antoinette was no dope. She knew her son. Who else had seen him every day of his life, except for those three weeks when he had gone to live with that *scifo* Nicky, and Amadeo Pavese's son Salvatore. She told the girls later that day when they all congregated for afternoon coffee and cake, before they trudged upstairs and down to their own apartments, that she knew something was up with their brother.

"You worried, Ma?" Rosina said.

"Of course I'm worried. How many times can I save his life?"

"Well," Albina said, "he's not gambling. He hasn't got a pot to piss in and there's no one on the East or West Sides who'll lend him a dime."

Filomena sighed. She dunked her almond biscotti in her coffee cup. "It must be a girl."

"Whatta you talking about?" Antoinette turned purple. "How could he have a girl? Someone would see, no? Someone would tell me? Everybody knows everything in this neighborhood. They don't miss a trick."

"Hey, Ma, wake up. It's a big world out there," Angelina told her.

"You mean, a girl that's not from here? Somebody we don't know?"

"Unlikely," Raffaella said. "I don't think Jumbo has universal appeal."

Antoinette smacked her shoulder. Raffaella spilled her coffee and wiped it up without a word. "Any girl in her right mind would kill for a man like your brother."

"C'mon, Ma," Rosina said. "We love Jumbo, but he's no Cary Grant."

"Oh, please . . . Cary Grant, Cary Grant. Why? Your husband looks like Cary Grant? Who cares about Cary Grant, anyway? He's a *riccone*. I read it in the newspaper, him and that one that wears the tights, the pirate."

"Errol Flynn?"

"Yeah, him." Antoinette cleared the table around them, pushing at their hands and elbows. "Go home now. I gotta make supper," and she piled the dishes and cups and saucers onto the ones from breakfast that were still in the sink.

Judy wanted to take the train but Jumbo borrowed Luca Benvenuto's car, which cost him a day's pay, and they set off early in the afternoon. He had gotten Luca to leave the car on Varick Street and Jumbo had gotten dressed in the back room of the bar. He wore a suit and tie and he had wet his hair and pomaded it until the teeth marks of the comb were as clear as furrows in a plowed field. Judy was waiting downstairs for him on Seventy-third Street and he noticed that she was very nicely dressed with a scarf around her hair and gloves and a pocketbook made of alligator that he had never seen her carry before.

They drove with the radio on and the windows open. Judy smoked cigarettes and blew the smoke out the window. Jumbo was sweating. He could feel the wet creeping through his shirt and suit jacket and hoped it was all in his imagination. He would have to leave his jacket on. He hoped they wouldn't stay too long.

The house was bigger than he had expected. He actually hadn't expected anything. To him, a house was a house, but this place looked like something out of the movies, nothing like his uncle's house in New Jersey where his family went for Fourth of July. There was a Cadillac and a Mustang convertible parked in the driveway of the three-car garage. Judy said they sold her car when she moved to the city. The Mustang was her mother's. Jumbo was impressed that Mrs. Bernstein had her own car. He was impressed that she could drive it. Antoinette didn't even take the bus. She only went somewhere if she got picked up and dropped off door to door and even then only for weddings, a trip to the cemetery after a funeral, and those Fourth of July parties in New Jersey.

Judy rang the doorbell and Jumbo wondered how come she didn't have the key. The door opened in a split second. They had been standing there, Mr. and Mrs. Bernstein. He saw right away that Judy favored her father, the nose and the hair and the height. Mrs. Bernstein—"Oh, please dear, call me Sylvia"—was tall and slim in pale green silk pants and a printed silk top that was a Pucci knockoff. It seemed like a classy getup to Jumbo.

Mrs. Bernstein, or Sylvia, as she insisted he call her, didn't remotely remind him of anybody's mother. He suddenly felt bad for Judy. He thought about how she wouldn't be able to help loving Antoinette. He felt better about the whole thing now, seeing how poor Judy had grown up. This big house but a mother who walked around in silk pants on a Sunday afternoon. How could she possibly cook anything?

Judy kissed her father and mother on the cheek and followed them into the living room. Jumbo went to sit on the couch but the Bernsteins just kept walking, through the dining room, and the den, and the kitchen, out to the patio by the pool.

"Did you children bring suits?" Sylvia asked. The smile on her face looked pained. It seemed to Jumbo like her mouth was paralyzed.

"Swimsuits," Mr. Bernstein, or Harvey, as he insisted Jumbo call him, explained. "The pool's heated. You could go for a dip."

"Oh, I don't know, Mother," Judy said.

"I'd love to go for a swim," Jumbo said. He was a wonderful swimmer, and a wonderful dancer, the myth of all fat men, light on his delicate feet always shod in the best of shoes. He turned to his beloved. "Gee, honey, you shoulda told me there was a pool."

Sylvia cringed just slightly at the word *honey* but her smile stayed put and she got up to serve iced tea in tall glasses with little paper umbrellas. "Just like a nightclub," Jumbo said to her when she handed him a glass.

Sylvia hated him. She had hated him on sight. She hated him with every breath, every pore. She could see the circle of sweat forming under the arms of his jacket. It was hot in the yard. She would have suggested he take off his jacket but the sight of a sweaty fat man in shirtsleeves was more than she could bear at this moment. Sylvia Bernstein hated fat. She tolerated a slight potbelly in Harvey, who only really enjoyed his food at lunchtime on Grand Street, away from Sylvia. He had the genes, she told him, to be a balloon and he had passed them on to Judy. Sylvia had mercilessly kept them in check as best she could but she couldn't be everywhere. She looked her daughter over carefully. She had definitely put on weight since the last time she saw her. Sylvia wasn't surprised, seeing the company she was keeping.

Come help me in the kitchen, darling," she said to Judy. "Let the men chat."

Judy didn't have to ask but she did. "What do you think?" she said when they were alone.

"About what, dearest?"

"Jumbo. What do you think? Isn't it sweet how he got all dressed up to meet you? I told him it was casual but he wore a suit and tie anyway."

"He seems like a nice boy."

"He's not a boy, Mother. He's a grown man and I'm going to marry him."

Sylvia panicked; her smile cracked. "But Judy, who is he? You don't know anything about him. He could be the Boston Strangler."

"They caught the Boston Strangler."

"Well, I still think you should be careful, that's all. You waited this long."

Jumbo came through the kitchen, Harvey behind him. "Your father's got a bathing suit for me, honey. I'm gonna go for a swim before we eat. Otherwise I gotta wait an hour. I don't wanna get a cramp and drown in your pool, Sylvia."

Sylvia thought that was a great idea, Jumbo drowning, but she retrieved her smile, weaker than before. With her lips pressed together, no teeth, she glared at Harvey, who excused himself and disappeared. Sylvia kept arranging the plates on a tray along with the little sandwiches she had had catered in town, cucumbers and watercress, the crusts carefully cut off and the bagels and Nova and cream cheese and blintzes and pickles Harvey had brought from the city for their lunch with their daughter's fiancé. She asked Judy to set the table outside, explaining that she had to run upstairs for a minute. She found Harvey in the bathroom. She could set the clock by his digestion. She knew where he'd be.

"He's a nice boy, Sylvia," Harvey said to her through the door. "He looks like he's going to enjoy your lunch."

"Be honest for once, Harvey. He's an aberration and we don't even have to go beyond his physical appearance."

"He *is* a big boy."

"He's a fat boy, a big fat boy. Do you know one of my friends that has a fat son-in-law? How will I take him to the club?"

"Listen, he's a hard worker. Judy says he works two shifts at the bar. There's always room for a boy like that. Let's face it, Sylvia. She's our only daughter. If this is the man to make her happy, we can help out a little."

Sylvia bit a fingernail. She sat at the edge of the bed, carefully smoothing her knockoff Pucci top under her buttocks so it wouldn't be wrinkled when she stood up. "You know, Elaine Himmelfarb's daughter married a Hare Krishna. She had to sit cross-legged on the floor in an orange robe at their wedding. And Harriet's daughter married some mountain man she met in Wyoming when she was conducting AA meetings on an Indian reservation." Sylvia heard the toilet flush and then the water running. Harvey opened the bathroom door. "So tell me," she said, "where you found swimming trunks for an elephant?"

They went downstairs together. Sylvia was feeling better. In the end, it was Judy's life. Sylvia had her own. They could set certain conditions: a rabbi for the wedding, the children raised Jewish. At least the holidays wouldn't conflict. It wasn't like they were the first parents to put up with this sort of thing. When Sylvia started to think, she had to admit that it was definitely a trend. Inappropriate matches. She was sure it had to do with all this education. You never knew who your children would meet today when they went out into the world.

Jumbo was sitting at the table with Judy. They were waiting, he said, for the Bernsteins to come down. Sylvia softened. She loved good manners. Jumbo made sure Sylvia was served first. Judy thought he was even charming Sylvia a little bit. He relaxed and slathered cream cheese on half his bagel, piled it high with Nova Scotia, and added the top. He pressed it down carefully and bit in.

This wasn't so bad, Jumbo decided. He imagined every other Sunday by the pool, maybe a spin in the Mustang. All he had to do was win over Antoinette and he was set. He could tell Judy's parents liked him. He looked around. They were doing pretty good and she was an only child. He would have married her with nothing but hey, money didn't hurt. He imagined the satin and lace *busta* at their wedding stuffed with envelopes. He might even be able to square it with Fat Eddie Fingers and get the hell out of Benvenuto's. Jumbo reached for a bialy and covered it with butter.

"You didn't have your swim?" Sylvia said. Jumbo was wearing his shirt and the bathing trunks Harvey had given him. Sylvia recognized them as the extra-large pair Harvey had ordered for a window display when he added a line of swimwear.

"Nah, I decided to wait, but look at this, the suit fits perfect." Jumbo snapped the waistband to show Sylvia.

Harvey smiled. "I told him he could have them," he said to Sylvia, "or," and here he winked and touched Judy's arm, "maybe just leave them here for when he comes over."

Sylvia smiled, too. "They fit nicely . . . Alfso," she said. "That is your real name, Judy's told us?"

"Sylvia, you can call me whatever you want, just don't call me late for dinner."

Judy slapped Jumbo's arm. "Stop teasing," she said. Sylvia teeheed a little bit. Harvey guffawed. Jumbo stood up and pushed back his chair. He walked to the edge of the pool and began to unbutton his shirt. The Bernsteins sat watching him. He turned to face them. "You save me if I get a cramp, okay, Jude?" he said to Judy.

Sylvia looked up at him, shading her eyes with her hand. Her smile tightened until her mouth was a slit the size of a paper clip as Jumbo pushed the shirt off his shoulders, exposing his mammoth chest, smooth and hairless and unmarked as a baby's bottom, except for two words tattooed in inch-high blue letters over each one of his nipples. The right read SWEET and the left, SOUR.

Sylvia's eyes rolled to the back of her head. She pitched forward and before they could catch her, she fell with a splash into the pool.

It's a fucking mess," Jumbo told Nicky when he came to see him at Benvenuto's to find out how it went.

"Whatta you mean?"

"I went out there to Long Island to meet her parents. She insisted."

"And?"

"*Marrone,* Nicky, they got money. You had to see this house. Swimming pool, the mother all dressed up like Paddy's pig. I mean, you know she wasn't sweating over no hot stove. I'm a little, you know, kinda thrown for a loop with all this. Judy coulda told me something, given me a clue."

"So?"

"So, wait. We're by the pool and they were nice, you know? Judy's old lady was a little snooty but I know how to treat old broads. Forgive me for calling Judy's mother a broad, but she wasn't my idea of a mother. I would never call your mother a broad even though she hates me."

"Go ahead, Jumbo. I'm getting the picture here."

"Okay, so, they're liking me even. 'Call me Sylvia,' the mother says. The father gives me a bathing suit so I can go for a swim."

"He had a bathing suit for you?"

"Yeah, he's in the business. He had this suit, fit perfect, was even a little big if you can believe it."

"Yeah?"

"Yeah, so it's all going good until I take off my shirt. Those fucking tattoos, Nicky. I forgot about the fucking tattoos. Sylvia takes one look at my tits and goes down like a redwood. Boom! She passes out, rolls in the friggin' pool. Stop laughing, Nicky. This is serious."

"So what happened?"

"What happened, what could happen? We got her up and Harvey got her upstairs and dried her off and put her in bed. He said it was food poisoning. He blamed the cream cheese but I know it was those fucking tattoos. Am I nuts? Who gets tattoos like that? It just wasn't a good start, you know? It wasn't a good introduction."

"Well, forget the mother. What did Judy say?"

"She says don't worry. But now she wants to meet *my* mother. She ain't taking no for an answer."

"Well, Jesus, Jumbo, she's right."

"But my mother don't know nothing yet."

"Well, you better say something."

"I thought you and Salvatore was gonna help me."

"What do you want us to do?"

"I don't know. Voodoo? Maybe Salvatore can get Magdalena to do something?"

"What about my mother?" Nicky laughed.

"Give me a break, Nicky. I'm looking for love here, not destruction. I'm cursed. I really am cursed."

"Sally said he'd be down tonight. His wife's up in Connecticut with her family and he's got to do work so he's in town. We could have dinner."

"Good idea. Three heads are better than two."

They met, Jumbo and Salvatore and Nicky. They started at the Kettle of Fish on Bleecker Street, where Pauly Rizzo worked behind the bar and bought them all a drink. They walked over to the Ninth Circle and listened to the folk music and Jimmy Burp, who worked behind that bar, bought them a drink and on around the Village and then uptown where the neighborhood boys had fanned out to work the nightclubs and bars. Jumbo knew all of them, from Domnick in Max's Kansas City on up to Pauly in the Copa. By 2 A.M., they were back downtown at the Page 3, to watch men in gowns sing torch songs on the stage.

The last stop was a place that didn't have a name, deep down on Broadway where they checked you out through a peephole before they opened the door and the men wore dresses and the women wore pin-striped suits and they all wore makeup as garish as a drunk's imagination.

Nicky woke up the next morning and couldn't remember how he'd gotten home. It made him so nervous that he left his apartment to come back down to the neighborhood and sit in the last pew in St. Anthony's Church on Sullivan Street before he went to his mother, who made him drink hot water and lemon juice and said terrible things about his ex-wife Gina.

Jumbo slept the sleep of the dead. His mother beat egg and milk into a soup dish, dipped a loaf of Wonder bread, slice by slice, into the mixture, and fried the slices one by one in a pan of butter. She stacked the pieces neatly into a pile just the way Jumbo liked his French toast, soft and wet in the middle, dripping with butter and syrup. Antoinette could smell the alcohol coming through Jumbo's pores when she went into the narrow bedroom to wake him up but it only made her sigh. Every once in a while Antoinette expected her boy to let off a little steam. As long as he ended up in his bed and her kitchen she could forgive him anything.

Out on Long Island Judy's mother hoped her daughter's affection for "the Italian from the city" (Sylvia had buried her Bronx roots long ago) would end with time. It wasn't about money, she told Harvey. It was about class. Jumbo had none.

Harvey rubbed Sylvia's freckled shoulders. They were spotted with black and brown dots from her bathing beauty days at Raven Hall in Coney Island, "the world's largest saltwater pool," where Sylvia would stretch out next to old women from Eastern Europe who sunned naked in the rooftop solarium, their bodies brown all over except for two narrow half moons at the backs of their thighs that their sagging asses had hidden from the sun.

Harvey dug his fingers into the muscles at the base of Sylvia's neck and told her that this should be the worst they ever had to worry about. Italians made beautiful babies, he said, which was the last thing Sylvia wanted to hear, and when Judy called with the news, Sylvia blamed Harvey, convinced his words had jinxed their only child.

"From your mouth to God's ears," she told him and took to her bed. The blinds were drawn, her bridge club was left looking for a fourth. Harvey closed the store on Grand Street and went on suicide watch. He sat by Sylvia's bed alternately holding her hand and patting her leg. He tried not to fall asleep in the chair he had pulled close to the bed but his eyelids drooped and he would wake up stiff and bent and go down to the kitchen only to make Sylvia coffee. She refused to eat and drank the coffee black.

Secretly Harvey was pleased. He thought a grandchild, even a half-Italian grandchild, was a blessing. And just this morning, Judy had promised him they would raise it Jewish.

Jumbo's reaction to Judy's news was not so far from Sylvia's. If he could have fit himself out the window that faced the back alley, he would have jumped. He knew from Matty J's experience that any attempt to fling himself from the window facing Spring Street would never work. At the first sight of him, and Jumbo would be sighted, between the time and effort it would take to squeeze himself out onto the sill, and the pigeons he would send flapping off the window ledges, half the neighborhood would be in his house pulling him to safety. The other half would be standing in the street looking up, hoping in their heart of hearts that he would jump or fall or in some way complete the drama he'd started before the cops came and put in their two cents.

When Nicky called to see how he was doing, Jumbo cried into the phone. He begged Nicky to come by and when Nicky did, that afternoon, Jumbo brought him into the men's room at Benvenuto's and locked the door. "You know, Nicky, if Luca Benvenuto comes by and finds us in here with the door locked he's gonna think . . . you know what he's gonna think? He's a small-minded guy."

"Then what are we doing in here?"

"I don't give a shit what he thinks about me, but you're a detective. You gotta worry about these things. I want you to know what you're getting into."

"Jumbo, what is it?"

"What am I gonna do about Judy?"

"Whatta you wanna do?"

"Kill myself."

"Besides that."

"Nicky, would I drag you over here if I knew?"

"Marry the girl, Jumbo. Isn't that what you want?"

"You're forgetting about Antoinette. My mother, Nicky. She's gonna kill me. She never even met this girl. How am I gonna hit her with this?"

Nicky shrugged. "Antoinette will come around. One fat baby and you're home free."

"What makes you think I'd have a fat baby?"

"Unlock the door before Benvenuto comes by, would you?"

Antoinette was having serious suspicions that something was not right with her son. He had started picking his underwear up off the floor and making his bed and sometimes even putting his plate in the sink, not normal behavior for a boy as coddled as the crown prince of Austria. Antoinette, not the best of housekeepers, noticed these things.

And his appetite was down. Antoinette was a brilliant cook; she held her reputation even in a neighborhood brimming with brilliant cooks, and she very carefully noted when someone did not eat, or in Jumbo's case devour, her culinary efforts. Just last Sunday, she had made a *bonsette,* stuffing the pocket of the veal shoulder with egg and bread crumbs and parsley and cheese, sewing it closed with a needle and white thread, breathing in the fragrant steam when she took it out of the oven, before she sliced it into thick pieces.

Jumbo had nibbled. Rosina was the one who couldn't stand it anymore. "Jumbo, what's wrong with you?" she asked him with a poke in the ribs, and a red flag went up for Antoinette. She looked around at the round pink faces of the others: Albina, Raffaella, Angelina, and Filomena. They all remained with their forks in midair and then Antoinette knew. If her girls noticed, it wasn't her babying him. It was serious.

She kept quiet until they gathered together that Monday for coffee, the time of day when they all sat in Antoinette's kitchen, their children put to nap on couches and beds and chairs, the last moments they had together before their husbands came home, before they had to go home and cook dinner.

"Something's wrong with your brother," Antoinette told them.

It was Filomena who twisted her mouth to one side and said, "We've been through this, Mama. I'm telling you. Jumbo's in love."

"Why d'you think that?" Antoinette said. "I only wish he would find a nice girl. I'm not gonna be here forever. You girls got your own families." Antoinette put her hand to her heart. "I know, I know how you feel about your brother, but you gotta think about your kids. They have to come first."

Filomena pushed against her sister Albina's elbow and the two of them smiled and let Antoinette's sighs settle into the air fragrant with garlic and oil. "He does have a girl, Mama," Albina said.

"And it's about time," Angelina chimed in. Rosina sat to Angelina's left and she pushed at her sister's elbow.

Antoinette sat down, heavily, carefully, in the vinyl kitchen chair that barely contained her. "What makes you say that? If he had a girl he'd bring her home to meet the family, no? If he was serious?" Antoinette shook her head. She got up and started to make more coffee. "I think you're *pazze*. All of you. Jumbo had a girl, he would tell me, or somebody would."

"Times change, Mama. You think this neighborhood knows everything."

"Pshew . . . I can name ten people who would give their eyeteeth to let me know something like that. Besides, if your brother had a girl, wouldn't he say something? Jumbo and I are like this," and Antoinette held up her hand, the second and third fingers intertwined.

"Just tell her, for God's sake," Raffaella said.

"What? Tell me what?"

"He's got a girl, Mama. Tony Four-Heads saw him uptown in Jilly's. That's where he met her."

"So, Jumbo goes with a lot of girls. Nice-looking boy like him. Why not?"

"This is one girl, Mama. She's a Jew, a schoolteacher from Long Island. He's been all over uptown with her."

Antoinette backed against the wall and steadied herself on the tin cabinet where the toaster sat under a floral cover that matched the doily underneath. She moved a chair out from the table and fell into it. "*Madonna mia!* Whatta'm I gonna do? Rosina, Albina, Filomena, Angelina, Raffaella . . . *aiutami!*" Antoinette started to breathe heavy. She pulled her dress up and the girls rushed to undo the garters that held her stockings over her knees and cut off her circulation. They fanned her with their handkerchiefs. They pressed a cool washcloth to her sweat-beaded forehead and they held her hands while she cried and raved and they watched the clock. They had to be in their houses by five to have dinner on the table on time.

Antoinette calmed down, sobbing into her hands, wiping her nose with a fist like a giant child. "You go," she told her daughters. "If I need you, I'll yell in the hall." They left in tandem, all five of them, asses and arms and knees bumping against the table and chairs and cabinets that cluttered the kitchen that was big for a tenement kitchen but small for the Mangiacarne sisters. Fifteen minutes of confusion and they were gone, outside in the hallway, dragging kids and bundles up and down the broken marble stairs of 196 Spring Street, and Antoinette was left in her kitchen, alone with the news that her baby boy was seeing a girl, a Jew, and he was keeping it secret from her.

She wouldn't ask him about it. Antoinette was too clever to switch the balance of power. This she knew. Let him perspire. Life was long. Anything could happen. And in the meantime, she would do her best to adjust fate.

The next day when she heard Nicky's mother, Teresa, climbing the stairs, she called out to her through the open door. Antoinette didn't like Teresa, was afraid of her ever since she blamed Jumbo for Nicky falling the three stories into the yard all those years ago, but everyone knew Teresa had experienced a miracle when Nicky had walked at his father's funeral. And Antoinette believed, like everyone else, that Teresa had the knowledge, that she had tapped into some higher power. White or black, it didn't matter which, as long as you got what you wanted.

Teresa stopped when she heard her name and looked up to where the voice was coming from. She was surprised and waited to hear it again before she climbed the extra flight of stairs and went to Antoinette's door and looked inside down the narrow inner hall that was the entrance to the apartment. "*Chi è?*" she said.

"Teresa, come in, Teresa. It's Antoinette. Come. I've got *crespelle*

I just made. Here, with the powdered sugar. Use as much as you like. Everybody waits for Easter but I make them all the time. I just took out the last one. Look, the oil's still hot. Maybe you like them with honey? I got honey, too, but come in. Sit down. How long you're not in my house?"

Teresa entered on the theory that you never show your enemies your true feelings. She accepted Antoinette's invitation to sit at her big kitchen table covered in flowered oilcloth. Antoinette moved the ironing from one of the chairs and wiped down the spot just in front of Teresa. She took a chipped cup from the pile of dishes in the sink, ran it under hot water, and dried the bottom before she poured Teresa's coffee. She offered her the carton of milk and a jelly jar filled with sugar lumps and pushed the tower of fried dough across the table to her. The fluted edges of the delicate pastries caught the powdered sugar, which Teresa insisted she preferred over honey.

"These are good, Antoinette," Teresa said, taking small bites.

"Ah, not thin like yours, I bet, Teresa. Yours, I hear, are like tissue paper." Teresa smiled at the compliment. Her *crespelle* were as thin as tissue paper but these weren't bad.

"It's so good to see you," Antoinette went on. "You know, all these years in the same building and we don't talk, all because of our boys. They're men now and still we don't talk. Silly, no?"

Teresa didn't answer, being a woman of few words and great action, and unlike Antoinette, secretive. Only the saints knew her heart. She sat very still, looking around under her eyelids. It was a very messy house. Teresa had always known this. It was a very messy family. Everyone knew this. But when Antoinette started crying, big fat tears that soaked the front of her apron, Teresa forgot the state of Antoinette's house and listened. They were, after all, both mothers. Weren't all women the same under the flesh?

They had both been blessed with one son, only one. Shouldn't this bring them together? Antoinette told Teresa. And their boys, they had always been close and, thank God, the terrible thing that had happened to Nicky had been fixed. Thank God he had walked.

Teresa nodded. She crossed herself, her right hand going from her forehead to between her breasts, from her right shoulder to her left in the sign of the cross, ending at her lips. She kissed her fingers and opened the thumb and forefinger of her hand to complete the benediction and she leaned back waiting for Antoinette to go on. She knew this was a prelude, that Antoinette had something on her mind.

"How did Nicky walk? How, Teresa? What did you do? The miracle . . . how did it happen?"

"What is it, Antoinette? What do you want?"

Antoinette pulled a handkerchief from her apron pocket and filled it with tears. It was a scrap of cotton in her big red hands. She pulled a second handkerchief out and blew her nose. "I want my son back, Teresa. He's got a girl, a . . ." and here she lowered her voice, "a *mazzucriste!*"

Teresa shook her head. "Antoinette," she said. "I can't do nothing. My Nicky married an Italian girl and look, she left him with nothing. I don't even have a grandchild and he has to pay her money! Count your blessings. Maybe she's a nice girl. Did you meet her?"

"I don't wanna meet her. I know what happens. I'll never see him no more. The girls pull. Jumbo don't have a chance. My brother-in-law, remember Jerry? He married a girl from down South. After that, who saw him? My mother-in-law got cataracts from crying. This woman, she didn't even want kids. 'Ugh,' she told my mother-in-law. My mother-in-law was a saint. You knew her, Teresa. She had fifteen kids and Jerry's wife tells her 'Ugh.'"

Antoinette leaned over and Teresa put her arms around her and forgot for a moment that Antoinette had spawned the *mortodevame* that had crippled her son. Teresa let it go. She patted the hump of Antoinette's back and muttered something about the woman on Bedford Street who was dead now and had left no heirs. "What about Magdalena?" she said into Antoinette's ear. "She comes from the other side and I've heard things, about a Madonna, a Black Madonna, that she brought with her when she came."

On Long Island, Sylvia spoke secretly to Harvey. There were things that could be done, she whispered. Ira Fleishberg's daughter had taken a weekend in Puerto Rico. Maybe Harvey could ask. Didn't he have Puerto Ricans working in the store? Weren't there a lot of them on Grand Street?

Harvey was horrified. "A child, Sylvia, our grandchild."

"Harvey, please, think of it. Our Judy tied forever to that . . . Oh, please. Meet my son-in-law Dumbo. Oh, Harvey . . ."

"Jumbo, his nickname is Jumbo, Sylvia. Be fair."

Judy, too, was getting edgy. She refused to see Jumbo unless he set the date and here she was getting bigger and bigger faster than she had expected. It was three months and then four. She spent weekends at her parents' house in tears. Her mother moaned that she had waited too long. Her father held her in his arms and said she could have whatever she wanted. If Alfonso was the boy for her, then they would embrace him like their own son. Judy cried harder, tearing at her hair. Sylvia would leave to put a cold compress over her eyes and lie down in the darkened bedroom until one weekend when she took Harvey aside and shook his arm until it hurt.

"It's four months, Harvey. Is this putz gonna marry her or what? Enough is enough. Talk to him. Make him do something."

Harvey and Sylvia went into Judy's room and told her to call the father of her unborn child and have him come out to Long Island. "No swimming," Sylvia said. "And definitely no lunch. Tell him to eat before he comes. We have to settle this once and for all."

When Jumbo got the call, he borrowed Nicky's car and drove to Long Island, where the Bernsteins sat him down in the living room and said they were willing to let Judy marry him for the sake of the child.

Jumbo was a little bit stunned at their attitude. Judy was pregnant. If he didn't marry her, who would? Wasn't he holding the cards here? He took a pack of cigarettes from his shirt pocket, tapped one out and put it in his mouth. He waited for Sylvia to get him an ashtray. He asked Harvey for a light. Judy sat at the end of the couch near her mother, frowning one minute, sobbing the next.

Jumbo wanted to tell her everything would be okay and that he loved her and of course he would marry her, but he wasn't going to let her parents push him around. If he showed weakness now, they'd crucify him. He was practically on the cross already. He wasn't going to give them the hammer and nails, too.

"What are you doing?" Harvey said to him. "You have a responsibility here. Are you going to be a man about it or what?"

Jumbo blew out the smoke he had inhaled lighting his cigarette. "Harvey . . ." he said, but Sylvia had had enough. She jumped up, threw aside Judy's hand that had crawled into her lap, and pulled the cigarette out of Jumbo's mouth.

"Listen, you fat greaseball," she said. "You don't deserve our Judy but she wants you so she's going to get you. She's going to get exactly what she wants. A rabbi's doing the ceremony and the baby's going to be Jewish. Understand?"

Jumbo looked at Judy, who turned her face away. "Sure, Sylvia," he said. "Anything you say."

"Mrs. Bernstein."

"You said . . ."

"Never mind. All bets are off. I'm calling our rabbi. Sunday. You be here in a suit and tie. You wanna invite your family, some friends, it's fine by us but you be here on time. And you don't see Judy until then. She's leaving her job and she's staying with us."

"Okay. I'll be here. Like I said, Sylvia . . . Mrs. Bernstein. I love Judy. I . . ."

"Goodbye, Alfso."

"Judy . . ."

"Never mind Judy," Sylvia said. She walked over to the door and held it open. "Three o'clock Sunday, suit and tie. And I don't want to hear your voice or see your face until then."

Jumbo drove back to the city, one hand on the wheel. He decided to think about what suit he was going to wear. He left the car parked on Grand Street and went up the house. It was too early for dinner so he ate Antoinette's meatballs and sausage right out of the gravy pot. He ate like his old self, which made Antoinette believe he was getting better, that his foolishness with this Jewish girl was a thing of the past.

Even though Antoinette was sure that Magdalena had played dumb when she had gone with Teresa to ask her for help, to ask her to take the love curse off Jumbo, seeing her Jumbo eat like this made her think that maybe Magdalena had taken pity and made the miracle. Carmella Lispinardi had told her years ago about Magdalena in the top of her house, under the eaves. Carmella had seen through her windows, had seen Magdalena pull the shades but not before she had caught a glimpse of a shrine with flowers and candles. She couldn't see much, she had whispered to the women on the stoop, but it had looked like church, except the curtains were black and Magdalena had pulled them across the windows when she came into the room.

Magdalena had welcomed Antoinette and Teresa. She had been curious to see them together after such a long feud and was amused that the mother love that had torn them apart was bringing them together. She knew they didn't believe her when she said the rumors of her dark powers were false but she told them that she would pray to the Black Madonna for Jumbo's happiness. She promised Antoinette that she would remember him in her prayers.

When they sat down to eat and Antoinette served Jumbo his sixth meatball and poured gravy over his bread she was convinced the prayers had worked. Jumbo was back, the old Jumbo who belonged to her was back in her kitchen filling his belly, filling her soul.

The Sunday of the wedding, Jumbo wore his best suit and a custom shirt and the solid gold watch he had gotten from Maurizio the jeweler on Spring Street who sold swag from the back of his store. Nicky drove with Jumbo out to Long Island. The ceremony was short and he understood none of it and everyone cheered when he broke the glass wrapped in a napkin under his foot. He kissed Judy, whom he hadn't seen all week, and they danced at a party right there in the synagogue and spent the night in a motel near her parents' house and he struggled to carry her over the threshold because she had gained a lot of weight. Nicky decorated the car with tin cans and white crepe paper tied to the bumpers, which mortified Sylvia, but she couldn't complain about everything. Harvey drove Nicky to the train, since Jumbo and Judy had taken his car. Nicky liked the old man a lot, he told Jumbo when he came into Benvenuto's later in the week for a drink.

"So how does it feel to be married?" Nicky asked him.

"Great, just great. My wife's out in Long Island with Harvey and

Sylvia and I'm here with Antoinette. And somehow everybody's happy but me."

"Well, what the hell are you doing?"

"I told them I gotta work double shifts this week. I can't get out there. They're happy. They got their daughter in their clutches and the baby's got a name, even if it's not such a great name, they can cope."

"Jumbo . . ."

"I know . . . I'm gonna tell her. I swear to God."

"Good. That's good, Jumbo. I'm proud of you."

"Yeah . . . you better be ready to come and get me when she stabs me with a bread knife."

"I'll be there. I'm a homicide detective, remember?"

Antoinette did not take the news sitting down. She threw a pot, one of her big macaroni pots, across the room and missed Jumbo's head by inches. She screamed so loud that doors flung open throughout the whole building and all her daughters came running from their apartments at once. The sisters convened. Jumbo had not thought to ask his sisters to be there, to support him. He knew at the first sound of trouble they would come in anyway, and take his mother's part.

Rosina held Antoinette's hands. Albina cleaned up the mess the flying pot had made, breaking the frame of silver dollars, a souvenir from Antoinette's twenty-fifth wedding anniversary. Filomena wiped her mother's tears. Angelina patted her mother's shoulders. Raffaella yelled at Jumbo after Antoinette had stopped. Then they all yelled while their mother cried.

"How could you do this?" Albina said. "Say nothing and then hit her with this. Who do you think you are? Poor Mama. She works her fingers to the bone for you, you big chooch, and you do this?"

"Knock up some Jew and come home like nothing happened?"

"Married? Just like that?"

Rosina kissed her mother's face. "It's okay, Mama. Look on the bright side. He's not married in church. He's not really married. He can always do it again, the right way, to the right kind of girl."

Antoinette pushed her away and sobbed into her hands. "A *mazzucriste* . . . a *puttana* yet . . . carrying my grandchild . . . ahh-hhhhhiyeeee."* She cursed Teresa for taking her to Magdalena and giving her hope. She cursed Magdalena for not making things right. She knew Magdalena had the power, everyone knew it, but she, too, was just another *puttana.* Antoinette raved. Jumbo took his mother's hand and kissed it. He held it until she got quiet. He put her head on his shoulder and scowled at his sisters, who had retreated, disgusted with their brother, with their mother, so weakly cradled in his arms.

"Please, Mama. it's gonna be nice," he said. "You're gonna love Judy. She's a good girl, smart, quiet." He spoke softly into Antoinette's ear so that only she heard. "And there's money there. You know how you always say you don't wanna go in the ground. You know how you're afraid of the dirt on top of your head in Calvary?" Antoinette's huge back heaved as she nodded her head, hidden in the crook of Jumbo's arm. "Well, the first thing I'm gonna do is buy you a drawer. I told Judy already and she said okay. I'm gonna buy you one of those drawers in New Jersey. Whatta you think?"

Antoinette lifted her head, her eyes red and swollen. She patted Jumbo's face. "You're a good boy," she said. "Which way the drawer is gonna go? Longways?"

"Longways. You can sleep on it."

"And this baby. You're gonna baptize it? It's gonna be Catholic, no, like us?"

"I swear, Mama."

"You're gonna name it after your father it's a boy? Salvatore?"

"I promise."

"Antoinette after me it's a girl?"

"Yes."

"I love you, *figlio mio.*"

Eh," Antoinette said later on the stoop. "You do the best you can. My Jumbo got married quick," she told the women, "because the girl didn't want no fuss. You know, these girls with money, it don't matter to them a big wedding. Everything they do is big. They go to big parties all the time. They don't need no *cafone* show, you know what I mean? But we're gonna have a big christening. Jumbo wants to do that. If it's a boy, it's gonna be Salvatore, a girl, whatta you think? Antoinette!"

"Hmmm," Aggie Mancuso said. "She's pregnant already?"

"Ain't that something? My Jumbo don't fool around. He's a real man, no blanks. On her wedding night it happened."

"How long they're married?"

"Well, you figure it out. She's due in six months, unless she's early. That happens a lot. So they're married three months. Can't you count?"

"We can count, Antoinette," Aggie Mancuso said. "We can all count real good."

"How come they're not living together?"

"Her mother wants her out there until they get settled. They got a big house, a pool. Jumbo don't want to live just anywhere so they're gonna take their time. What's the rush? They got everything."

"You met the family?"

"Sure. Of course. They're coming Sunday. I'm gonna cook. Their eyes are gonna pop out when they taste my meatballs."

"Maybe we'll see them then."

"Could be. You see a big Cadillac on Spring Street, you know my son's in-laws are here."

True to Antoinette's word, the Bernsteins arrived on Sunday. Harvey pulled up in his white Cadillac and saw that the only parking spot was taken by a white-haired man sitting on a vinyl upholstered kitchen chair in the street. Harvey pulled up beside Dante and Sylvia leaned over and stuck her head out Harvey's window before Harvey could say anything and demanded to know what he was doing blocking the spot. Dante knew immediately his mission was accomplished.

"You the Bernfelds?"

"Yes. Yes," Harvey said. Sylvia hit him in the shoulder.

"Don't volunteer, Harvey. How many times do I have to tell you? You'd volunteer for the Cossack army if I wasn't here to save you." She leaned over Harvey and spoke out the window to Dante. "Maybe we're the Bernsteins," Sylvia said. "Who wants to know?"

Dante got up out of the chair and moved it to the sidewalk. "She's all yours," he said to Harvey and guided him into the spot, which was tight for a big a car like Harvey's Cadillac. Dante opened the door for Sylvia. He tipped his hat. "I was hoping you was gonna come soon," he said. "Antonina's got the food waiting for me. I don't usually eat this late but I promised Jumbo I'd wait."

Sylvia raised the corners of her mouth in a semi-smile and stood on the sidewalk looking up, her eyes shaded, trying to find number 196. She was slightly appalled, she told Harvey, on the way up the stairs, and when he mentioned their first apartment in the Bronx, Sylvia looked at him as though he had two heads. "What does the Bronx have to do with it? Why do you always have to drag up the past?"

"Stop it, please," Judy said. She had sat without a word during the ride and the exchange with Dante but the stairs were a struggle for her and she just wanted to get this over with. She didn't really care about Jumbo's mother and had already decided that he could come here to visit her by himself and she wouldn't give a damn.

The stoop had been empty. Jumbo had purposely made it a Sunday so the women would be home from church, stirring their gravy, too busy to gather one above the other. But they were not too busy to hang out the windows, and when Dante had yelled up to tell Jumbo and Antoinette that the Bernfelds had arrived, they had all heard and they were leaning out now, elbows resting on the pillows that covered the window ledges so that they could sit comfortably and watch the street.

Sylvia found the steps tricky. They were steep and worn in the center. She struggled in her delicate high heels to make the five flights of stairs, holding on to the grimy banister, ignoring the occasional urchin who stood by an open door to watch the procession of the Jews from Long Island. They had been waiting, the women, to see what Jumbo had married because they had been convinced, as they were about Dante, that he never would marry, never leave his mother or the building on Spring Street where all his sisters lived with their husbands and children.

Jumbo was waiting on the landing to meet them. Judy rushed into his arms and he held her for an embarrassed moment, glad Antoinette was inside. He shook Harvey's and Sylvia's hands and led them into the apartment.

"Good trip in?" he said to Harvey and Sylvia. "Did you hit traffic?"

"No, not much," Harvey said. "That was nice of your friend to save us a parking spot."

"Yeah, well, Dante's always outside. It must be fifty years he hasn't left Spring Street." Sylvia raised an eyebrow but was looking at the wallpaper pattern on the kitchen walls, big plaid patches in red and white with teapots and spoons and plates.

"Here they are," Jumbo announced to the kitchen filled with Mangiacarnes. The five sisters descended. They kissed Judy and Sylvia and Harvey in a round robin. One would grab them and pass them on to the next sister, the next husband, the next child. Sylvia was dizzy, Judy was shy and grateful, Harvey was covered with lipstick, his hands filled with the flesh of arms and waists and occasionally boobs and behinds. By the time he had kissed and felt up all of Jumbo's sisters and embraced their husbands and children, he had tears in his eyes. He liked this, the smell of the gravy cooking on the stove, the heat of the bodies, the steam from the boiling macaroni pot. Sylvia was horrified. She gritted her teeth and closed her lips, terrified someone would slip a tongue between them. The touch of each sweaty hand made her cringe. The worst was when Jumbo smothered her in his arms and whispered "Mama" in her ear.

The sisters insisted they couldn't stay, they just couldn't. They were just too many. Sylvia was glad to see them file out. There certainly were too many of them, she thought, and they were all too big. They left through the narrow entranceway, patting and pinching as they went until there were just the five of them: Judy, Sylvia, Harvey, Jumbo, and Antoinette.

Antoinette wiped her hands on her front apron. "Come into the parlor," she said. "Sit down. Have a drink."

They moved the few steps into the living room, which was separated from the kitchen by a wall with a square cut into it and dressed with a curtain as though it were a window. The living room had two windows that faced the street. There was a couch, a coffee table, two chests of unmatched drawers, a television set, and a chair with a hassock. There was barely enough room to get around all the furniture, and Jumbo guided the Bernsteins to the couch, where they sat like three blind mice facing Jumbo in the chair with the hassock.

Sylvia looked around carefully, wondering where on earth they slept and how on earth the group that had just left had ever fit all together in these miserable rooms. She didn't know that Antoinette was very proud of these rooms, that they faced the front, that they were square, and that she actually had two bedrooms, one tucked off the living room, one off the kitchen, each with a cardboard closet and a window. Antoinette had nothing to be ashamed of. She did notice how skinny Sylvia was and she wondered if she might be sick. It looked like cancer to her but she knew enough not to ask. She offered the Bernsteins a highball, which Jumbo got up and mixed in the kitchen in a cocktail shaker that had instructions printed on the glass.

"Nice place you've got here," Harvey said. "Reminds me of my mother's apartment in the Bronx." He had to, Sylvia thought, refer to the Bronx. He just couldn't let it go, and when Harvey launched into a rhapsody about the old neighborhood, Sylvia pulled her dress down over her knees, plastered on a smile, and sipped her highball.

Antoinette got up and Harvey followed her into the kitchen. She took out a meatball from the pot and put it into a small dish for him to taste. Sylvia scolded from the parlor, but Harvey was gone. He asked to use the bathroom and Antoinette pointed to a door in the corner of the kitchen. Harvey opened the door and looked into a room the size of a closet with a toilet inside. He closed the door and turned back to Antoinette. "Excuse me," he said. "There's no sink."

"What do you want?" Antoinette said.

"I want to wash my hands."

"Well, why didn't you say that? I thought you had to go. There," and she pointed to the kitchen sink next to the stove and the big gooey bar of brown soap in the saucer on the drainboard.

Jumbo laughed from the living room. "That's funny, Harvey," he said. "Did you think someone stole the sink? Get it, Ma?" Sylvia held out her glass for a refill. Antoinette raised an eyebrow. She didn't know Jews were drinkers. The Irish, yes, not the Jews. Antoinette liked the father. She had given him the dish towel to dry his hands and he was at the table, tearing off a piece of bread, mopping up the gravy from the meatball. She thought the girl was plain and she thought that was good but she wouldn't have minded beautiful grandchildren. She knew that good looks were more trouble than they were worth in a wife. Nicky had married that beautiful Gina Gandalfo with the long black hair and the big tits and had lost her just as fast, although Nicky was not Antoinette's idea of a man.

Antoinette looked Judy over carefully, especially her bulging stomach. She seemed quiet and definitely pregnant. Antoinette calculated: six Mangiacarne women to one of her. The mother didn't look like much competition. Sucking Judy into the family or, better yet, leaving her behind should not be a problem for the

Mangiacarnes. Antoinette was thinking these thoughts, about to call the Bernsteins to the table, when a huge crate swung outside the living room windows.

"What's that?" Judy said, pointing. She went to the window and looked down; there was a piano movers' truck parked downstairs. "Look," she said, "they're moving a piano."

"It's not a piano," Antoinette said, putting the bowl of macaroni on the table. "It's Lucy Petrazzini. She passed away last night." Antoinette crossed herself.

"Oh, I'm so sorry," Judy said. "Was she ill?"

"She had everything. Diabetes, heart condition, psoriasis, asthma. She was four hundred pounds. Dr. Vincenza told her, 'Lucy, you're digging your grave with your own fork.'" Antoinette shook her head. "She wouldn't listen."

Sylvia estimated Antoinette to tip the scales at way over two hundred pounds herself. She shuddered to imagine Lucy. "That's a shame," she said.

"Yeah, Nucciarone, he's our undertaker, the one the Naples people use, he came last night but he took one look and said there was no way he was getting her through the door, forget down the stairs."

"That was smart," Harvey said, "calling the piano movers."

"Oh, he's smart. Did you ever meet a dumb undertaker? Now we're all thinking, what's he gonna bury her in? A piano box? Eh, we'll see tomorrow when they lay her out."

Sylvia held out her plate for Antoinette to fill and pulled it back so quickly a meatball rolled onto the table. Jumbo speared it and ate it off his fork. Harvey sat, his shirt covered with a huge cloth napkin that Antoinette had tucked into his collar after she made him take off his jacket, which she hung on the back of the bedroom door off the kitchen where Jumbo slept.

"You're not eating, Sylvia," Antoinette said. "Something wrong?"

"Mother has a delicate stomach," Judy said.

"I knew it was something but I didn't want to ask," Antoinette said. "That's why you look so sick, huh? So skinny. Poor thing. You want me to make you pastina? That's easy to digest."

"No, no," Sylvia said. "Please, I'm fine. This is delicious."

"Well," Antoinette said, "Harvey here made up for you. You want to take some home? Jumbo can bring me the bowl next time he comes."

"I'd love some to take home," Harvey said. And Antoinette shuffled macaroni and meatballs into a green Pyrex bowl, telling Jumbo just to make sure she got the bowl back because it was part of a set.

Sylvia stood up as soon as she could, edging toward the door, hoping to avoid the physical contact she'd endured when she arrived. "Traffic is terrible on a Sunday night," she said. "We should be going." Harvey stood up with her and then Judy, who got up and stood behind Jumbo. She ran her hand along his neck and up under his hair. Antoinette noticed.

"Where you going?" Antoinette said. "There's more food. I got roast chicken, potatoes, salad, coffee, cake. Where you going so soon? The kitchen was hot and she wiped her face with the dish towel.

"We'll come another time," Sylvia said. "This was wonderful. Thank you. We loved it. But you know, Judy gets tired. You remember."

"Let's go, sweetheart," Judy said to Jumbo. She bent down and kissed his ear.

"Where's he going?" Antoinette asked.

Judy looked at her mother, at her father. "Home," she said to Antoinette.

"Home?" Antoinette looked at Jumbo. "What's this? This isn't home?" She took in a breath. "Whatta you doing?" she said to Jumbo. "I just meet this girl and now you're going home with her?" Antoinette turned to Sylvia. "I don't know about you, Sylvia, but I don't think they should rush things."

Judy bit her lip until there was blood. "We're married," she said, "and we're living with my parents until after the baby comes. Jumbo must have told you."

Antoinette ignored her and spoke to Jumbo. "After the baby comes, sure. You get your own place. But now? Believe me, it's not healthy to live with parents. I know. Didn't I do it for six years? Wait, *caro*. Stay here until you get set. Let her go with her parents. It's better for now."

Judy dug her fingers into the flesh of Jumbo's shoulders. "You choose," she said. "Me or her."

Jumbo stood up. "I gotta go, Ma," he said, and followed the Bernsteins out the door.

Antoinette put on black. She had lost her son, the only one she had ever had. She sat in the kitchen for three days after meeting the Bernsteins with her arms folded in front of her on the kitchen table and her head buried. The girls came one by one and all together. They shook her forearms, the size of hams, and they talked to her head since her face was hidden.

"So, Mama," Rosina said. "It had to happen sometime. She's a nice girl. They're gonna have a baby. You should be happy."

"I'm not happy, Rosina. I want to kill myself," Antoinette said, her voice muffled by her arms. "I want to die. You tell me, how's she gonna take care of him? How's she gonna feed him? How could she do this to me? I'm a widow. She took him away from me to God knows where . . ."

"Ma, Long Island is not God knows where. You can get there by train. And he's still working across the street in Benvenuto's."

"A daughter's a daughter till the end of your life. A son's a son till he finds a wife," Albina said. She had four daughters. She thought she had all the luck.

That made Antoinette raise her head. "Leave me alone, all of you. If I'm not here in the morning, call Nucciarone. Lay me out in the blue dress. It's in the back of the closet in Jumbo's room." And she put her head back down and sobbed.

Raffaella made her coffee and patted her hair. "Drink something, Mama. It will work out."

"Call your brother. Tell him what's happening. Tell him I'm dying."

Jumbo came. Luca Benvenuto let him leave the bar. His mother was calling, after all, and Fat Eddie Fingers was in Miami. Jumbo came into the kitchen with apple crumb cake. He got a dish and put the cake in the middle of the table. He called for his mother but she didn't answer. He called again and then sat down and cut into the cake with a knife. He heard moaning from his old bedroom, the one off the kitchen. He could see her lying on the bed from where he sat. "Get up, Ma. You wanted to see me, I'm here. I got crumb cake."

Antoinette came out of the bedroom. She pulled his hair, then kissed his head. "You're gonna kill me, Jumbo. How much can I take?"

"C'mon, Ma, Judy's a nice girl. I'm married to her, for chrissakes."

"Can she cook? Is she gonna let you see your mother? Take care of your sisters? Will she spend all your money?"

"Ma, whatta you want from me?"

"I want you to swear this baby's gonna be ours. You're gonna baptize it. We're gonna have a big party. You cheated me out of a wedding. You're my only son. You disgraced me. You gotta make it up."

"Christ, Ma. Didn't I promise you the drawer?"

Antoinette folded her arms across her chest. "That's separate. I'm talking about the baby. The name, if it's a boy, Salvatore, after your dead father." She crossed herself and kissed her fingers. "He should be a saint in heaven by now the way I pray. If it's a girl, you know what to do."

Jumbo could feel the sweat under his arms, down his spine. "Ma. I told you yes already. I promised."

"Promise again. I want to hear it!"

"Ma, what is this? Calabria?"

"Swear to me!"

Jumbo could feel the crumb cake dry in his throat, caught, like a dead fish. Antoinette unwound her arms. She poked the back of Jumbo's head. "You swear and you promise. Now!"

"I swear. I promise."

"What? Tell me what you swear and you promise."

He went through the litany for her. When he finished, she took his head in both her hands and kissed his cheeks and his mouth. He was soaking wet, as though he had been caught in a summer storm, as though the heavens had opened up and tried to drown him. After Antoinette, Fat Eddie Fingers was the least of his worries.

Jumbo's knees buckled on the way out. He held on to the banister to get down the five flights of stairs and when he got out in the street he asked Dante if he could sit in his chair just for a minute while he caught his breath. Dante went and got him a Coke from inside Benvenuto's. Luca made him pay for it.

Jumbo shifted between his mother's house and the house on Long Island where Judy, huge with the baby, sat by the pool in maternity shorts and a white cotton pleated smock. Sylvia said she should stay at home, it was summer and her ankles were swollen, but the truth was Sylvia had always been embarrassed by Judy's figure or lack of it, and she didn't want her waddling around the country club with the varicose veins that were starting to climb up her legs like grapevines. Harvey stayed by Judy's side, doting, carrying trays of fresh-squeezed lemonade in colored glasses and rubbing her ankles. "Her husband should be doing that," Sylvia said, pouting, but Harvey ignored her.

"He's working, Sylvia," he told her and he was happy Jumbo was working and away from there. He liked taking care of Judy. Jumbo was working every night, and on the weekends when he did double shifts he stayed on Spring Street with his mother.

Antoinette was happy to have Jumbo back, even if it was just for weekends. It was the least he could do. She had wanted him to marry, she told her daughters, but not like this. She had wanted to dance at his wedding to "Son of Mine." She had wanted a dress with beads and a matching hat and shoes, an orchid on her shoulder. She had wanted to be the mother of the groom and walk down the aisle of St. Anthony's on the arms of her sons-in-law and have everyone admire her dress and matching hat and shoes. Jumbo had cheated her.

So every Friday night he pulled up to Spring Street in Harvey's Cadillac and got dressed up his mother's house and went to work across the street in Benvenuto's. He called Nicky to tell him what was going on and Nicky gave him the news that their mothers had seemed to bury the hatchet, but he didn't tell Jumbo that Antoinette had asked Teresa if maybe Nicky could do something, like arrest Judy Bernstein, give her parking tickets, anything to maybe make her go away, to open Jumbo's eyes. And Nicky didn't tell Jumbo that they had gone together to Magdalena looking for magic spells to get rid of Judy.

"So now you're friends?" Nicky had said to his mother. "After all these years, the two of you are looking out for each other?"

Teresa had ignored this. "So what can you do, Mr. Big-Shot? Can you help?"

"I'm a homicide detective, Ma, not a traffic cop. If Jumbo's wife commits murder somewhere between here and Canal Street, I could arrest her for murder." Teresa sat down and put her head in her hands, her fingers splayed across her temples. "If she committed murder . . . maybe if Magdalena asked her Madonna. If only people would help each other, life on this earth would be easier."

"You tell your friend Antoinette she's gonna love this girl if she gives her half a chance."

Teresa puffed her cheeks and blew the air out of her mouth in disgust. "These girls today don't have no respect," she said. "Look at you, with that Gina. If I had known . . ."

"Weren't we talking about Jumbo?"

"So now I gotta tell Antoinette. I gotta tell her there's nothing you can do and she's gotta live with it."

"Right, Ma. She's gotta live with it."

"Her only son. I know how she feels. Even if he is a *mortodevame,* he's her son." She softened. "Like you're my son." She raised her hands to hold his head. "Ah, Nicky, I worry about you all alone."

"I got you, Ma. You're all I need."

"This year I'll do Our Lady of Mount Caramel for you to find a girl to take care of you when I'm gone."

"Where you going?"

"Ah, Nicola, nobody lives forever . . . not even your mother."

When Judy Bernstein had the baby, Jumbo was uptown at Jilly's with Nicky and Salvatore. They had picked him up after work and gone to have a few drinks. Judy had been frantic trying to call his mother's but Antoinette kept hanging up the phone when she heard Judy's voice. Finally Sylvia tried and then Harvey but by then Antoinette wasn't picking up the phone at all and Harvey said they might just as well go to the hospital without him. He'd find out sooner or later.

Jumbo had a big fight with Antoinette when he found out but she denied everything. The phone never rang, Antoinette told him, except for some crank calls. But when Jumbo told her about the baby, a boy, Antoinette's face changed just a little. She hid the expression that slipped across her eyes and mouth when she heard the word *boy.*

"A boy," she whispered, and clasped her hands together and eyed heaven. *Grazie, Madonna,* she mouthed, and turned to face her son. "Salvatore, remember? You promised, you swore. Salvatore." And she cried big fat tears that rolled down her face. Jumbo put his arms around her and they sat together on the couch. "Salvatore, after your father, like he was named after his father, Salvatore." She kissed Jumbo on both cheeks. "You'll bring him here. So I can see him, right away, and you don't wait too long to baptize him. Right away. You never know."

And after Jumbo left Spring Street and went to Long Island Jewish Hospital and kissed his wife and faced the puss of his mother-in-law and the scowl of his father-in-law, he held his baby in his arms and was as proud as if he had done this all on his own.

Harvey put his finger to his lips. "Judy's happy, Sylvia. We have a grandson here with us. What could be better?"

Sylvia thought a nice Jewish doctor would be better. She was sure the one who had come in to see Judy after the delivery had noticed Judy's big brown eyes and sweet nature. If only she had met him before.

I don't know what I'm gonna do now," Jumbo told Nicky the next night. They were sitting in Benvenuto's. Jumbo had locked the door and was closing out the register. He had also broken out a bottle of twenty-five-year-old scotch to celebrate.

"What now?" Nicky said.

"I promised my mother I'd baptize the baby. I promised her I'd name him Salvatore. I promised Judy's parents I'd raise the kid Jewish. I promised to name him Sol after some dead guy. The Jews name after the dead, did you know that? What kind of custom is that? How you gonna get money from a dead guy?"

They hatched the plan the next night, the three of them, and even Salvatore had to admit it was a good one. Of all of them, he was uneasy, because Magdalena had always made him know there was a greater power, an omnipotent one, and though he moved out in the world in custom pin-striped suits and slept with a

golden blond woman who could ride a horse with an English sad-
dle, he knew there were lines you didn't cross, so when Nicky
came up with the idea of the bogus priest he had arrested at the
San Gennaro feast on Mulberry Street, Salvatore wanted to tell
them to leave him out of it. But magic was for women and Salvatore was a man, so he listened while Nicky and Jumbo schemed
and when the part about the priest came up he excused himself
and went outside into the street to check on his car.

So we get Father Jerome to baptize the kid," Nicky said.

"But where?" Jumbo said, pouring himself a shot of scotch.
"Antoinette's not gonna buy a ceremony in her living room I don't
care what kind of collar this guy is wearing."

"Will you relax?" Nicky looked over his shoulder. "Where's
Sally? He was just here."

"He wanted to check the car or something. Keep talking. He
don't have to hear this. We can tell him later."

"Father Jerome's a professional. You know how many years it
took to nab him? He's retired now but he's still got the collar. I
think he works a door-to-door scam in Florida in the winter."

"Nicky, I don't need a history. I need a baptism."

"Okay, so we get Father Jerome and we do it in St. Pat's on
Mulberry Street. Tell your mother this priest did you a favor. It's
sentimental. You want him to baptize the kid. She'll like that you
got a priest for a personal friend."

"I know a priest I never mentioned before?"

"Jumbo, you tell your mother everything?"

"Okay, forget it. How do we get into the church?"

"My ex-wife's Aunt Geraldine takes care of the altar cloths
down there. I still stake her at Christmas. I'll get the keys. If there's
any surprises, well, I'm a cop, no? We'll play it by ear. It's quiet there
Sunday night. Tell your mother it's a private baptism. Make it
something special, just the principals."

"What principals?"

"For chrissakes, Jumbo, the main parties: you, your mother, the godparents, and the baby . . . the principals."

"Good. Then what?" Jumbo looked around. "Where the hell is Salvatore?" The light from outside cut the darkness of the bar for a second as Salvatore came up alongside them and sat down.

"The car's okay?" Nicky asked him.

"Yeah, I just wanted to make sure I didn't get a ticket."

"Christ, Sally. It's the neighborhood. You're parked outside Fat Eddie's and Nicky's a cop. You been in Connecticut too long. Lemme feel your head."

"Just pour me a drink, will you? And bring me up to date."

"The baptism's set. All I need are godparents. I'll get one of my sisters to be the godmother."

"Which one? How you gonna pick? You got five."

"The one with the biggest mouth, the biggest ass, the oldest, the fattest, I don't know. My mother can take care of that. And I need a godfather." He looked at them. "You wanna flip a coin?"

Salvatore stood up. "Choose Nicky," he said. "You almost killed him. Now he'll be the godfather to your son. It's appropriate."

"Geez, these words, Salvatore. You're giving me a headache."

"That's nice, Sally," Nicky said, "but . . ."

"No, I think it's only right. I'll stand up for him when he gets confirmed. With Jumbo for a father, by the time he's twelve, he'll need me."

Jumbo put an arm around each of their shoulders and they stood there, the three of them, in a huddle. "We got it," he said. "All we need is a party. I should have it here, no?"

"Perfect. Fat Eddie Fingers can take a piece of the kid's envelopes and make on the party too."

"Christ, maybe this kid will get me out of debt finally. So I can get a real job and move out of Harvey and Sylvia's house."

"You gonna come back to the neighborhood?"

"Well, Antoinette's been making noises. I hear she's got two hundred in an envelope for the super when he clears out Big Lucy's apartment. One more Mangiacarne in that building and we may as well own the rattrap."

"What about your wife?" Nicky said.

"*Gita, git,* you know what I mean? A little at a time. I think Antoinette and Judy are gonna be crazy for one another. My sisters are gonna forget she's even Jewish. And hey, double holidays, more parties, more envelopes. *Gelt,* they call it. I'm in heaven."

"It's okay to name the baby Salvatore?"

"No, Christ. I promised to name him Sol."

"Sol? How's he gonna live in the neighborhood with a name like Sol?"

"When he's here, he'll be Sal. Sal, Sol, who can tell the difference? Smart thinking, no?"

"I think you just got lucky, Jumbo. Suppose you had to name him Irving?"

"Suppose, suppose. Suppose I drop dead and don't have to worry about nothing? Hey, things work out. Who used to say that? Who used to tell us that the end it all balances out?"

"Magdalena," Salvatore said. "Magdalena used to tell us that."

That night Jumbo went out to Long Island early. Luca Benvenuto let him go since he had booked the christening party for the next week. Jumbo held Judy's hand in the living room after the nurse had put Baby Sol to bed and whispered in Judy's ear how happy he was. He made love to her on the couch after Sylvia and Harvey went upstairs. Jumbo told Judy to be quiet, to save up all those screams for when they had their own place. If Judy had known how quiet she'd have to be on Spring Street, she would have screamed till her lungs burst.

On the planned Sunday, Jumbo said that he wanted to take the baby to see his mother and his sisters. Judy said she would come. He took her aside and said if she didn't mind, he thought it was a good idea for his mother to have some time alone with Baby Sol. He didn't want Antoinette to feel left out. After all, Sylvia had the baby all the time. Her girlfriends had come bearing gifts, raising their eyebrows in private. Except for Elaine Himmelfarb, whose daughter had run off and become a Hare Krishna, they whispered, no one had done worse with their children than Sylvia Bernstein.

Judy was nervous. "Could the baby nurse come? Just to make sure," she said. "Antoinette hasn't had a baby in years."

"Oh, Judy, c'mon. It's like riding a bicycle. And what about my sisters? C'mon, honey, you gotta give her a chance. She's the grandmother, too, and she ain't hardly seen him. He'll be back tonight safe and sound."

So they put Baby Sol in the portable carriage in the back seat of the Cadillac and made Jumbo promise he'd pull over right away if Baby Sol cried. They armed him with bottles and diapers and diaper pins and rattles and dressed him in short knitted baby blue pants with knitted suspenders and a white shirt with a Peter Pan collar with rabbits embroidered along the edges. They needn't have bothered.

On Spring Street, Antoinette had the christening set ready. A long satin and lace dress and matching cap and booties. She had even cleaned the house for the occasion and when Jumbo arrived he made her sit down in the living room chair before he'd put the baby bundle in her arms. When he left to go downstairs, his sisters came and they undressed little Sal and counted his toes and his fingers and eyed the size of his penis and the width of his chest before they dressed him, layer by layer, in his christening outfit. "Not as big as Jumbo," Antoinette said, "but then no baby ever was. Salvatore," she crooned, "little Sal . . . if only your grandpa was here to see you . . . his little namesake . . . his little Sally. He's gonna be smart," Antoinette said, looking up at her five daughters. "Jews are smart. You gotta give them that." She snuggled him up near her face; she cuddled his head in the folds of flesh at her neck and she started to sing.

Jumbo waited for Nicky downstairs and when he showed up, Jumbo put his head back and yelled for his mother to come down. Antoinette had wanted the baptism in St. Anthony's but Nicky had been right. Antoinette was excited that they would have the church to themselves, even if it was St. Patrick's on the East Side, and that the priest was a friend of her son's. Nicky chauffeured them over and Antoinette was impressed enough with Father Jerome to kiss his hand.

The main doors to St. Patrick's were open and the church was lit only by the altar and at the baptismal font. Antoinette leaned heavily on Rosina's arm, the daughter she had chosen to be Baby Salvatore's *gummara* because she was the her favorite. Rosina wore a light blue satin suit with a white lace blouse and a small blue hat that ended in points on her forehead. Antoinette had put away her mourning clothes and wore beige, from her stockings to her pearls.

The East Side neighborhood watched the procession enter the church after hours. Nicky waved and stopped to talk to some of the old men on the chairs on the sidewalk. He knew them by name and they knew not to ask. Father Jerome had slipped away and met them now at the font, the white-and-gold stole draped around his neck, his Bible open. He said the prayers for baptism and made the sign of the cross over Baby Sol/Sal's head and dripped the water on the forehead. The baby squirmed but never cried and then fell back to sleep. Nicky and Rosina recited their Apostle's Creed and Father Jerome blessed all of them standing together and Nicky handed him a white envelope with a C-note inside and shook his hand.

"You're coming to the party, no?" Antoinette asked. "You sit by me."

"Of course," Father Jerome said, and Nicky took him aside and told him if he got drunk or touched one woman at the party he was going away for minimum three years, and Nicky would make sure it was someplace cold and dark, someplace like Dannemora.

They drove back to Spring Street, and for once in a long time, Antoinette was happy. She was getting out of a white Cadillac holding a brand-new baby boy, the heir to the Mangiacarne name, dressed in a satin-and-lace christening gown from Italy. She had bought it on Grand Street, not far from Harvey Bernstein's underwear store, and she would have stopped to see him if she could have remembered his last name. Antoinette walked into Benvenuto's slowly, waving to the women who stood outside in the summer heat, to the people on their way to her grandson's party. She moved slowly, because of her size and because she wanted to savor every minute of her ascendancy. She had produced the biggest baby on Spring Street and now, she was sure, she had the *smartest* baby on Spring Street in her arms.

Luca Benvenuto had done the place up like a palace with silver and white crepe paper and blue cardboard baby shoes and Italian and American flags he had borrowed from the American Legion hall on MacDougal Street. BENEDETTO SALVATORE hung over the main table in big blue letters and the food started at one corner and went around to three sides of the room. Sugared almonds sat in glass dishes on the bar. Antoinette insisted Father Jerome and Nicky sit at her table and she held a seat for Teresa. "We're family now," she told her, and she let Teresa hold Baby Salvatore and then he was passed from arm to arm and back again and Nicky never bothered to bring in the portable crib from the back seat of the Cadillac.

When they asked where the mother was, Antoinette said she was resting. It had not been an easy birth, she whispered to the women. Girls today were delicate. The women nodded and Anna Giacometti said the baby seemed small. "Maybe," Antoinette said, "but he's gonna be smart. He's half-Jewish. You know anybody smarter than them?" The women nodded their heads some more. "And how come he's so quiet now?" they asked, and Antoinette pinched his leg so he howled and then she sat back in satisfaction. Oh, her Jumbo had done good.

Magdalena came in to wish Jumbo well. She had sent the cake, a tower of marzipan in blue and white, filled with cannoli cream and rum. She had a girl with her, Marilena, from her village of Castelfondo. Marilena didn't lower her eyes when Magdalena introduced her to Nicky. He noticed the strange amulet she wore at her throat on a black silk cord. He couldn't have known it was the polished black bone of a goat. She was very young, and when the music started, she danced a tarantella with a white handkerchief held high over her head. Magdalena stood to the side watching, holding Salvatore's arm. His wife wasn't there. She always preferred to stay in Connecticut.

Antoinette waltzed with her son to Jimmy Roselli and when she sat down and fanned herself with her beige handkerchief, her knees apart, her thighs meeting, Teresa leaned over and spoke softly in her ear. "See, Antoinette, Magdalena's prayers to the Black Madonna were answered. You got a daughter-in-law, that when there's a wedding, your son can take you. She won't care about what's important to us. On Sunday, they'll eat in your house because this wife, she'll never cook better than you. She won't even try. And you've got a grandson. Come fall, you'll be on the stoop with this baby in your arms."

"And you can hold him, Teresa. Anytime you want."